A MAN WHO LOVED TOO MUCH
A WOMAN WHO LOVED FOREVER

It was a very special marriage—tenderly
beautiful yet dangerously blind. A crisis looms
before Joshua, a crisis so tragic he cannot bear
to reveal it to Sarah and he quietly begins a
scheme to protect her.

But Joshua has overlooked the greatest
obstacle in his plan to spare his young bride
any pain—the honesty, passion, and depth of
Sarah's love for him—a love that will not die.

SARAH AND JOSHUA

J.J. McKENNA

AVON
PUBLISHERS OF BARD, CAMELOT AND DISCUS BOOKS

SARAH AND JOSHUA is an original publication of Avon Books. This work has never before appeared in book form.

AVON BOOKS
A division of
The Hearst Corporation
959 Eighth Avenue
New York, New York 10019

First Avon Printing, August, 1979

AVON TRADEMARK REG. U.S. PAT. OFF. AND IN
OTHER COUNTRIES, MARCA REGISTRADA, HECHO EN
U.S.A.

Printed in the U.S.A.

For Barbara

Let not thy divining heart
Forethink me any ill,
Destiny may take thy part,
And may thy fears fulfill;
But think that we
Are but turn'd aside to sleep;
They who one another keep
Alive, ne'er parted be.

"Song"
John Donne

CHAPTER ONE

My Sarah stood with her creased nightdress billowing out around her in the warmth from the electric heater. Beneath, her trousered knees huddled together. She said, "This place is too bloody cold. England's too bloody cold. My lips are cracking and my nose is all dry." She leaned to the dressing table and took a finger dab of white cream from a pot without a lid. She pulled a small hair out of the grease before rubbing it on her nose.

"Come to bed then."

"It's warmer here. Do I have to undress the rest of me?" She giggled. "Poor Josh, what a letdown. I mean, in the south of France or Nigeria, where you were, I could be languishing before an open window in the flimsiest of negligees, martini in hand, feeding you ripe figs and succulent grapes. Here, well . . . a brushed nylon nightdress and too cold-lazy to take off my Levis. Climate is a magical thing, my love. Consider how it affects us all."

"I'm considering. Come to bed."

"Is it warm in there yet?"

I stretched a tentative toe to one side and retracted it quickly as a tortoise's head. "No. We ought to get an electric blanket."

"Where was I?" She rubbed her nose thoughtfully and moved so that the updraft of comfort reached her back. She prefers that heater to me. "Yes. Climate. People from hot climates have time, don't they? Perhaps that's why they are underdeveloped."

"There's this African I know whose—"

"Economically! They don't race, it's too hot. Gives other things a chance to flourish, no doubt. Who is this African?"

I smiled back at her sly grin. "No one you're going to meet, I promise."

"Spoilsport. Am I right, though? Us cold types, we twitch and rush and—did you know that's why Lancashire was considered a good area for cotton mills, one of the reasons anyway. They had to work hard to keep warm. True! It lifted the output no end. I'm cold, my feet are cold!"

"So are mine, girl. Get in and I can put them on your back." Sarah screamed softly. "This weather is too cold even for working," I added. "This is when our typists sit on the storage heaters and children put their hands through those old lukewarm radiators and the school milk is solid."

"Was, my love. Was."

"Yes, and it looked like the top of Everest poking through the metal caps."

"You remember that? A Canadian immigrant?"

"Don't be cheeky. I was nine when I came and I went to one of your country junior schools, which is more than you did. It had a coke boiler that gave us low-grade carbon monoxide poisoning."

"How warmly nostalgic. I'd forgotten how cold . . . playing hockey in cotton shorts with snow on the ground and never, never getting hot. Our poor little blue hands that hurt like hell when you just touched them. They were cruel, you know, running around in thick tracksuits while we striving little scholars got frostbite. We didn't catch pneumonia, strangely enough."

I watched her eyes, great luminous gray discs; the first attraction I had ever felt for Sarah was to the huge sadness of those eyes. Contrarily, she is not sad, but her eyes know something she doesn't. Across some crowded pub they had stared and put an imprint on my mind that has never faded since. Her face is so overshadowed by them that her other features have little importance. One day when she is old my Sarah will be beautiful.

She hugged the heater one last time like a departing child, then sat on the bed to take off her jeans. "Look," she said. "No, don't. My skin looks like wrinkled waxed paper. I put cream on when I think of it. Oh ghastly legs! Oh morbid legs! Do corpses' legs look like that, Josh? Don't tell me. To think I have corpses' legs is different from knowing it."

Sarah smiles, what have you done to me that I am incomplete without you? Eighteen months married, when men begin to look around and wonder what they have become and why, and I still see you. "You haven't changed," I said.

"I always had corpses' legs? How unkind. May I come in beside you, Joss-stick?" I pulled back the covers and watched her kick off her slippers. She is just tall enough for her head to fit under my chin and she is soft in outline, but like a cat, strong beneath and scratchy if prodded from sleep. Sarah takes the world away with her when she sleeps, my dreams and hers,

3

and she is separate and isolated and doesn't need me then. I didn't want her to go to sleep yet.

"Oh, that grin, that sweet grin," my wife giggled. "I'm jealous I have to share it with anyone. Your lady students must adore you, Joshua Steel." She got in beside me, squeaking cat noises at the cold sheets, and turned on her side to face me. A soft crease of skin ran between her neck and shoulder, always the same. "Warm me, Josh," she said. "I'm cold as the sea."

Sarah shut her eyes and slept almost immediately, as she does when she is warm and self-satisfied, and took her soul away to dream. I stared into the dark, breathing sharply, unable to relax yet fatigued beyond reason. I felt ill, cold, and nauseated. I shut my eyes tightly to blot out the pale oblong of the curtained window and its paler reflection in the top of the looking glass and listened. My heart banged its metabolic rhythm, more felt than heard, through the length and breadth of my body, and fast, far too fast. With each thump my head expanded and forced perspiration from my skin in minute fountains. The noise feeling was deafening. I snapped open my eyes, scared, and sight was quieting. The rushing, hot sounds receded as the cold curtain light invaded. I reached up a shaking hand and pushed the sweat back into my hair. Night is not the time for reason, so be reasonable, Joshua Steel. You are thirty-one, slowing down a little, not so adept at exertion, overworked, underpaid . . . ill? A flock of possible diseases flew across the bedroom air on well-remembered textbook pages. I looked at one or two. TB? Simple anemia? Sarah, am I ill?

Faintly behind my thoughts I heard her even breathing and imagined the colored dreams flowing from her nostrils like smoke. The pale light was grow-

ing as the moon rose and soon a shaft of whiteness
would lean across our bed, cutting between the curtains that have never quite met in the middle. I turned
toward my wife, curled kitten-tiny with her nose above
the sheet and her hair, black ink now, blotted on the
pillow. I wondered what Dad would have thought of
her, and remembered the old man. Pictures elbowed
in; the tough stocky frame in short-sleeved shirt and
baggy gardening pants, puffing his pipe over the rose
bushes. What a garden our home in Westwood had
had! We had moved to Los Angeles when I was six,
from an insignificant dot on the coast of New Bruns-
wick. It was cold in Canada in winter and the sea was
pewter, I remember that. But my other memories from
that time are of people in a quiet, rural setting—of
the town itself I can recapture very little.

California was kind to plants and the children who
played among them. My father had looked like a
farmer in his garden, wide brown-eyed and ruddy
complexioned with a broad, slow grin. He looked like
a farmer until you saw the hands that caressed a rose
so gently or spread in quick explanation; they were
strong and long-fingered, the tapered, clever instru-
ments belonging to one of the best orthopedic sur-
geons on the West Coast. He was modest about his
work. "I do what I can," he used to say, but he developed a new prosthesis that is now used all over the
world. I guess I thought he was God until my mother
died. He couldn't save her, couldn't mold and snap her
bones and put it all back straight. So at five years old
I had no mother. I can see her face sometimes and
feel her warmth, but Dad lives strongly in the memory,
ruddy and smiling and quick, strong-handed. He
brought me, his only child, to England to live with my
Anglicized aunt in the West Country because he felt

I needed a woman's influence. "Kids get all screwed up without gentle people around." Those had been his words, so we came to Aunt Gale and learned to be British in the small village of Somerfield. I gained a lot and left a lot behind, too, including relatives I loved and most of my accent. Sarah says I sound sort of Canadian now, but better. I smiled in the dark. Sarah says a lot and means the unlikely half of it. Even now I have to pause sometimes and look at her eyes. She is an island; man may not be but some women are, lush and green or cool and blue, inviting but discrete entities. I wanted to wake her and bring her back from that far-off place where no man can follow, but I didn't.

I stared at the blackness and the shaft of moonlight, and shivered. In the looking glass reflection I could just make out the picture of Greta Garbo that Sarah had pinned up, "Because she was the most beautiful woman in the world and so far above me that I don't feel at all jealous, that would be like being jealous of Michelangelo, or you." My heart slowed down now and I relaxed reluctantly, waiting for it to start up again. Reality faded into jumbled reruns of the past day, and at last I was dreaming. I never remember my dreams.

"Joan and Alan are coming to dinner." It was eight-thirty and still cold, the kitchen window shrouded in condensation. I looked around the room and it seemed I had never been there before. It is good in summer, very good as garden flats' kitchens go, big and cool gray-tiled, with Sarah's pot plants along the window's edge. Today it was cold and full of dampness and unfamiliar.

"Who are?"

"Joan and Alan. We went to a party they gave about a month ago, remember? Oh Josh, come on, wake up. She's a good friend of mine, even if she did give you the odd sidelong glance."

"Who?"

A bowl of porridge landed heavily beneath my tented arms. Sarah turned back to the grand new cooker which had come with a free tin of poor caviar, and flicked dials angrily, her cold red hands protruding from the sleeves of her old wool dressing gown.

"I'm sorry, oh woman mine, for being obtuse. Is Joan the elderly lady with bleached hair?"

My wife brought her cup of coffee to the table and sat opposite, wiping a spot from the yellow plastic top with a wetted finger. "She's a good friend," she said. "And she's only thirty-five." She waited for me to speak but I smiled instead. She chuckled suddenly. "You are a mean devil sometimes."

"And you're a slut. Look at you. Hair all curly and a robe a tramp might have thrown away."

"I can't help that! This place is so cold! If you won't ... Joshua, it's too early for me. Eat your porridge."

"Porridge! Por-ridge. Poor idge. Alas, poor Idge, I knew him well." I tapped the spoon on the oats and looked at her. "Come here, slut."

"No. I told you, it's too early. You'll be late." But she moved around the table slowly and came into my arms. Her mouth tasted of unsweetened coffee and her skin smelled of sleep. The old robe warmed both of us and reminded me of the one Dad always wore at breakfast on Sundays, a checked, moth-eaten creation which, like his gardening pants, fitted his soul and his disposition. My Sarah knows my body well; she stood up. "Time to go, my love. Don't forget about dinner, will you?"

"Promise, rosebud, promise! I'll try to get home early. May I bring you something? Lark's tongues, cakes and ale, the perfume of musk or a boxful of distilled rainbows?"

"Fool. Drive carefully." She always says it, a charm to keep me safe on the road, and if for some reason she misses, she worries all day though she thinks I don't know it. I love the little ritual, feel the spell and am grateful, but I have never spoken of it. That would break the magic. "We shall have duck Provençale for dinner," she added.

"Mmm! What a wife I have in thee, oh ancient-named Sarah. Wine too?"

"Go along. Let it be a surprise."

"A surprise to be relished. I shall sip of its honey all day. My students will love you, I shall be kind to them."

"As if you'd be anything else. Fool." I saw her eating my porridge like Goldilocks as I passed the window.

My car has a recalcitrant streak; it is an old Morgan with a mind of its own, to be respected and cajoled. Its engineering has quite a few years' advantage over me and the old girl knows it. So do I. I never lend her to anyone except Sarah, or leave her parked insecurely, or flatten her battery or swear at her except on the rare occasion when she dies miles from civilization. There was one particular and pertinent time when . . . it made me smile. Sarah hadn't believed me, of course, until I had walked two miles through pouring rain to an AA box. Even then she had been doubtful and hadn't let me near her. As a first date it had been a travesty. I had shouted at her because I was soaked and cold and she had silently refused to acknowledge my presence in the car, despite the cloying smell of wet jacket. I had wondered aloud what had happened to the permissive society and she had snapped back that if I were a member of it she sure as hell was not going to join. Like most disasters, it had been funny after a while.

The car started second time, the low drum of the exhaust flattened and absorbed by the breezeblock garage walls. It is a tight fit and there is a round black patch on the rear wall where the carbon spits. I have been going to clean it off for at least a year. I drove slowly along the driveway, frozen gravel exploding under the tires.

The Kensington High Street traffic was dense, as always, and the car hiccuped and coughed like an asthmatic. I blew on my fingers and turned on the heater but it breathed icy air on my knees. I must buy a new thermostat. Good morning, commuters. Come along, hurry, hurry. Run for that Tube, that big snarling bus, tote that barge, lift that bale. Blue noses, purpled cheeks, flying black shiny feet, plaid mufflers and thick gloves the color of clotted cream, all twitch, jerk, hurry, hurry. To that office to sweat all day in central heating, to that big store with Father Christmas in the middle of November. Perhaps, as Sarah said, it all has to do with climate. On a warm summer day faces aren't quite so hard, not even in London where the year-round expression is self-centered and so very different from my old home in Somerfield where people smile and have even been seen to stop and speak.

I coughed and tasted the tang of sulphur and traffic exhalations in my throat. It could be that this is part of the reason for the set faces, the slow poisoning each morning and evening, the gentle suicide everyone including the oil companies only pretends to notice. Soon we will be wearing masks and dropping like flies as they do in Tokyo. It matters, I feel, it matters. Old Marker and young Alfie call me unreasonable and even Sarah, who shares my apprehensions when she has time, ignores me when dinner is to be cooked. "You have to have a sense of proportion," they say, but they never say whose proportion. It does matter. "You're so intense about everything," Sarah said once. "It makes you true and open, but—" and she stopped because the roast chicken was ready.

I ran up the stone stairs two at a time, the quiet University building jumping at the sound of my feet. Industry is here, but quiet and hidden behind closed office doors, in roomy lecture theaters and cramped, machine-packed laboratories. As I neared the top of the flight the checkered edge of the steps began to leap out at my eyes. I grabbed at the rail, panting, waiting for my vision to steady. The black mosaic squares jumped and danced in time with my pulse and a silly waltz tune jangled in my head. Slowly they settled back in their concrete and slowly I moved on upstairs, each step a mountain. Sweat ran down the inside of my thighs. I tried to ignore the whole thing, but left a wet palm print on the bannister.

The familiar corridor was longer this morning, the brown wooden doors spaced more widely in the neutral walls, the overhead neon higher and harsher. First door, *Nutrition Dept. Secy. & Main Office*, always standing open. The two girls were there already, one leaning against the electric heater, one typing, cold-fingered. "Good morning, Doctor Steel." As usual, early bright smiles for me, especially from Julie. I have heard from our intricate and ubiquitous grapevine that tall and fair Julie is fond of me. Poor girl, with small blue eyes. I treat her gently because I am flattered, knowing it is unkind to be kind, but would she care less if I were rude and unpleasant? Women are not built that way, not the ones I have known.

"Good morning, girls."

Next, gold letters on a black plaque: *Prof. S.C. Eyles* and the room behind the door empty. He is an old gray man with an old gray complexion and a jutting strawberry nose with hairs sprouting from it, which I confess fascinates me. Whenever we talk I cannot take my eyes off it. He never arrives before eleven. Next are two labs with glass panels in the doors, also empty, then *J.M. Steel, M.D., F.R.C.S.— Senior Lecturer*, the first M for Matthew, my father's and grandfather's name, and the Senior not so impressive as it appears because we are a small department and have no lecturers.

When I went in Alfie Corbett was already there, sitting on my desk and flicking through a folder of close-written notes. "Good morning, Doctor Steel." He leaned heavily on the title as if he didn't believe it or didn't want to use it. Alfie is in the final year of his Ph.D. Soon he will be a Doctor, too, but Alfie hasn't seen that far yet. I smiled at him. He is brilliant, sharp as acid, and limited. The development of a philanthropic attitude had been arrested in Alfie at birth and anything he does he does for Alfie. I don't think he'll ever make a true scientist; a true merchant banker, perhaps, but he lacks the philanthropic spirit which impels the best of scientific inquiry. "You promised we'd start at nine," said Alfie.

I hung up my coat and slumped into the chair behind the desk. Suddenly depression hit me like a breaker. "Get off my desk," I said. Alfie cast a sly glance over his shoulder. His face is made for sly

glances, with eyes of indeterminate color locked together above a short, thin nose. He has a woman's
cupid mouth that sneers easily. I had long ago labeled
him with an inferiority complex, then retracted it because I'm no psychiatrist, but the initial impression still
raises its head on bad days. "Get off my desk," I
repeated. It wasn't looking like a good day.

"Okay, okay. You Yanks can be touchy, can't you?"

I put my head in my hands. Alfie knows I'm not a
Yank. Stupid boy, ridiculous man. What pleasure does
it give you? In the wide world why pick on me this
morning? "I'm your superior," I said. Now why pull
rank? It saves time. "Do you want this Ph.D. or don't
you?"

"Aw, come on, Doc," Alfie smiled and was charming.
"You know the work is excellent, you said so. Will you
look at this last set of results?"

"No, not now."

"But you said—"

"After coffee break. Not now."

Alfie grinned and was unpleasant. "Bad night, Doc?
Too much hard work?"

"Not now, Mr. Corbett, not now. I don't think I
would judge fairly, do you?"

Alfie left, taking his small hurt dignity away with
his folder of papers. I leaned back in my chair and felt
sorry, fighting away threatening indigestion. I wondered whether I was developing a duodenal ulcer.

The shelves of books stared down indifferently and
listened to my thoughts. A gray winter light picked
out the torn, used corners and the flaking gold paint
of the titles. "Good morning, troops," I said quietly.
"My silent army that armed me for the job. Step up,
platoon of J. Sci. Food Agric., don't laze against one

12

another! Come along all, to attention! Straighten those pages, get that print in line! It's an interesting job, isn't it? Don't you relish being opened and turned and studied? Let me drag out a few more facts for the devouring students. Do they care, I wonder? They eat knowledge like there's no tomorrow but where does it go, what do they do with it? Will what *I* say change them, or are they using me? Tell me, army. You should know, you bottomless repositories, you're always being used." I stopped at the sound of a door opening. Desmond Marker, Reader, called through the connecting door of our offices, "Morning, Joshua!"

Must you shout it? Every bloody morning whether I'm here or not. Morning, Joshua! And you don't give a damn if I hear or if I care about being shouted at. The familiar monotonous morning sounds continued. A thud as the rolled black umbrella dropped in the stand, a slight groan of effort as the camel overcoat was hung on a hook too high for easy reach, a creak and another groan as the office chair took its nine-thirty A.M. fill. "Good morning, Doctor Desmond Marker, fifty-five, candidate for a cardiac arrest if ever I saw one. Now you take out your pipe, pat yourself in all pockets for matches, and open the desk drawer for the spare box because you left the others at home." The drawer slid open.

"Did you call me, Joshua?"

"Often, but you never heard."

"Eh?"

I went to the door, swung it back and said, "Good morning," very quietly. The acrid smell of pipe smoke caught my throat and reminded me of the traffic fumes. "Could we have a word?"

"Far too busy now, old chap." Marker rustled

13

papers from one side of the wide desk to the other. "Important? Well, it'll have to wait. Now, I'm taking the discussion group this morning. Can you take the afternoon practical; starts at four. Good." He puffed like a chimney at the pipe, his little fat hand clasping the bowl tight, his long sharp fingernails with the lines in them like corduroy, overlapping each other. He had dismissed me.

"We arranged that I should take the discussion."

"Uh? Oh, that can't be helped. I happened to have time last night to prepare a jolly good subject for them. Yes. 'Contraception and child nutrition—discuss the relationship.'"

"That's a bit vague, surely, and they've already covered the effects of contraception on community nutrition in Indian villages of up to five hundred people. I was going—"

"I think it should be dealt with more widely. You take the practical, will you, old chap?"

"They won't finish until six-thirty. I promised to be home on time. We have dinner guests."

He looked up severely. "Joshua, this work is important, vital. If we let the brains of tomorrow down every time we had dinner guests, how would the educational system function at all? Now, I really am busy. You must have work to do, too."

I stared down at him for a few seconds. He is short, a gnome when sitting down, with a pointed balding head and pink, close-shaven jowls with the fluff from the towel still clinging. Behind rimless glasses his eyes are pale blue, short-sighted, and blandly mean. His body is shaped like his head, an avocado, narrow-shouldered and wide-waisted. Oh, you ugly old bastard. You have an ugly mind, too; it looks just one way. Inward. I went back to my own room and drew a line through the proposed discussion notes. How would my father have reacted now? Dad would never have been here. "There is no point in knowing medicine unless you practice it," he had said, turning brown spadefuls of earth with his surgeon's hands. "Use it, it's your talent. Piano players don't stand around telling you how they can play. They find a piano and get right in there." But if you can't find a piano you grind a barrel organ.

I sat glaring at the row of pens and pencils in the plastic tray. There were two Biros from the stationery cupboard, a pencil marked Oxoid from a traveling representative, and a Sheaffer from Sarah for my last birthday. This was for Sarah, the job, the money. She doesn't want it, she says, but I want it for her. No point in trying to shift the blame. She has never asked and rarely complained, but there are many little things. The dressing gown, the cold flat, how delighted she had been with the new cooker. She loves the things this job can buy and I can't stand to see discontent in her gray eyes.

"Are you coming to coffee?" The tall, fair Julie stood in the doorway, her face nervous and smiling.

"Yes, Julie. Thank you."

"I thought I'd remind you, Doctor Steel. You know how you are about time and things. I thought I'd remind you."

She has never come to my room on unofficial business before. It was proving to be a strange day for me, and strange for Julie perhaps. I stood up and went to her. "Come along then." I smiled and squeezed her thin shoulder briefly, knowing as soon as it was done that it should not have been. I was near enough to

15

feel her loneliness. She walked on ahead quickly, hiding whatever it was that she felt. Loneliness keeps a woman slim, her bottom and waist trim, her breasts taut. It keeps her hair shiny and her clothes becoming and she hopes the effort will win someone to break the loneliness. When this someone comes and there is security, then Sarah's curly brown hair and old gray robe. My wife would have killed me to hear my thoughts. She always makes, what is it? the best of herself. The best of my Sarah isn't seen, certainly not by Sarah.

The refectory was crowded, but our usual table in the corner under a print of Vermeer's beautiful *Music Lesson* was still empty. Two technicians from our department followed Julie, me, and the other typist, Shirley, to our seats. Pattie, the waitress, saw us and came at a varicose-veined run, pressure of orders making her tetchy. She fled with our requests.

"Say, I'm the center of a bevy of beauty this morning," I said. "It'll make Doctor Marker jealous."

The younger technician, seventeen and pert and permissive-society personified because she is afraid to be anything else yet, blinked preposterous eyelashes at me and said, "Of what? At his age he's past it anyway."

"And I'm knocking at the door."

"Eh?"

"Being past it is a state of mind, young woman."

Julie tucked in her lips as if she knew better and passed my coffee. "You don't take sugar do you, Doctor Steel?"

"Thanks, no. With three-quarters of the world underfed, why should I?" I smiled. The technician piled three cubes into her cup and Julie pushed the bowl aside. I'm sure she hates bitter coffee, but I like it. She drank and flinched.

16

"Did you see 'Top of the Pops' last night?" asked the other technician, a greasy, ungirly girl.

I acted as old as I felt. "Mmm? Is that the program with luv in every song? All those hermaphrodite persons gyrating around luvving themselves and having it off with their guitars?"

Julie blushed and the others giggled. I felt I must appear to them as another, randier Marker. I picked up my cup and grinned all round, excusing myself. Little Julie's face changed as I walked away and I wished I could kill her feelings stone dead.

Bob Alice, who hates his name, sat alone two tables away. I sat opposite, spilling my coffee in the saucer. "How are you Bob?"

"Awful." Bob's health is a continual source of pleasure to him. "My stomach's been playing hell these past three weeks." He was eating a doughnut. "Wish the medics could find out what it is. One day, nervous dyspepsia. Next, hiatus hernia. Next, peptic ulcer. I'm on so many diets I can eat what I like. Have a doughnut?"

I smiled a refusal. "Uh, I feel a bit off-color myself. Can I come over?"

"Why not? Happy to take your blood. It becomes compulsive after a time. Most of us take our own samples every couple of months. What's up?" He ate messily, leaving traces of highly colored jam round his mouth.

"I don't know. It could be psychosomatic. I keep feeling hot my pulse races, I feel exhausted climbing stairs. I probably need a tonic."

"We'll look at it. Drop in after lunch. Hematology at your service."

"Okay, thanks. Be seeing you." I left my cup and walked back to my office. Marker passed me in the

17

stairwell, staring straight ahead, unseeing. Am I a ghost, am I invisible?

When I got home at seven-fifteen Sarah was working at the kitchen table, clad in a butcher's striped apron and looking delectable.

"Don't shoot! Don't shoot! I'm sorry, headlamps. That miserable old man asked me, commanded me, to take the practical. I was quite superfluous, but 'Someone has to be there, Joshua.' Have they arrived yet?"

Sarah smiled without warning. She has the smile Helen of Troy left behind. "You have three-quarters of an hour. Have a bath and change, yes?"

"Angel goose-bump. Can't I help with dinner?"

"Nope. It's done. What's wrong, Josh?" I have grown to respect that quick change from banality to depth. She draws a curtain aside and there she is with all her intuition ends out, probing my skull. "Oh, don't frown at me so, man. I only asked."

"But why did you ask, my Sarah?"

"You looked tired, that's all. Go and bathe before I really get to work on you."

I kissed her forehead lightly on the way. "Promises, promises." I hung my coat in the hall, turned the taps on in the old white tub in the bathroom and went to undress. Sarah had left the heater on so the bedroom was warm, and laid out my new pants, sweater, and the new good shoes that pinch my feet. Perhaps she wouldn't notice if I wore the old ones. Of course she'd notice, she always notices. Maybe I'd make a stand on my awkward feet this time. Who were Joan and Alan anyway?

The bathroom had the cold damp feel of steam and old china tiles but the water was hot and I lay in it, wriggling my toes at the taps. Sarah sits the other way round, so she can see the door, she says. I realize I don't like my feet, my toes are irregular. I hunted through my mind for something to look forward to, some pleasure to anticipate. At work what was there? Marker's retirement? Ten years is too long for pleasant anticipation. Alfie's longed-for entry to the ranks of the well-paid and out of my hair? The end of the course for the post-grads who take all the knowledge and leave nothing behind? To be followed by another batch and another.

I sat up suddenly, throwing water up the wall at the foot of the bath. It has to stop, it really has to. I can cure and heal and mend. I can save and touch and feel. I am fed up with money-grabbing when half the world has none and never will. But Sarah. Sarah, how will you feel? I lay back and pulled bits off the bath sponge. I promised security and you need it so much.

I shaved, standing to one side of the mirror because the other side is spotted in the shape of a horse, a rusty, rearing horse, though my wife says it is a cat. Widely spaced brown eyes with a frown above drawing the eyebrows into a straight line, stared at me, earnest and critical. God. I look like a second-rate poet viewing a deep mystery of life. I grinned and wondered whether that smile was the one Sarah calls ethereally randy. Needless to say, I have never been in the position to rush out of bed and look in the nearest mirror to check. I cut my chin and swore and the earnest expression reappeared.

"Will I do kitten?"

Sarah had taken off the apron and was arranging nuts on the coffee table. She looked around absently and I guessed she was deciding whether to put the sherry in a decanter or impress the guests with the

19

"Dry Fly" label. "The shoes," she said, deciding on the decanter. "Don't you like them?"

"You're incredible. They hurt."

"All right." She set out four tulip-shaped copitas, examining them for bits of cotton from the tea towel. "Can't have you grumbling and groaning all evening because your toes are all crossed up. You've got funny feet, you know. It's not the shoes."

"Yes, dear." The doorbell rang.

"Oh! Josh, let them in."

"Yes, dear."

"And Josh—"

"Yes, dear?"

"Don't get on your war, pollution, population thing tonight, please? They're not the sort."

"I don't have a thing!" The bell rang again. On the way to answer it I decided to create a pleasant anticipation. Tomorrow we would drive down to Somerset and stay with Aunt Gale for the weekend. That would hold my evening together.

CHAPTER
TWO

Somehow Alan Slater got to my favorite armchair after dinner so I had to take the sofa, next to Joan. Now I had nowhere to put my cigarettes and lighter, no wide expanse of knobbly tweed arm to rest my glass on. Still, Alan wasn't a bad guy; thick-skinned, as I imagine insurance agents have to be, and proud as a camel of his new car, but amicable and interesting.

Sarah smiled a nervous hostess smile and asked what they would like: Scotch, gin? I went to give her a hand. "You do Joan's gin and tonic," she said, "and don't move the tray. It's covering that burn mark you made."

"Yes, dear," I whispered back. "Silly Sarah so sublime, I'll do greasy Joan's gin and lime."

"Tonic! And it doesn't scan."

I watched her firm hands, tendons tightening as she lifted the full whisky bottle, nails whitening. Tendons tightening, nails whitening, that scanned if you said it properly; I tried. I looked round for the bottle

21

opener to de-cap Joan's tonic and Sarah passed it over. She looked straight into my eyes and our hands touched and my stomach bucked as it had done the first time. "Hey," I said softly. "I really fancy you, ma'am."

She cut off a giggle and turned to our guests with full hands and a smile that should have been for me. "Enough soda, Alan?"

"Just right, ta." His voice still has the habits of the North though the accent is all but smothered by newsreader English. I handed Joan her glass and bottle.

"Thank you, Joshua." She made full use of her good teeth in her smile. "You've made my horoscope come true. It said a tall, dark man would give me something I appreciated."

"And that could cover a multitude of sins," added Alan, with a smile both affectionate and vicious. I wondered how hard he had to work to keep his wife contented. "You can't really believe in that stuff. Some poor little office lad jotting down the forecasts between running errands and making tea?"

"Give it a rest," said Joan. "We all know the daily papers give us so much eyewash, but the people who really study the subject, like that Kevin Bastedo in Kew, they know more than you'd care to admit."

Alan wobbled his Adam's apple frantically, trying to swallow the whisky before he laughed. "Kevin Bastedo in Kew! Some creepy little poof from Putney, I wouldn't wonder. I bet he took you for a right Charlie!"

"You went to him?" interrupted Sarah. "Oh, Joan, tell us what he said!" I sipped my straight Scotch and lit a cigarette, old thoughts rising. Aunt Gale has always followed the advice of fortune-tellers and believed avidly in the tea leaves, all much to my father's amusement when he was alive. "You mark my words," she would say when he laughed, and wagging a strict, unfunny finger at him. I am not sure that I have inherited either my father's or Aunt Gale's attitude. There are times when coincidences frighten me because they haven't the texture of coincidence. I watched Sarah listening to Joan.

"Well, he wasn't a poof, you can take it from me," she paused to drop a scathing glance at Alan and I could see the heavy wrinkles beneath the blue eyeshadow. They fell into place so easily she must have used the look a thousand times before. "He was tall and distinguished and very well dressed like someone in the City. Not that I'd have trusted him with the lights out. He kept his hands nice, I can always tell. Still, he knew his business. He took my birthdate, and palm prints with this thick black ink on a roller—terrible stuff to get off. You have to use a special green soap that stinks like cats. He gave me a full reading."

Sarah stood up to refill the glasses and Joan interrupted herself to finish her gin with a practiced throw. "What did he tell you?" Sarah pressed.

"Oh, lots of things, past, present, and future. He said my life would remain on an even keel for quite a while but that I must be careful about money."

"Now I agree with that," Alan nodded emphatically. "Especially when it's my money. Obviously a poof after my own heart."

"Shut up. He told me I have one child, a son, that's Donald, and about my operation last year."

"He probably plays golf with the surgeon who did it," Alan retorted. "How much did that cost?"

"None of your bloody business," snapped Joan.

Sarah said, "Josh, Joan can read hands. She did mine

23

the other day; she's very good." I sensed what was coming and wondered why she wanted it.

Alan said, "Then what did you go spending my hard-earned cash on Kevin Bastard for?" He gazed incredulously from face to face, expecting agreement.

"It wasn't your money! And I can't read my own hand, never could. I'm biased."

"You'll be more than biased if you go on putting gin away at that rate. Don't give her any more, Sarah love. She'll get morbid." Sarah hesitated, the gin bottle in her hand, and I stepped into the embarrassment by turning to Joan as she was about to reply and holding out my right hand, palm upward.

"You'd better look," I said. "Sarah's smiles will make my life a misery if I refuse." Joan gave an upward glance that women have used since Eve and took my hand on her lap. I could feel the heat of her wide thigh and caught Sarah's eye to wink, but she was only interested in Joan's words.

"Mmm, nice hands. You're a sensitive type, long fingers and palms. Impulsive thumbs, though. What's your sign?"

"A rusty scalpel rampant under two pound signs flanked by a black cat named Sarah and a shield bearing the motto, 'Thou shalt not do thy thing.'" My wife's eyes burned the side of my face.

"Scorpio," she said, abruptly.

"Ah, yes." Joan took a firmer grip. "A water sign, deep, reflecting others' moods. A dreamer, idealistic, committed, very determined but prone to depression; very practical in some ways."

I laughed. "Sarah, you have a very long tongue."

"I didn't tell her, Josh. She knows from your sign." Joan went on looking, murmuring.

"Your hand says you are trusting and ambitious. People might let you down, Josh. Your heart line is long and unbroken; you will marry only once."

"There you are, my sweetness. I'll never desert you for any of my mistresses, no matter how hard they beg." Sarah tut-tutted at me. I don't think she believes a word I say. She simply makes up her own mind, presumably on what I do rather than say. Suddenly Joan dropped my hand and picked up the glass Sarah had refilled.

"That's all," she said.

"Oh, come on, Joan," Sarah sat down with her drink on the arm of the sofa, leaning against me to reaffirm her claim. "You told me more than that."

"Okay, his heart often rules his head, he will have a —have children, and he must watch his health. That's all I can say." She knocked back her gin and put the glass aside. "I'm not that good, you know." She smiled a bright, false smile.

"You got life insurance?" Alan inquired loudly. Sarah jumped and a strange, shocked look colored her gray lamps. I touched her hand and she smiled down at me, hiding behind her curtain smile. I grinned back quickly. Oh Sarah, what came into your mind? What horror crossed it then like a shadow? What rare two and two made four and shook your being? She touched her lips to my frown.

"No," she said to Alan. "Should we have? I loathe insurance on principle."

"Now, now. Think a bit. What would you do if something unforeseen happened to Joshua? What would you live on?"

"My wits," said Sarah. "If I wanted to, and I wouldn't. There are more things in life than money,

25

romantic and old-fashioned as the idea might be. I'd just live and die and go on round until I found him again."

"Uh?" Alan's thick eyebrows knitted and Joan wired him to be quiet. "Oh, uh, you believe in life after death, all that sort of mystic thing, um? Well, we're all Christians but . . . "

I smiled. "My wife has various pet theories," I said kindly, and I'm afraid the kindness was faintly derogatory.

"Which Josh doesn't understand because he doesn't know what they are," added Sarah. "He smiles and pats my head."

"Typical bloody man," inserted Joan. "What do you believe, Sarah?"

"It's difficult to explain simply. You could call me a fatalist. The difference is that I think we have more than one chance at life. It's not a new idea. When I first met Josh I felt I had known him before, long ago, many times. I think we'll always be destined to meet again, everywhere. That part is very simple."

"How did we get to this from insurance?" said Alan.

Joan leaned forward to help herself from the gin bottle, her face a disc of concentration. She even forgot to silence Alan. She spoke with assertion and intensity. The gin was at work. "But could it be you're kidding yourself, Sarah? I mean, would you remember, even if it were possible to—to go round again? If you didn't, it wouldn't mean a thing."

Sarah's eyes were full of private knowing. "I remember," she said. "I remember." Sometimes I envy that tranquility, even if it is homemade, just to fend off the world.

"I think it might be a good idea to get myself insured," I said. "What's the premium, Alan?"

"No, Josh. Not for me."

"Yes, Sarah, for you. Look what happened to Dad's money just because he thought he'd be a British citizen next year, and next year; and next year was too late. Alan?"

"Uh?" I think he'd been working at mental arithmetic. "Oh, we have various policies, various premiums. There's a very good one just come out called the 'Anyman,' or—"

"Not now, Al." Joan had seen Sarah's bored, irritated face. "Make a proper appointment for your business."

"Tomorrow?" Alan nodded encouragingly, his bluff, salesman's cheeks glowing with eagerness. He has short, wide graspy hands with black hair on their backs, lush as spring grass, and they fastened on my chair arms.

"No. We're going away for the weekend." Sarah glanced sharply at me. "Come round on Monday evening," I said, returning her gaze. "About eight." Sarah frowned. "And now, would you care for a last drink?" My wife grimaced at my bad manners, a small threat pursing her lips. Joan looked hungrily at the gin bottle, now half empty, but Alan stood up and pulled her to her feet.

"Come along, Jo. I expect these good people have to be up early in the morning. See you Monday."

When they had gone Sarah banged out to the kitchen to wash dishes and I settled myself into my chair and lit a cigarette to go with the nightcap. The seat felt funny; it always does after a stranger sits in it and I have to fidget it right again. The room was warm, softly lit by a pair of Victorian oil lamps converted to electricity by Sarah, who has a knack for doing that sort of thing. The brass gave out its own light. The sofa is brown leather with a sheepskin seat,

27

a wedding present from Sarah's Uncle George. It has wooden feet and weighs a ton, but it is good and luxurious and cosy for two when we lie on it in the long winter evenings to watch TV. The electric fire in the grate was humming through its three kilowatts; the framed photograph of Sur, my big, silly mongrel dead ten years now, faced me from the mantelpiece. Loving as a woman, old Sur had been, big and orange-colored and soft, with adoration naked in his bright brown eyes. Dogs give more than they take, and that's the way to be. I need you now, old Sur, but what and why . . . I have a good job, good prospects if I persevere, good health, good teeth, a good home. And Sarah, who can be delightfully bad. If I hadn't Sarah I'd have no need of the rest. If I hadn't Sarah, who else would matter, who on earth would want me? Marker? Huh! The big joke. Marker wouldn't notice my passing after five minutes. Writ upon water I'd be. The students? Huh, again. A computer could fill them full of facts on the conveyor belt. stick the little lids on their little cardboard knowledge boxes and seal them with a strip marked "Course completed." They could even have a Christmas variety with holly and reindeer. But if I were to go back into general practice again . . . Now that's not fair, that shouldn't have popped up even in thought words. that was only a ghost idea with no business materializing. No. Sarah wants a house, her own centrally heated place. She would deny it, has done so vehemently, but I saw her eyes when we went to Marker's wedding anniversary party last month. Those delightful thin radiators, that spacious staircase, the four bedrooms and gold Axminster. Her eyes had swamped her face in admiration. Be secure, Joshua Steel, be secure. In this country a practice can be too risky.

Sarah came in frowning, looking for glasses.

"Was I rude to them, Boo? Did I do wrong?"

"Yes, Joshua." A sure sign of annoyance, "Joshua" and her bland expression. Her hands moved quickly. "I wouldn't mind, but you lied about the weekend and they knew you did."

"Ah, but there you're wrong. Come and sit on my knee and forgive me for pretending to lie."

She came over slowly, kicking her shoes off on the hearthrug. "Do you mean it? A surprise?"

"A surprise. Tomorrow morning we will call Aunt Gale and tell her we'll be down for the weekend. Okay? It'll only take three hours or so." I pulled her into the chair with me and she wriggled comfortable.

"That's impertinent, Josh. She might not want us. She might be busy. You know Aunt Gale, always out being charitable somewhere."

"It'll be okay, I predict it. She'll be charitable to us and love it. We haven't seen her in six months. Remember the house? Warm as summer and toast for tea and that gigantic feline mammal that hits you like an affectionate lion."

"And your old room under the roof."

I turned in the chair so we faced and dropped my head back to focus. How did you know? "Yeah, my old room. I never told you."

"No. You didn't show it much either. Oh, I hope we can go. You've convinced me now. Time for bed, my lovely man. Finish your drink while I switch off the fire." She struggled out of the chair, entangling our legs. "Ow! Josh, let go, you're breaking my shin!"

"Come back here."

"All right." She fell across me, a hand to each side of my face. "I submit. What else can I do when you're such an impish bully." She examined my face closely.

29

"Did you know you've got a new line? Parallel to that dimple. You're the only man I ever met with one dimple in his cheek, you know that?"

"I know it; the bane of my life. Aunt Gale said it was cute and Dad teased me about it until I was fifteen."

"What happened then?"

"Girlfriends."

"Ah, we women see beauty where men don't, or can't."

"Nonsense, child. Who have all the great painters been?"

"You've fallen for a great painter then?" She laughed as I grabbed and tickled; squirming, sinuous, soft cat Sarah. Then she relaxed and held on tightly. "Josh, don't leave me."

"What a bunch of contradictions you are. Did it feel as if I wanted to?"

"No . . . I just remembered how it felt to be lonely. Like your cold feet on my back. Let's go to bed."

Unusually, Sarah went to sleep with her head on my shoulder and her arm across my chest, her fingers tucked secretively between my body and my arm. Normally she lies a little apart, trailing a foot or elbow to be sure I am there. Whenever I get out of bed in the night she knows immediately. I don't think she wakes but her breathing becomes silent; her eyelids like smooth halves of nutshells stay closed and when I return she never stirs or speaks, but I'm sure she knows. Night is her private time, not to be intruded upon, but this night was special and different and I didn't know why, though it was nice to feel the warmth of her body along mine and the coolness of her toes on my instep.

The moonlight cut the bed in two, easing between

the curtains. Tomorrow would be fine and beautiful. How long could such rosy anticipations last? For our children, for theirs? But even without Sarah to remind me, I drove away the thought and fought for sleep.

The Morgan considered the day suitable for a long drive and Aunt Gale, even at eight A.M., enthused over the prospect of seeing us again after so long, too, too long. The weather consented to join the fun by producing a crisp apple and cellophane morning in blue and white with shiny edges on the office blocks and palest gold in the window panes. Even the London trees stood tall and proud despite near-winter nakedness. Early people walked briskly and breathed deep of the diluted, stinging air, their clothes brighter, their forms deeper and more real, the gold in their eyes, too. Everywhere I felt the beauty of life, even in its hibernation, and it made me angry. Why should we let it be destroyed? When we can still feel it, appreciate it, why let it go? Who in his right mind could pour smoke into a clean, sweet morning, but that huge diesel ahead hammered out darkest gray behind it and left a smell like hell. When I commented on it to Sarah, she said, "Well, you're driving a car, aren't you?" Then I was angry again and amused and flattened.

"Did you mean it about the insurance?" Sarah watched the truck drop behind and her voice was sugar-soft, its most dangerous.

I threw a quick look at her face and knew the small tilt of one lip against the other meant she wanted her own way. Sarah, Fairah, you give yourself away, and I suspect you know it. "No arguments today, flower child. It's too beautiful."

"Who's arguing?"

"We will be if you don't drop it. Light me a cigarette, honey."

"Don't call me honey!"

"All right! Okay! If you want to row, let's have one and get it over before we reach Gale's."

"What about, Josh?" Her innocence was genuine, to an untrained ear. "I'd hate you to upset Gale. You know how you sulk when we row. For hours at a time."

"I do not sulk!"

"You do." She lit a cigarette and placed it between my fingers. "You're doing it now. On such a lovely day, too." Laughter bubbled under her voice like a submerged spring.

"I'm not!"

"Yes, you are, Joshua lemon squash." She tugged my hair gently. "Joshua, Joshua, I could take a walk on that bottom lip." Her laughter broke with mine. "Oh, Christ, that grin, that sweet, sweet grin!"

The sun sailed up slowly, a giant kite held by invisible strings, and the singing surface of the motorway shone below it. I saw a signpost. "Hey, Sarah, shall we go and look at the Severn Bridge? I haven't seen it since it opened and it's quite a beauty. It'll remind me of the Golden Gate. Shall we?"

She nodded. "Can we see it without crossing it?"

"I should think so. Keep your eyes open for a turn off to go down beside the river." I eased off the throttle and the Morgan quieted. I felt her sigh as her pistons slowed, her tappets eased, her heavy crankshaft dropped its revs. She is an old lady and likes a rest. We found a road and ran immediately from one of man's latest achievements in the way of transport to one of his earliest. The narrow country lanes still followed the contortions of old farm tracks, made

when people went round things, not through them,
and the drone of traffic faded into the calls of blackbirds and thrushes. It seemed an intrusion to bring a
car this way at all; but that was false, a myth. These
local folks had big noisy tractors and Daimlers for
Sundays, they were part of the real world too, the
same one as mine. They escaped to the bright lights
of the cities when they could, just as we escaped to
the quiet and the darkness where the stars are visible
and the earth smells of earth.

The road came to an end in a ragged pool of grass
and gravel under a few tall trees and our horizon
was bounded by a shelving bank ahead, a high stone
wall to the right and a drab, forgotten shack of a
boathouse on our left. On a short, rotting post some
hand had tacked a sign with a pointed end, *To the
River*. We got out of the car silently, moving round
the front and coming together below the bank. "Let's
discover a new world," I said, taking Sarah's hand.
"Let's peep over the edge." I pulled her up the slope,
the grass still crackly and slippery underfoot, untouched by the sun. The tarmac path at the top was
wet with thin dew puddles. Away to the right the
suspension bridge dived across the estuary in a perfect curve, incongruous and gleaming.

Sarah tired of its austerity quickly. "I'm cold," she
said, looping her arm through mine. "Shall we walk
along there?" She pointed to our left where the path
followed the top of a stone-built retaining wall with
its feet in the river mud to an outcrop of uneven turf
that ran down to the water's edge. We moved along
slowly.

"That's Newport across there." I pointed at the
dark gray-green hills across the estuary. "Hey, look
at that water!" The wide river was palest buff and

33

shiny steel under the sun's gentle hammer and flowed a hundred ways at once over the submerged banks of silt, some of which showed their backs like encrusted, petrified whales. The colors darkened, deepened, brightened, faded as the river ran. "It's just like that dress you have, Sarah. The one with the sleeves I like. It shimmers just that way."

She nodded. "I don't think I'd like to live there," she said. A dismal concrete cottage stood on the inland side of the wall, below river level, with tough too-green grass struggling quietly to uproot the foundations. Pinned to the door was a *For Sale* sign so old I had to screw up my eyes to read the faint yellow print.

"Poor lonely little house. I guess others must share your opinion. It must have rising, falling, and every other kind of damp."

Our footsteps echoed flatly on the path and disturbed no one. We could have been the last two people on earth. I stopped. "Oh you sickening bastards! Look what they're doing, Sarah." Way ahead, a couple of miles down the river, the pencil stacks of a chemical plant grew out of the distant haze. One trailed a streamer of acrid orange, the other a pennant of yellow-green. "Look at the colors! You can smell them from here. That can't be innocent. When I was a kid that place didn't exist."

"Let's go down by the water," said Sarah.

We climbed down to the muddy turf and found it littered with cigarette butts, strands of barbed wire, empty bottles from some nighttime drinker's pocket, plastic trash, and two dead rats. It had looked so pleasant from afar; now I shuddered. "All the world's a dustbin." I found a dry stone above the water line and sat down, opening a new pack of cigarettes. I rolled the wrapping into a small ball and dropped it in my pocket.

Sarah stood before me, looking about. "Josh, I don't like it here. It's surrealistic, all right on the surface until you look deeper. It's as if the whole place has a disease it's keeping hidden, only one or two ulcers are breaking out and the skin is sloughing in patches. I don't like it. It's threatening somehow."

I glanced up at her. You can't tell a woman, you have to let her feel it for herself. "Listen," I said.

She did, with her eyes. "I can't hear a thing."

"No. No birds. No seagulls, not even a sparrow. It's dying, Sarah." I stood and stepped from stone to stone to the water's edge. The river eased past, clear and black and empty. I ran my fingers in it over the rock at my feet. There was no soft green slime, no estuary seaweed. I wiped my fingers on the inside lining of my coat pocket and wondered whether the drops might burn the material so that at some future time the money would fall through the hole. One of our technicians has a lab coat like that, all ragged pockets where she wipes off the acid. What's the point? A voice, dismal and my own, came from deep inside where I keep my loneliness. Why rush and fight and procreate to inherit the debris of the rushing and fighting and procreating? Too late, said a colder voice. Too late here, too late back in North America, far, far too late.

Sarah came close with wobbly steps, her arms outstretched for balance, and fell against me, sharing my stone. "Josh. Josh, it can't really die, can it? Not just because of that plant down there and all its brothers, Josh? Listen, believing defeat is wrong. I can't explain. If you think it's inevitable, it will be."

I spoke into her brown hair. "If you don't think

35

about it at all, it will still be inevitable. If I hadn't met you, all I'd have would be this; the earth and the trees, the birds. Now look at it. It's shaming, Sarah. I couldn't have lived with it."

"Don't! You sound like Geoff."

Geoff! Less than two years ago and I'd forgotten already. Forgotten with the part of my mind that lives in the real world. Dear cousin Geoff who couldn't cope either and found only one way out. A snapshot image of a young kid with a laughing face and tragic eyes chasing old Darcy the dog round the California garden, his shirt hanging out like it always did; never could keep a shirt tucked in. And another, with older, wilder eyes, fighting for freedom in any way he could, shoulder to shoulder with students, shouting from some campus dais for compassion, leading crusades against injustice. "It beat him," I said. "I didn't realize you knew."

"I only met him those four days when he came over, but he had an aura, Josh. A kind of mercurial un-reality, as if he wasn't quite human, half a ghost al-ready. Or perhaps he was too human and the rest of us are half plastic."

"That's interesting, goose-bump. Maybe someone should have told him that before he shot himself."

"Don't be bitter. That's when you're most like him. Not mean bitter but sad bitter. It makes me cold." Her forehead had the crisscross look it always has when she's backing away.

"Okay, petal, I'm sorry. At least the sun is still shining. Come on, let's leave the river to rot in peace. It was supposed to be a good weekend." I smiled and she smiled back quickly. "Race you to the car?"

"No. No, I want to walk quietly with my husband

and hold his hand and tell him how incredible I think he is."

What man could ask for more. I shivered happily. "Talk on, child of the moon, talk on."

Creosote and roses, that is Aunt Gale's house smell. The garden fence is black and thin with the golden oil of thirty years. The knots have dehydrated and fallen out so each plank has a peephole or two, and though the wood is sound it has shrunk and warped and stands like a row of crooked teeth. Behind and over the fence trail the roses, still with a few late blooms browned at the edges by last night's frost, still with the full perfume of summer lodged faintly between the leaves and spiked on the thorns. When I was small, the fence and the roses were tall, tall as my father who trained and molded the rambling bushes as he would set and straighten and bind a broken bone. The scent was heavy then, the ancient real rose smell from great, near black blooms and small creamy flowers. The colors were right, too; no flash of Superstar, no burnished oranges with vermilion streaks, just rose colors. Velvet brown reds, brown pinks like a baby in the sun, palest bleached lemon yellows, and whites that were never snowy. Aunt Gale and my father believed in roses like a religion. The garden has vegetables all year round and daffodils in spring and snowdrops before anyone else in the district, but the roses are like people. You talk to them and hold their hands and breathe them in face to face.

I remembered how I had hated Somerfield for a whole month after we arrived. The locals talked strangely, and their cars, when they had them, were small and shabby without any chrome. The children called me Yankee in their wide country tones and giggled at my new American clothes. They'd never heard of jeans and wore short pants of gray serge or scratchy tweed. Their down-to-earth blend of innocence and evil quickly cut the pomposity out of me and it hurt at first, until I changed. Soon they were pestering bemused mothers for jeans like Joshua's. The roses had been a help until then, my father pottered among them just as he had in Westwood, puffing at his pipe, serious, absorbed. The world couldn't be too far wrong if Dad and his flowers were still the same in it.

Gale came out of the back door as Sarah got out of the car and I tugged our overnight bag from behind the seats. She ran down the path, calling our names. The wooden gate creaked on its hinges, it always has —with or without oil—and slammed shut behind her. She is a tall, well-boned woman of sixty who always wears expensive sweaters and skirts in precisely matching shades, and at her throat a string of pearls or a silver locket with my father's picture inside. Only her smile tells of our family relationship. Her face is long and narrow, her eyes myopic chips of sky, her forehead high and domed like that of cousin Geoff, who had been her sister's son.

"Sarah! How nice!" She kissed her cheek soundly. "And Josh!" A special, big hug despite the overnight bag. "I'm so glad you came. I was only wondering last night how you were, and this morning, lo and behold, here you are wanting to visit! Come in, it's cold out here. The frost caught the last of my flowers but they've been wonderful this year so I mustn't complain. Come along, Sarah, in you go." She fussed us up the path into the kitchen, warming us with hospitality.

For all her outward show of pleasant vagueness, Aunt Gale is a strong woman at heart, and terrible when crossed; maybe it comes from having been a schoolteacher. She is the only mother I have known and I have loved her for that strength and loved her for that rare, well-hidden temper since I was old enough to appreciate them. She has never tried to be my mother, she has always been Aunt Gale and a little distant, loving but scared of her own love in case it overwhelmed both of us and left Matthew out in the cold. On our wedding day she told Sarah, "I was so glad Matthew brought him to me. I never married, you see, so I was lucky not to miss looking after a family. Even though it wasn't the real thing, even though I had to pretend . . . "

Lunch was almost ready on the old gas cooker in the kitchen, the same cooker that has stood in the corner beside the sink unit for about seventeen years. Natural gas, self-ignitors, easy-clean burners can all come and go and leave Aunt Gale unimpressed. Every suggestion my father made about that gray, dangerous heap of cast iron was turned down flat or plain ignored. Once he'd called in the Council refuse collectors, arranged for delivery of a brand new, white machine, and attempted the switch while Gale was away for a day's shopping in Taunton. But she'd come back too early, rescued her precious old cooker, and refused to speak to him for a week. "It suits me," she always insisted. "I know it and it knows me." But Dad swore it deliberately stuck out one of its short, curved legs for him to stub his toe on whenever he passed.

I looked around the room for changes. "Where's the Christmas jar gone?" There was an empty space on the shelf above the freezer.

"Um? Oh yes. It was that awful Samson. He got up there, you know how he does from the windowsill, and tried to chase his tail round it. It made a dent in the refrigerator and broke all over the floor."

"It was a treasure trove at Christmas," I told Sarah. "Full of sweets and nuts and sugar mice and candy cigarettes."

After lunch Gale took Sarah away for a chat over cups of tea in the sitting room and left me to please myself. I had indigestion again so I went out to walk it off. The village had changed little in six months. A couple of new and very elegant houses had appeared where old Cider 'Arry had once lived in his tumble-down shack with the empties stacked outside the front door, but otherwise the place was the same. Old Cider 'Arry hadn't been old at all and was only forty-two when alcoholism brought its tortured end. We children had lived in mortal terror of him, though our fear was exaggerated when we talked of him and subdued when we met him in the street and stared at him, wondering how his face got so red and why his hair stood up straight like a scrubbing brush. He walked the village, a scarlet-cheeked clockwork doll, muttering to himself, his bleary eyes permanently surprised and vacant, his mouth open and dribbling slightly from one corner. He wore a brown coat that reached his ankles, tied round the waist with string, and no one had ever seen him dressed differently, summer or winter, snow or heatwave. In its one capacious pocket the gold-hatted, brown-necked lover, friend, ally, murderer always lay. He was a mystery man who peed in the hedgerows, an enigma, and nobody ever talked to him or he to them.

I learned years after he died that Harold James had once been the prosperous manager of a drapery store. He had married the pretty cashier who died of diphtheria shortly afterward. And Cider 'Arry had been born then. That was how the story went and that was all anyone knew. I passed the pristine houses standing on the spot where Harold James had drunk his sorrows into oblivion.

The smell of lemon thyme still pervades the lane that leads to the school. It is the smell that used to mean sticklebacks in jamjars, buttercups for shining under chins to see if you liked butter, glass marbles sharing pockets with white mice, bubblegum that somehow always got round to your ears, footballs that leaped over walls and had to be pleaded for from mean old Mr. Williams who ate boys for supper. Here in this narrow lane I had sworn eternal friendship with Jamie Brown who had a squint and a pet grass snake; just along under the ivy my father had belted me for copying Cider 'Arry and peeing against the wall; at the end by the rusty hinges where no gate has ever hung I had kissed Chrissie Bates on a dare for a prize conker and she had smelled of toast from her breakfast and mothballs from her winter coat.

The school was empty and Saturday-still, but the same innocuous things were written on the gray stone walls under the pointed arched windows. *Jane loves Paul. True.* Funny how I'd always believed it implicitly when the writer added *true*. I wanted to peep through the windows at my past, hear the echo of high voices, the scuffle of running, playtime feet, the sharp instructions of teachers, but I knew it had changed.

I'd seen before the rows of new yellow desks, the modern wall charts; the boxes of felt-tipped pens where there had been brass nibs and powder ink that never mixed properly and got up your sleeves.

What had changed in twenty years in me? Inside, the boy still exists, built upon and around, but still there. He sings a different song now, a song with some of the hope gone. I breathed in the tang of lemon thyme to dilute the uncertainty.

I followed the path behind the school alongside the playing fields where a rough football pitch was marked out in the lumpy turf. Makeshift posts stood at each end, drunken and netless. Football! What a strange game that had been. No pads, no body tackling. I was probably the only boy in the school who couldn't play football at nine years old. By ten I was pretty good. And rounders, a feeble baseball played by the girls who called the pitcher "bowler" and screamed when the ball got near them. I trod the gritty path that always scagged knees and palms unmercifully, and presumably still does, toward Vivian's shop.

It is a small, dark place of uncertain hygiene, a shop holding mysterious secrets in big brown jars and dusty black tins, a shop with no bottom to its stock, no limit to its variety, a drab, cheap Aladdin's cave with mice. The sign over the door has been repainted twice in twenty years, the same black on gray. Young Miss Vivian, who is seventy, looks exactly like old Mrs. Vivian, who ran the shop until her death twelve years ago. Mr. Vivian had been one of the shop mice, a pale, shadowy man who carried the heavy goods and never dared speak to the children when his wife and daughter were around. The Vivian women were tyrants with soft hearts and sharp tongues, tall gray hairstyles like coiled fiberglass and round glasses with black metal frames. No man could ever compete with them and in Miss Vivian's case none has tried. They were straight-backed, straight-laced, greedy, and patient with children who clutched burning coins, eyes penny big, not knowing what to choose. Should it be a twist of licorice, four chews for a penny, two gobstoppers, gum even though Mum said you mustn't, sherbet tubes with straws that always blocked solid, or pineapple rock that had to be broken with a minia-ture silver hammer and made your tongue sore it was so sharp. Over the years the Vivian women must have seen a million rounded, hungry eyes and taken a penny or two for each, their patience rewarded.

The brass bell jumped on its spring as I went in. A rubber mat on the floor still advertised Capstan cigarettes, almost worn through with eager feet; and the smell, the smell! Pictures you can conjure in your mind, but a smell is always new and brings its images independently. Stale cheese, chocolate and tobacco, Oxo cubes and matches, bleach and apples, mouse droppings and cat fur, old varnish, talcum powder, dirty windows and drains. A sweet, evocative, happy-sad combination. What confectionery fads there had been; Horlicks tablets one week, with all the kids rattling tins in their pockets, licorice allsorts the next and black mouths, tiger nuts, Wagon Wheels . . . I stood still in the empty shop. A skinny white cat with dirty fur watched me lazily from between yesterday's bread and an open tin of broken biscuits; the sweet jars were the same, orderly glass cylinders with round black lids; the cigarettes still ranged untidily on the shelf behind the wooden-drawered till.

The door to the house at the back had the same glass panels in night blue with white etching at the borders, though one pane was cracked. I had never peered into the cave beyond. Once I had been too short to see and now I did not want to, in case it was just an ordinary storeroom. The door opened and I looked away until it closed and Miss Vivian was behind the counter. She surveyed me from behind a beaky nose and a baggy gray cardigan, her bespectacled eyes black in the gloom. "Yes?" I asked for cigarettes and handed over a pound note. She put the pack on the counter beside the bags of crisps and gave me a sharp stare. "You're Steel, aren't you?"

I smiled. "Yes, Miss Vivian. How clever of you to remember."

She opened the till and counted change expertly. "No. You haven't changed much and I'm good at faces. Remember most of the children, going back fifty years now; though most of them pretend not to know me. Perhaps they think it's best to forget their childhood." I felt I might just have been caught with my hand in the aniseed balls again. The old lady gave me my change and went back into her murky interior.

The cellophane on the cigarettes stuck momentarily to the old wooden counter thick with the sticky, metallic grime of a couple of lifetimes.

The afternoon had mellowed just for an hour before winter sank its teeth in again. Yellow leaves on the narrow pavements lifted before my feet, golden autumn currency; the air held still and sighed a lukewarm breath to itself, a village dog sniffed his after-lunch round, excited by the movement of a leaf, the scent of a gatepost. It was good, had been good. All the bad parts had faded, tolerable with time, unimportant. Who cares now that Johnny Arthur punched my eye because, mindful of my father's profession, I had tried to operate on him with a penknife and had

cut a gash in his knee that had turned septic. If we
met now we'd laugh about it. Even the dreadful things
like setting fire to Mr. Williams' garden shed not
knowing that the dog was inside—they were in proportion now though my skin still creeps a little at the
memory. I had cried and gone to Old Williams with
two cigarettes in a pack stolen from Aunt Gale, and
offered to replace the dead mongrel with Sur as soon
as he came out of quarantine. The Welshman had
taken the cigarettes and refused the dog. "There are
always things we can't see and don't expect," he had
said, and I hadn't known what he meant. On my way
out of his gate a group of friends had passed, so I
had to pick up a stone and throw it back up the path
and swear, in case they suspected.

There was toast for tea, do-it-yourself on a toasting
fork over the lively coals, and the room was warm
and smelled of bread and Aunt Gale's favorite perfume. "It's lovely to be warm," said Sarah over her
teacup. "That flat is an icebox, Gale, it's a positive
string vest and costs us a fortune to heat."

"I hadn't noticed it was that bad," I said.

"That's because you spend all day in a centrally
heated building. Remember, I'm sitting at a type-
writer for hours on end. I can't walk about typing
theses, can I?"

"You work at home now, Sarah?" Aunt Gale put a
saucer of milk down for Samson, who dribbled as he
lapped.

"Josh's idea. I was quite happy at U.C.H. as a
medical secretary, but he doesn't like his lady wife
doing nine to five. I can earn quite a bit by copy
typing at home. Josh gets me clients, makes sure I
don't have time to laze around doing nothing."

It is an old discussion and every argument has been

dragged out and repeated at least twice. "Pass me the paper, Gale," I said.

"It's yesterday's. Mostly local news."

"It'll do." I turned the pages, my eyes catching words, "Killed in . . . " "Farmer sues motorist . . . " "Girls arrive for contest . . . " my ears listening to Gale.

"I thought for a moment, when you said you were at home, I thought you might—" her freckled fingers entwined with her pearls. "Oh, Sarah, I'm being extremely rude, it's none of my business."

"It is." Sarah smiled at her, the wide, reassuring grin that shows her gums. "And I'm not, unfortunately. We both want it but things don't always go the way you want them." I watched her over the paper, remembering only last month when she had been five days late and so unwillingly hopeful.

"I'm sorry, my dear." I think Gale understood. "But there's plenty of time yet. I guess you've checked there's nothing wrong?"

"Apparently not. According to our Ob.-Gyn. friend it's a trying-too-hard syndrome." She laughed suddenly. "Not that it isn't fun."

Aunt Gale smiled a little uncertainly. Naturally, being of a medical family one knew the facts, but joking about them?

"Excuse my wife," I said. "She's a wicked woman but she has her good points. Sarah, see if you can find my old copy of Omar Khayyam in the shelves there. I'd like to read it again."

"Unabridged? Edward Fitzgerald?"

"The very same."

"And I'm a wicked woman?"

I smiled behind my paper. Gale excused herself to do the washing up, refusing our help, and the room fell quiet and relaxed. I read remotely. It was yesterday's news anyway, appropriate, soporific reading. An advert caught my attention. I said, "My lady, listen to this. Somerfield Cottage Hospital wants a Registrar for their Children's Department. Permanent position, um . . . six beds . . . experience in E.N.T. Less money than I get now, but then it's cheaper to live here. Write, giving relevant details to the Secretary, Regional Hospital Board, et cetera . . . "

Sarah put away one book and pulled out another. The fire coughed as a coal slipped and Samson whimpered in his hearthrug dreams. A faint rattle of china came from the kitchen. It was an important moment. It had arrived without warning, I had spoken without preparation in hasty truth, and now I had to wait. Someone outside us both had walked in, dumped down a crossroads with big signs and gone again. I found myself breathing shallowly, aware of the pulse in my throat, the newsprint tacky under my fingers.

"It's nice down here, but very quiet," said Sarah, turning pages.

"Um? Yes, I suppose so. Not much life except the two pubs and the church hall."

She nodded to herself. "Oh, that's beautiful. Listen, Josh, 'I wonder by my troth, what thou, and I did, till we loved?' Isn't that just right, captured?"

"Donne," I said. " 'The Good-Morrow.' I knew it by heart when I was a kid."

"Yes. That piece that you quoted me once. Here it is. 'For love, all love of other sights controls, and makes one little room, an everywhere.' Remember that room? You were the first man I ever knew who recited poetry to me."

"It was a very moving moment, flower child. Very moving."

"Don't mock. I thought it was at the time. Then I discovered you were an ape with an angel's tongue."

"It worked though, didn't it?"

She made to throw the book at me but caught the movement half way. Two little puzzled lines showed between her eyebrows. "Is that true? Just a fancy line?"

"I married you three weeks later. What do you think?"

"I think I'd like to borrow this book."

My old room at the top of the house is too small for two to share but I went to look at it while Sarah bathed. It stands at the head of the second flight of stairs, stairs that creak unless you walk on the left side for two, the middle for four and the left again for six. I climbed without making a sound. In the room the ceiling slopes steeply on one side and the bed stands underneath the angle, sheltered like a cave. A desk, a mirror, and a heavy wardrobe that must have grown there make up the rest of the fittings. The walls are white, the curtains with brass rings, green and faded, long ago seconded from the sitting room.

I sat on the bed, minding my head. The collection of *Boy's Annuals* still shares a shelf with *British Birds*, *The Hobbit*, and Hilaire Belloc's *More Beasts for Worse Children*. I'd once had the *Bad Child's Book of Beasts* too, but it had been loaned or lost; or did I dream it? Maybe it was Geoff's. On the windowsill lies a collection of pebbles, argued for from holiday beaches on lapidary grounds and never touched since. They had looked so colorful when you wet them with spit, deep and magical, and they were to be polished in a cocoa tin with carborundum to look that way forever. They lie on the windowsill, uniformly gray, hiding their magic. I didn't touch them. The world has changed so much since then, not only because I am older, but of itself changed. Once you could rely on it, knowing it would last forever; now it seems to be looking to us to rely on. Sitting in this very bed I had once wanted to know, "When will I be grown up, Dad? Aunt Gale says I can't have a real gun till I'm grown up." The smell of pipe smoke was still in the air as my father puffed and thought, his head forward like an inquisitive bird's so he didn't hit it on the ceiling. I coaxed his reply from my memory; something about, if you're sure you're grown up, don't buy the gun . . . or was it the other way around?

Sarah called and I went downstairs, creaking the treads.

She lay awake longer than usual, the contentment of sleep far away. She listened to my breathing and I knew she was thinking hard, trying not to toss and turn, and tense because of the trying. "Josh?" she whispered, in case I was asleep.

"Yes, Sarah?" My voice was big and loud and strange in the darkness.

"Ssh! I thought you were sleep." She amazes me, she really does. "I've been thinking." I waited, not prompting. "Well, don't you want to know?"

"Aren't you going to tell me?"

"Yes. That job. I think you ought to apply for it."

After several happy nighttime seconds I rolled over and embraced my doubts. Do I want to, should I, what if it doesn't work out, all that sort of thing. "You think I should?"

"I think you need to."

CHAPTER
THREE

Monday was glassy wet, a day for going nowhere. Ugly clouds swam over London, impaling their bellies on the Post Office Tower and spilling sheets of cold rain from their insides. Josh watched it stream down the window of his office. The lights were on and the room was drab, the rows of books asleep on duty. He picked at the loose corner of the mock-leather desk top and wondered whether it had been a good idea to post that application yesterday.

The door of the office next to his opened, there was the umbrella thump, the coat hook groan, the "Morning, Joshua!" and suddenly he was filled with relief and a kind of wonderment. Of course he should have posted it, thank God he had posted it. He locked away the four pages of notes for his eleven o'clock lecture—Marker had been known to take such things away, scrawl comments in the margins, and return them with instructions on delivery—and quietly left the room. He put his head round the Main Office door. "I'll be down in the library if I'm wanted," he told the girls.

"Unless Doctor Marker wants me." Julie nodded and understood with her eyes.

On the second landing he remembered he had to see Bob Alice and changed direction, away from the peaceful call of the library to the tattered, hissing day outside. It was a very short dash across the greasy road to the hospital block, but he arrived panting and with muddy splashes up the back of his white coat. He took the lift to Hematology. The main lab was empty, hooded microscopes on the benches, racks of slides waiting to be stained, racks of stained slides waiting to be viewed, but there was a light on in Jock McCleary's office and a moving figure behind the frosted glass door with *Hematologist* written on it. Josh knocked and went in.

"Morning, Jock."

The Scotchman looked up from the papers on his tiny, crowded desk with a quick, unhappy frown. Then he smiled. "Hello, Joshua. Sit down. Bob said you'd be over."

Their relationship was only professional but Josh liked Jock McCleary more than some who were supposed to be friends. He was a tall, thin man with cow bones, bird eyes, and a voice like Dundee jam. His once sandy hair resembled a graying doormat and his large Adam's apple moved his woolly tie up and down as he spoke. "How's your wife? Sarah, isn't it."

"Fine. And yours?"

Jock nodded vaguely, lighting an inch of cigar salvaged from a full ashtray. It smelled like a burned-out coil. He watched Josh with bright slits through the smoke.

"Is Bob around?" asked Josh. "I left some blood with him on Friday; I've been feeling a bit off lately."

"Aye." Jock stared some more, the big bones of his forehead a portal for his eyes. "No, Bob's over in Bacteriology somewhere. I said if you came I'd tell you."

His voice was flat and careful and his eyes unhappy again. The words themselves were innocuous enough but some cold, unspoken thought hung in the air and Josh caught its shadow. He glanced around the office; the Gallenkamp calendar, the Baker microscope, the dented wastepaper bin, a stack of slide trays, the bleary-eyed window with the heavy reference books below it. All as usual, a bit untidy, a bit worn like Jock himself. "Tell me?" he said.

Jock scratched his head and stared into the smoldering end of his cigar. "How have you been feeling, Josh? More precisely."

Josh lit a cigarette for company. "Uh . . . well, I get very tired. I've had one or two bouts of pyrexia and dizziness and I get out of breath easily." He waved the cigarette. "This, and advancing age, I shouldn't wonder."

Jock nodded again. "You're a doctor," he said. "An M.D." He stopped and cleared his throat. "I think you'd better see the blood films." He moved a stack of papers and pulled the microscope to the middle of the table, then opened the desk drawer and laid out a tray of slides. As he watched him place the first slide and focus, Josh felt a tiny tremor of apprehension in the fingers holding his cigarette. He waited, and it was like waiting for a lift to drop. "You remember your hematology?" said Jock.

"Well enough," Josh said quietly.

"That's the Giemsa." Jock moved aside to let the younger man sit down, and his calm, sad voice went on as Josh refocused, "You'll see a high proportion of

53

granulocytes in all stages, mostly neutrophils, occasional basophils. Here's an LAP." Relentlessly he removed the first slide and replaced it with a second. "A typical picture, Joshua. Negative polymorphs." There was a short silence, then he added gently, "I'm sorry."

Josh stared unblinkingly down the eyepieces, seeing the cells with their contorted little nuclei and not seeing them, feeling sweat on his eyelids. The top of his mind was reeling off medical data and reaching conclusions like the trained machine it was; symptoms, blood picture, diagnosis ninety-nine percent certain. The middle part was incoherently crying out along with his sweating forehead and reaching lungs, "It's not true, it's a mistake, it can't happen to me, it's not true, it's a mistake . . . " And the deep, deep part had already known it long, long ago and had accepted, "I'm dying and Sarah will be alone; I'm dying."

The Scotsman saw his face pale slightly, his body tense, and that was all. "It's myeloid leukemia, Josh. I wish to God I didn't have to be the one . . . "

In a voice that sounded like his own but far above his head, Josh said, "There's no mistake? It is my blood?"

"Positively no mistake. I checked and double-checked. Here, have a cigarette." He found a box of Players in the drawer and offered them. Josh lit one steadily. "We did a WBC and a hemoglobin as well," Jock added. "They fit in. At the moment it's not too severe, Josh, it can be treated, you know. We've records of cases living several years with chemotherapy."

Several years. The middle part of Josh's mind exploded and flooded his head. He stood up quickly, breathing hard.

"I think you ought to see Mr. Ford," said Jock. "He can do a sternal marrow, recommend a course of treatment."

Josh went to the door. "Can you make an appointment?"

"Why, yes, of course. I'll do it now." He reached for the telephone.

"I'll come back later."

"But—"

"I'll come back later."

Jock McCleary wondered how the man could smile. He watched the door close softly, then picked up the phone and asked for Mr. Ford's secretary.

Josh crossed the road without looking and in complete safety. He wasn't aware that a bus might have knocked him down and wouldn't have cared if it had, but the narrow gully of a street was momentarily and inexplicably empty. He climbed the stairs one by one, each step the last, went to his office and exchanged his lab coat for his outdoor jacket. Before leaving he unlocked the desk drawer and took the sheets of lecture notes in to Marker.

"Would you give this for me, please," he said, and his voice was ordinary and breathless. He left, and Marker's words followed him, an unintelligible jumble.

The only awareness of Josh was inside his head. He knew with the top, analytical part of his mind that his feet were striking the pavement, that people were passing him facelessly, that the rain was soaking his shoulders and running down his neck from his hair. His scalp was cold and raindrops hit his wide eyes but he did not blink. His mouth was slightly open, still grasping for the breath that had gone so suddenly as he looked down the microscope. His hands were clenched in his pockets, the fingers of his right hand mangling an old theater ticket. All this he knew and did not know.

The shock, the personal shock and the terrible fear of what would happen, that was it. Or was it? What would Dad have said, felt? But Dad's picture would not come, nothing would come except I . . . I . . . I am dying . . . soon, and I don't want to. Oh, I'm so cold. All the others, all the people in the world, they don't know, they don't have to die by inches and live through the dying. They don't have to watch and wait for every new sign, cat and mouse, they don't feel each backward slide, gain an inch, lose two, until there are no more inches. Why do I have to know? Why me? Why did that bastard McCleary tell me? Deep breath, another, another. Rain in your eyes, that's all it is, rain in your eyes, lead-filled, sulphur-dipped London rain. There should always be something to laugh at in the worst situations and here it is—I've been concerned about that London rain and where am I now. Laughing. "Sarah!" A woman glanced at him haughtily, scared of the wild brown eyes and the muttered name, and hurried away.

Sarah . . . with the thought another, deeper consciousness arose. Lovely, quick Sarah. They weren't even thoughts now, just snatches of old times woven in a strange way with Donne's poetry, "Only our love hath no decay." No, but I have. I want to stay. "Remember the room, Josh?" One love letter on blue paper folded in his wallet; her absorbed expression when she watched television, and "Fool. Drive carefully!" Brown hair and gray headlamps, the curtain smile, and taking the world away to sleep behind the half nutshells of eyelids. "I'd live and die and go on round . . . " Sarah, Sarah, that's not so. We live and die and our sons go on round, not us, and there's an end. What will we do?

The rain had stopped and he found himself standing over a park bench in a strange other world that didn't exist. Tired, he sat. New thoughts came now, knife-edged thoughts of Steel. How long? With transfusions and chemotherapy, those devitalizing cytotoxins like methotrexate, how long, and in what condition? Each remission, how long? And how long before the remissions got shorter and shorter? And if the disease didn't get you first then the chemicals surely would. How much time, and time for what? Time for what, for Chrissake? Everyone is bound to die, it's not knowing when that makes all the difference, makes sense of living at all. Who in hell perpetrates death on me, *I* shall decide, me, Joshua Matthew Steel, I'll decide. A gun to my head, my time, my way, like Geoff. But Sarah . . .

The raindrops in his hair ran over his fingers, his knuckles were warm and wet against his face, the pulp of the theater ticket screwed in one palm; the bones of his elbows dug into the muscles of his thighs. His body was tingling and deep in its marrow malignant cells were forming, invading the blood, distending the spleen, he could feel them, see them behind his eyes.

A child ran past because running is always better than walking, even when you are going nowhere. There is the wind to race, the puddles to catch and banish with both feet, a tree to be touched before counting ten and dropping dead. The boy reached the tree, had a fight with it and won, dusted his cowboy palms on his suede chaps and pulled his holey gray

57

socks up to his rough knees. He had been aware of Josh as a potential audience, but now glancing up through his wet spaniel hair he saw that the man wasn't looking. A child's intuition told him that this was not the type to avoid, not one of the dirty pervs his Dad talked about, whatever they were, but an intriguing subject for study. He pulled his school cap over one eye, turned up his blazer trench coat collar, and shuffled with big spy's feet along the edge of the forbidden grass, eyes furtive and beady on the suspicious character with his head in his hands. At the crucial turn, just in front of the subject, James Bond slipped on the gutter leaves and sat down sharply and suddenly, the soft earth unpleasant through his thin school trousers. He used his best curse and stood up. He and Josh watched each other, the boy with cat insolence, pulling the muddy trousers away from his backside, the man with unfocused eyes.

The boy moved closer, brave Wyatt Earp with one hand hovering over a Colt .45 and the other holding his pants' seat. He stopped two feet from a sleeping Bengal tiger that could pounce and eat him head first with his legs sticking out unless he watched every single second.

"'Lo," he said.

The marble man moved his lips. "Hello."

There was a voice! A real cool voice with an American accent. The boy practiced it in his head for the next time they played *Star Trek*. Hello, hello, hello. "Hey, mister, are you American? Do you know Harry O or Starsky 'n 'Utch?"

The lips moved again but the eyes never wavered. "No, I don't."

"Mister, are you blind?" His Mum would have

belted him for that, but he had to know. The man's eyes were two empty gun barrels, invisible inside and dangerous.

Josh frowned them into vision. The boy was fair, freckled, and ugly, with a round nose and a broken incisor. "No, I can see."

"Are you crazy, then?" To say, I met a crazy man in the park, a real ravin' lunatic who sounded like a cowboy only different and he chased me all the way to Stepney, what a story!

"I don't think so. What do you think?"

He talked behind a frozen mask. The boy scratched a bite on his wrist and wanted to pick his nose but didn't. "I dunno. You sure look strange, Mister." It seemed only right to talk American to an American. "Kinda nutty, I guess. I thought you wuz blind."

"I can see," said Josh, quietly.

The boy picked up a packet of cigarettes from the ground beneath the bench and held them out, the first boy in the universe to feed a wild Bengal tiger by hand and live. "These yours?" The man turned his head by slow degrees and frowned at the boy.

"Yes," he said, not taking them. "Thank you."

"You're welcome." Was that what they said? He put them on the seat. "I've got a gun. Do you want to see it?"

The man moved his hand slowly toward the packet, as if he too were in the presence of a tiger, and his hair fell across his forehead and hid his frown. As he looked down to light a damp cigarette the boy drew, faster than the eye could see except it got stuck in his waistband, and Josh looked up along the plastic barrel of a cap pistol.

"Bang! Bang! You're dead!" said the boy.

* * *

The Museum Tavern had a blue sign with gold letters above a frosted window engraved with *Courage Beers*, and a green wall of china tiles stained by passing dogs. A fan blew the warm, beery breath of the interior out into the street. It was a pub Josh had never used though he'd passed it often enough. He'd always gone to the Blue Bowl because his colleagues used it. Why they ignored the Museum Tavern in favor of the Blue Bowl was hard to say. Both were typical oldish London pubs with the same glass window and the same smells. Now Josh wanted to know; now it seemed arrogant to promise himself to drop in one day, it seemed important to see the inside of a place that formed part of his working life.

He pushed through the heavy door, a cold, wet adventurer in search of the lost saloon. There was a long counter with toweling mats, a wrought-iron canopy with rows of suspended glasses, sticky bar-room carpet and plastic bench seats. The lighting was high and hard. An ordinary, ordinary pub, empty but for the man in shirt sleeves reading the *Daily Mirror* behind the counter. He glanced up as the door opened, then went on reading. Josh found some money and asked for whisky. The man's hand raised toward the glasses and groped until it fastened on one and brought it down. He finished his paragraph and reluctantly turned to the row of inverted bottles. The measure drained and he placed the glass on the bar, not quite slamming it.

"Thirty-three," he said. "Bloody awful day."

Josh nodded, his wet fingers sliding over coins as he counted. "Thanks." He took the drink and went to sit by the one-bar electric fire and watch his shoes steam. The whisky burned down with false comfort.

Drinking alcohol made one colder, but the illusion was happier than the reality. He emptied his glass, lit a cigarette, and went back to the bar. His feet were hot and wet now instead of cold and wet, and neither was pleasant.

"Double, please."

The barman looked up from his paper with more interest. "Keeps out the cold," he said, as the second shot went in. "Nothin' like a drop of whisky on a day like this."

Josh nodded, wanting to be alone. Then he changed his mind and sat on one of the bar stools. Being alone wasn't going to help. Let it all flow along behind the scenes and maybe something would resolve itself while the show went on out front. That's it, the show must go on, blah! blah! This work is vital, Joshua, blah! blah! "What are the headlines?" he asked, nodding at the newspaper.

The barman flicked pages with one hand while he searched about under the counter with the other. He found a mug and helped himself to a half of bitter, his forearm bulging as he pulled the pump. "Ninety-five killed in an air crash in Canada. Look," he turned the paper sideways. "Bloody dangerous things, airplanes, I always said so." The picture showed scattered wreckage in gray and black and white. It had nothing to do with people. It was a spreading jumble of unidentifiable bits.

"They say it's the safest form of transport," said Josh.

The barman drank some beer with his elbow level with his ear. "Don't believe it," he said with asperity, and belched softly. "Those things ain't safe. Never were, never will be. You should hear them out at Slough where my old mum lives—they've made her deaf. And they pollute everythin'. And look, ninety-five people killed, no chance of gettin' out like you'd have in a ship. Safest form of transport, my Aunt Fanny."

"I know. It's dreadful, but far more people are killed each year on the roads." Josh sipped his drink tiredly. *What am I saying, and why, for Chrissake?*

"Don't mean we have to have them though, does it? What good do they do me, mate? I've been in an airplane twice, went to Majorca on a package tour. What good are umpteen flights a day to America to me or half the people in the country? We only gets the bills to pay, mate, we can't afford the benefits." He finished his beer and pulled another, half angry, half philosophical.

"Does it matter?" said Josh almost to himself.

"Course it does. They'll get away with anythin' if no one speaks out against it. I got two kids, mate. I don't want them to grow up deaf from jets and blind from fumes. Course it matters."

"Supposing you had no children, supposing you were alone?"

The barman folded the paper and tucked it beneath the bar. "Dunno," he said thoughtfully. "I suppose I'd still mind for myself, but well . . . I'd probably make the best of it in case it didn't last long. But life ain't like that, mate. We've got what we've got, good or bad. Long as we don't hurt no one, like those bloody airplanes do."

Jock McCleary took Joshua down in the lift. Being naturally taciturn the Scot didn't search for words to say, but he wondered what Josh was thinking as he stood by his side. He smelled faintly of liquor, and who was to blame him. He looked unhappy and tired, and who was to blame him for that, either. Jock checked his watch. Two minutes to four, they wouldn't keep Bernard Ford waiting.

The consultant's office was spacious and contained a little-used desk with an onyx writing stand and a couch with a white sheet. Ford toyed with a pencil; he had been waiting for them. "This is the man I told you about," said Jock. "Doctor Steel; Mr. Ford. If you'll excuse me . . ." He left quickly.

The two men eyed each other silently. Ford was a distinguished man in more than his feted career. If an actor had been chosen to play the part of eminent consultant, he could have been no more impressive. His shock of prematurely white hair was arranged to perfection, his matching eyebrows jutted keenly above sympathetic eyes, and his voice when he spoke was as rich and soothing as honey. "Doctor Steel; sit down please." He pulled up a deep chair and Josh sat, watching Ford pace the room with long strides. "I'm very sorry to hear about this, Doctor Steel. McCleary has shown me the peripheral blood films and reports. It's an unfortunate thing to happen to a man of your age and prospects. However, as you probably know, there is much that can be done for leukemia sufferers these days. More perhaps than for other forms of cancer. I can't tell you not to worry," he smiled briefly with his eyes, "but I will assure you that we have every facility to help you and will use them as expertly as we can. Now, a houseman would normally take your past history, but I have an hour to spare, so . . . " He sat at his desk and took out some sheets of clinical notepaper. Josh saw and couldn't believe it. "Your full name?"

"Joshua Matthew Steel."

"Date of birth?"

"Eleven eleven forty-five."

"A.e.t.—thirty-one. Occupation?"

"Lecturer in Human Nutrition."

"Next of kin?"

"My wife, Sarah Helen . . . " *What will she say, what will she do? I can't break her heart, break my promise and leave her. What can I do? "Sorry?"*

"Your nationality?"

"Naturalized British." The questions went on. He could see his father sitting where Ford was sitting, with the same kind voice and illegible writing. He recited his symptoms accurately, then smiled as the consultant asked, "How do you feel now?"

"There's a hilarious TV program," said Josh, "in which one of the characters says 'my brain hurts.' It's very funny."

A brief silence, then Ford said, "Would you mind stripping for an examination? There's a gown in the changing room there." He watched Josh go and doodled on the clean blotter. It was always hard with colleagues who knew all about their own diseases. One couldn't encourage them like a child or a layman. There was so little to say except the stark truth and they knew that already. It was hard, too, to know how Steel was taking it; not knowing the man, he couldn't judge. He found he had written on the blotter, *? Problems of adjustment.* It might be worth following up. "On the couch, please," he said as Josh came back. He flicked the intercom switch and asked his secretary to send in Doctor Murphy. The houseman appeared at once and was introduced to Josh. "Take notes, please, Doctor," said Ford, handing over the incomplete sheets.

Josh stared at the ceiling, saying the words in his head as Ford's cool hands located the telltale facts. Spleen one and a half f.b. below costal margin and hard, liver down and palpable, less than one f.b. Nil else palpable. No glands as yet, CNS and heart NAD. Chest clinically clear. The stethoscope was cold. "Doctor Steel?"

"Mmm? I'm sorry, I was miles away."

"Doctor Murphy will take you down to the clinic for a sternal marrow and X-rays, you know the kind of thing. I'll see you again tomorrow at three if that's convenient, and we'll discuss a course of treatment. Yes? Good. Oh, and Doctor Murphy, will you give Doctor Steel some antibiotics?" He smiled the quick smile again. "Don't want you getting chest infections." He frowned suddenly. "Doctor Steel, is there anything I can do?"

Josh stopped. "Thank you. I presume you mean outside of medical help?"

"Outside my professional capacity, yes. Is there?"

"Yes. My wife mustn't know."

"My patients are treated in absolute confidence, of course, but Doctor, you'll find you have—"

"No. That's all I'm asking."

The consultant took in the weary, young-old face and knew it could stand no more argument now. Perhaps later. "All right," he said. "I'll see you tomorrow."

For the first time in his married life, Josh was afraid to go home. At five-thirty he was still at his desk, undecided. Marker put his head in, so Josh guessed he must have something more to say than the usual shouted "Good-night!" The short man had his coat on, and over his arm the umbrella with its tip dragging the floor. "I was rather disappointed that I had to give your lecture, Joshua," he said. "It was very short notice and very sparse notes." Marker always read his lectures word for word. "I hope it won't happen again."

"I'm sorry. Something important came up."

"I'm sure, but as I've reminded you before, personal matters cannot be permitted to take precedence over your work here. Lately you've become very lax; not that your work isn't satisfactory, but you're becoming unreliable and that's not a good thing in someone who could easily be head of this department one day. Think of it, Joshua. It would be a pity to ruin a promising career by letting outside matters interfere."

Josh laughed unintentionally. To his own ears it sounded harsh. Suppose I told you the truth, what would you say? We can't let outside matters interfere with our career? He laughed some more and it got out of hand. He could see Marker's little mouth moving, his piggy eyes disgusted behind his glasses, his long corduroy nails grasping the air, but he could hear nothing but his own laughter tearing the walls.

" . . . when you come to your senses. Good-night!" The door slammed.

"You stupid old bastard!" Josh choked and laughed again. "I won't be here long enough to get your job, let alone head of department, you bloody, insensitive bastard . . . " He choked again and his head was exploding and the hysteria turned to anguish with brutal abruptness and he couldn't control that either.

He became aware that his room and the others around it were silent. The clattering typewriters had stopped, and so had the rattle of glassware from the labs. He lifted his head from his arms and listened. Alone, Josh, like you'll be from here on in. A secret he could share with no one, not even Sarah. My God, Sarah! He reached for the phone and dialed his home number. While he waited for her to answer he rubbed his sleeve across his eyes and tried to think of something to say.

"Hello, goose. It's me."

"Josh, are you still at work?"

"Afraid so. Marker kept me." It wasn't exactly a lie.

"Are you coming home now? Josh, is anything wrong? You sound funny."

Half a dozen miles away and she still picked vibrations out of the air. Face to face, how would he manage? "No, my sweet, nothing much. I'm tired and busy. Can you give me an hour?"

"Of course. I'll wait dinner till you get here. Are you sure you're okay?"

"More or less, nothing to worry about. I'll tell you when I get there." He could see her frowning.

"Oh, Josh, have you forgotten Alan is coming round tonight to discuss insurance?"

Insurance! A whole new set of problems arose. "Uh, yes I had forgotten. Could you put him off?" Medicals, questions, false claims . . . please put him off and give me time.

Sarah chuckled. "You'll kill me for this, but I have already. Joan came round to lunch today and we talked about it and I, well, I told her to cancel the appointment. I'm sorry, Josh, but I loathe the whole idea. Are you mad at me?"

He sighed silently. "No, no, I'm not mad; but you are a contrary bitch at times, aren't you?"

"I'm sorry, Josh, really."

"See you in an hour. Bye." He hung up and sighed again. Leave them alone and they'll do what you want even when you don't know you want it. "I have a wonderful wife," he told the assembled books on the shelves. "Now, tell me, what would you do?" The deep, accepting part of his mind broke out and its presence was quieting. "If this is my fate, how do I use it? How

67

do I leave my Sarah happy? How can I blunt the pain and do I want to? To have someone mourn me terribly would be comforting. What a selfish idea! Should I tell her, just for that? Question, question, where are all the answers? I can't tell her, there's an answer. I can't tell her the truth and I can't just up and leave her without warning. I've got to leave her happy, or as near it as possible. Long as we don't hurt no one, wasn't that it?"

At home it was easy. There were other things to think of and the new shadow prowled behind and only raised its head when he let it. He was running away and he knew it. Dinner tasted good. Sarah looked good. Even the weather had changed and become warmer with the rain. Life had to be for savoring now.

After dinner he sat in his chair and smoked and watched television and even laughed at the funny bits, and the middle part of his mind was amazed that he could. He caught Sarah staring at him. "Have I grown horns, kitten?"

She went on staring and Josh prepared to lie, or at least bend the truth. "Your hair needs cutting," she said.

He laughed and stopped quickly. "Fetch the scissors then."

She went to the kitchen and brought an old newspaper, half an old cotton sheet—Sweeney's flag, she called it, and the kitchen shears.

"I hope you haven't been cutting up meat with those." He took the paper and spread it on the floor, then put one of the dining chairs on it.

"I have cleaned them and they're the sharpest pair I have. Take off your shirt or you'll get hairs down

68

your back and be itching all night." He did so with his back to her, then turned to take the sheet. "What's that plaster for on your chest?"

"Marker got so mad he bit me." He sat in the chair and Sarah began to snip.

"Your hair's gotten awfully long, Josh. It looks a mess when it's like this, it's not curly enough. What was Marker so mad about?"

Fragments of brown fell into his white lap and he moved his hands under the sheet to push them to the floor. "Usual thing, my love. Imagining that I should regard the department with the same degree of reverence that he does. Most of the time I can ignore him, this morning I couldn't. He had to take my lecture himself."

"I see. Put your head forward." She snipped some more. "You could do with a holiday. Get away from it for a while. Go fishing or something, like you used to do before we got married."

He turned to look at her and flinched away. "Mind my ear!"

"Don't jump about then." She turned his head back, tapping with the scissor blades.

"It was a strange thing for you to say. It sounded as if you wanted to get rid of me. Wouldn't you come too?"

"If you like. I just thought you might prefer to be alone."

"Stop cutting a moment!" He wriggled out of the chair and stood up, catching her hands.

"Don't, Josh! You're spreading hair all over the carpet."

"Bugger the carpet. What on earth gave you the idea that I would want to go on holiday alone, Sarah? I have no intention of doing such a thing."

"Well, all right! I'd like to come. I want to come. Now sit down."

He stared at her and couldn't read her face. Slowly he sat down and tucked the sheet around his neck. Somehow all the hairs had gotten to the inside. He fidgeted. "Sarah, what brought all this on?"

Snip, snip, she trimmed a sideburn level with his earlobe and he didn't dare move. "Uh? Oh, I thought you seemed fed up and Marker's been on your back and all that stuff about insurance. You were happier down at Gale's than you have been for ages, and I thought . . . I don't know. It does a man good to get away sometimes."

"That, sunshine, is just not worthy of you. It's not your style and it's not true. I like to be alone for an hour or two, not a week or two." Not now, especially not now. "Who's been influencing you? Ah, don't tell me. Insurance. I detect Joan's platitudinous little puddy behind that remark." He could not turn to look, but he knew her face was pink.

After a moment she said, "She's not stupid, Josh. She sensed you were unhappy and she knew from reading your hand."

"Sarah, that is arrant nonsense. She knows because she's nosey and keeps her eyes and ears open. But if she's talked you into believing it's your fault, I'll go round there and shut her big mouth!"

Sarah laughed and hugged his head with one hand and the scissors. "That's not you at all, Josh. You'd just be quietly rude and she wouldn't understand you. Don't worry." She combed a shower of cut hairs on to his shoulders and some fell on his nose and tickled. "Could we afford to have a holiday before Christmas, do you think?"

"Why not?" Why not except that his treatment

would start tomorrow and its duration was uncertain, and where would they go, and Marker wouldn't let him. He groaned and rubbed his nose angrily. "Marker. He hates people taking holidays. I have four weeks due to me but he makes such a fuss it's not worth asking. And we are busy until early December."

"I've finished now. Josh?" She prodded his shoulder with the comb. "Get up." He obeyed, and as she collected the newspaper, kneeling on the floor with her head down and her hair parted across her neck, she added, "I think you should ask him, busy or not. Early December would suit us and him."

"Nothing suits him."

"Then ask the Prof." She looked up. "I know I'm silly, but I think you need a break and it's partly my fault."

"Sarah, my darling, you talk the most delightful rubbish." He smiled at her.

"Put your shirt on and stop looking at me like that. Seriously, though," and her eyes were immediately round and important, "you will ask Marker, won't you?"

"I'll ask, my petkin, but I can tell you now what he'll say. 'We can't let outside matters interfere with this vital work, Joshua.'" His laugh sounded natural enough.

"Good morning!" shouted Josh at his books. "It's a beautiful morning, men. Washed and shiny, a beautiful morning for dying in confusion. Come along, lay down your pages in defense of learning, let me use your guts for student fodder." He ran a fingernail along the leather and paper spines and it sounded like soft machine gun fire. He selected two bound volumes of the *British Journal of Nutrition* and put them on the desk, flicking through the pages as he took off his coat. "Today we shall study the potato. Bring out your good old British spud. Let's see; we've separated and examined your constituents by chromatography, we've discussed your metabolism and studied your history. What shall we do with you now, you ugly, many-eyed tumor, um, tuber. Ah, what about the effects of fertilizers, insecticides, and water pollutants on your bulging little bodies? Yes." He hung his coat in the chair, picked up Sarah's pen and began to make notes on a clean sheet of foolscap. At first it was a pleasure to write neatly and roundly on unspoiled paper, then he made a mistake, crossed out, and it didn't matter any more.

Half against his will, the subject absorbed him. He got up, pulled a few more books out, his memory clicking, habit driving him even when his logic insisted it didn't matter any more and soon there were three pages of closely written, lucid information. He walked up and down followed by a trail of cigarette smoke, his frown in place, aware of nothing but the potato and its unhappy battle with the environment. His office door opened.

"Um, morning, Joshua. Fine morning."

Some of the ebullience had gone. All was not right in Doctor Marker's world. Josh half smiled in surprise at the overcoated and umbrellaed figure in the doorway. Had the sky turned purple, invaders arrived from Pluto, or the Welsh Nationalists gained Bexley? "Morning, Desmond." He couldn't stop the query in his voice.

"I wanted a word, please."

Josh decided it must be the Welsh Nationalists. "Can I do something?" He hesitated, wanting to continue his notes before the ideas stopped flowing.

"Uh—you seemed a little upset yesterday, Joshua, and I, well perhaps I wasn't entirely fair." He took off his glasses and polished them, though each lens was a perfect reflector of the morning window already, and his narrow forehead gleamed with embarrassment. "I think perhaps you could do with some time off, a short holiday. Get yourself fit and rested for next term. What d'you say, um?" His smile was a struggle, fought and lost. His eyes glinted shortsightedly and the polishing handkerchief fluttered like a flag in a gale.

Josh sat at his desk and stared unseeingly at the pages on potatoes. "It would be most welcome," he conceded, watching his fingers twine together. "If I can be spared. Sarah would appreciate it, too. We only had a week in June because of the symposium. That was a lot of hard work."

"Most of it fell on me, Joshua. I'm still not clear of reports, I've been up to my eyes for months. However, we can spare you for a week after end of term exams, providing you leave an address where I can contact you should you be needed." He nodded sternly to emphasize the conditions of surrender.

Josh grinned widely. A holiday? Under those terms? "Thank you, Desmond," he said quietly. "I'd hate to think I'd more or less forced you into letting me go simply because my temperamental presence is intolerable."

"What? Well, you always were temperamental, Joshua. It's an unfortunate trait. But I thought you should have a holiday."

"You did?"

"Yes, yes. Now I must press on with some work." He hurried out importantly.

Josh frowned at the door, then tried to pick up the

threads of pollution and potatoes. Perhaps the old bastard wasn't so bad after all.

Bernard Ford bunched up his impressive eyebrows at the younger man and ignored his bland smile. "I would like you to come in," he said.

Josh smiled wider. "But it's not necessary."

"Not essential, no, but methotrexate can be unpredictable stuff. You'll have a maintenance dose after initial intravenous treatment and with my luck we'll achieve a remission. But I'd like you in for twenty-four hours."

"Sorry."

There was a prolonged silence. Ford made and rubbed out fingerprints on the onyx writing stand. "I have to respect your wishes," he said after a time. "But I am your consultant."

"Yes. May I compromise? I promise to keep myself under close observation and report directly to you should I get adverse side effects."

Ford sighed. "All right. I can't force you. But may I ask a question? Why so tight-lipped, Doctor Steel? I understand your wife would be upset, anyone would, but that doesn't stop them knowing. Partners can help greatly, not only with the physical problems but by actually coming to grips with the situation. Women are a whole lot tougher than we give them credit for, their stamina can be extraordinary in crises. She's not an invalid, is she, your wife? Or mentally ill?"

Josh shook his head. "Since you ask, I don't know why she mustn't be told," he said. "I haven't had the inclination to find out, but there is a reason somewhere. When it shows up I'll let you know."

Ford smiled back. "She'll find out in the end," he

said. "But we'll leave it for now. It could be months before there's any real need for concern."

"For those few kind words, I thank you, Mr. Ford. Marker, my reader, has suggested I take a holiday. Will that suit?"

"When?"

"Early December, probably."

"Good. I'm glad he accepted the idea." Ford got up and went to the window. "It will be nice if this sort of weather holds. Where will you go?" He turned back to see Josh staring intently.

"What did you say?"

"Where will you go?"

"No, no. 'He accepted the idea'?"

Ford smiled, ruefully brief. "I can't resist running my patients' lives," he said. "Giving absolutely nothing away, of course, I tactfully suggested to your Doctor Marker on the phone last night that you were not entirely well you should be released for a week or two. Don't worry," he held up a large hand, "I said nothing more. He seemed concerned but we didn't discuss you. I hope you'll forgive me, but I thought you wouldn't consider asking on your own behalf."

"Crash!"

"I beg your pardon?"

"Just another illusion biting the dust. I thought sensitivity had at last blossomed in his heart. We live and learn." And that seemed a silly thing to say.

CHAPTER FOUR

"I've had a horrible thought!" Sarah stopped packing cold chicken and packets of crisps into her shopping basket. "Suppose this place doesn't exist. Remember that article in the paper about people who hire out nonexistent cottages. Oh dear, Josh, I hope it's not one of those."

"Have you seen my waders?"

"Josh, I'm saying something."

"I know, I'm ignoring it, silly Sarah. Finish packing our lunch and don't anticipate trouble. Must you always dilute your pleasures in advance?"

She put the thermos of coffee in. "Yes, I suppose I must. It's a defense. If it turns out all right I have double the happiness. That's silly, isn't it?"

"Yes. No. Where are my waders, Sarah?"

"In the broom cupboard. Is the car okay?"

I found the waders under the vacuum cleaner, flattened and dusty. Bending made me dizzy and I stood up quickly. Otherwise the treatment so far had been successful. I was better, my blood picture was good, I, we, the medical profession, had achieved a remission. I had a new, if slippery, handhold on life. "She's full of petrol and oil and water, her plugs and points are clean and I've even polished her."

"Liar. I did the elbow work. You only put the stuff on. It's nice, isn't it?" She looked up across the kitchen and smiled. "Exciting, like when I was a little girl and we went on holiday in the car. Dad did all the mechanical things and looked after his fishing tackle as you're doing, and Mum took a picnic and made sure we had all our clothes packed, and I got in everyone's way and wanted to take the cat and have the beach ball blown up before we left. It's not the same when you go abroad and have a taxi and an airplane. Today I can feel we are off to our country estate like rich people and the river you'll be fishing in will have big fat salmon for tea."

"Sarah bump, the game season is closed. But thanks for the thought. I'm going to try coarse fishing. Little Alfie, whom I abhor at times, kindly lent me his bait box and lures. People are surprising, aren't they?"

"That depends." Sarah poured milk into a plastic bottle and didn't spill a drop. She's like that.

"On what?"

"On what you expect them to be. Pass me that bag of sugar, please. Thanks. Well, go and pack your tackle, I'm almost ready. Oh, Josh, now I think it's going to be a good holiday. It feels happy already. It'll be time for us to think and plan and look ahead, won't it?"

"Yes."

Sarah frowned at me before she smiled. "Hurry," she said.

The cottage was there, where the advertisement in

the paper had said it would be, a gray outcrop at the base of a gray and green crag which was a mere bump beside the great swellings of Snowdonia. The river hurried down the hill into a pool like an eye in the earth watching the sky, then reluctantly slithered away toward the sea, only speeding where the narrow banks bunched it up like silk through a wedding ring. It was clean; river weed trailed in the currents, small fish reflected like pins and needles, the air held a sweet dampness above it as if only sheep breathed into it, and wood fires, and people like Sarah and me. The sky was high and white, misty with afternoon. If I needed tranquillity to think, I might find it here where there was no resemblance to London, to my daily environment, to the old Joshua who had been told he was condemned. Here, I might easily forget it. But I mustn't; that wasn't why I came. All those processes behind the scenes, all the strange swimming shapes in the murky aquarium I keep in my head, had to be brought out, looked at. Construction had to be done. But not yet, not quite yet.

"Tea, Josh!" My Sarah, in gray and blue, blended with the tiny house and the quiet landscape. They looked like a Seurat painting through the moist air, hazy yet distinct, a harmony of softest hues. For a moment that was real and this was dreaming. I was standing in some other dimension, looking through a telescope from a different world. Sarah was not calling me but a reflection, a ghost on her side of the mirror. Maybe it was the drugs, maybe not. "Come on, love! It's a funny old place with no locks on the doors and I've made some tea. Come and see."

She disappeared, seemed to fade rather than move, leaving her smile at the doorway like the Cheshire

cat. Who couldn't love Sarah, with her kind of magic?
I moved through the winter grass toward the cottage,
back to her side of the mirror, at least for a while.

"Can it be a second honeymoon, Josh? I always
wanted a honeymoon in a cottage with roses at the
door and an oil-paper tablecloth." My wife breathed
steam over her mug of tea.

"You're a dragon. When did we finish the last?"

"When you got the bill. There's nothing like a hotel
bill for bringing you down to earth. Poor Josh, it was
nice among the clouds, wasn't it?"

"It always is. All right, Aphrodite, it shall be our
first, second, and last honeymoon, all rolled together
for all time. We'll roam the countryside hand in hand,
feasting on berries and drinking spring water. We'll
run in slow motion through the meadows, leap from
rock to rock like mountain sheep, and at night . . . ah,
the still, breathing nights, my love, these will be our
voyages of love and delight."

"Fool. But I like you foolish. More tea?" She fetched
the chipped earthenware pot and poured milk from
the bottle. "Must it be our last honeymoon, too?"

"Perhaps it must. I may have no strength left afterwards. I may endure permanent flaccidity after a week
with you, sex pot. Be warned."

Sarah laughed, a different laugh from her amused
one. Brazen and provocative is Sarah, when she
chooses, and she says she chooses with infinite care. I
hope so. She loved a man once before I knew her, and
even now my soul feels a little heavy when I think of
it. I am not jealous, but from what she does not say I
know she gave all of herself without thought or cau-
tion and when he left he took most of her away. I
am my Sarah's second chance, last chance, and she
treats me with some of the reservation she learned.

Even I, and to me she is sun and moon, cannot pierce the thin armor she put on. All this, because she smiled at me in a dangerous way. "Come and see the rest of the place." She held out her hand and I took it.

When the description "two up, two down" is used, it isn't always accurate. Like the forty days and forty nights, it is a key phrase for the imagination. Our haven of peace for the coming week was the only true two up, two down I have ever been in. "Up" was one medium bedroom with the stairs guarded by black oak bannisters arriving in the middle of it, and a bathroom. "Down" was the kitchen into which the only door opened, and the parlor where the stairs began. Each room had a fireplace with a two-bar coal effect heater and each had a small square window set in the three-foot-thick wall.

"Like it?" said Sarah, bouncing on the double bed. "The geyser over the bath is a bit erratic. I tried it while you were eyeing that stream out there and trying to look like you think Isaak Walton might have looked."

"Your arrows of truth make my fantasies bleed. How did you know?"

"Try the bed, Josh. Will it creak, do you think?"

"Who will hear if it does? That unpronounceable village must be two miles away and we didn't pass another house on the way here."

"I just don't like creaky beds. Try it."

We sat one each side and bounced a bit, like self-conscious buyers in a Slumberland showroom. "I wonder how old Marker will manage without you," said Sarah.

I wished she had not spoken. I was less than a day free of Marker and all he stood for, free of the place where the biggest adventure had started. "He'll have to learn," I said, sitting still. "We all have to learn that we can't run the world the way we want it all the time."

"Just some of the time, like you and I now. I think we should all get a chance some of the time, with our own little worlds. Will Marker learn?" Sarah frightened me then. I'm sure she has a console in her head with telltales that wink when a vibration comes in and transforms it into what she calls her woman's intuition. "Would he learn to do without you, Josh?"

"The old, old tale, sweet flower. Adapt or die, and he has a strong instinct for self-preservation. If he missed me he'd never admit it to himself."

"Wouldn't you care what happened there if you left?"

"Not much. You can't buy loyalty and respect by paying wages. All you buy is time and work, anything else is a peak to be earned. Marker and I have no respect for each other. In fact I don't think he respects anyone. That would be a mark of servility. Listen, Sarah child, he's invading our holiday like poison gas. I don't want to talk about him or work."

"Oh. I thought you did."

"I'm going for a walk before dinner. Will you come?"

"No, I'm going to cook something special for our first night if that cooker will oblige. Did you bring some matches?" So rapidly could Sarah doff her siren hat and put on her Mrs. Beaton one. Women have a control never given to men.

"They're in the car. I'll fetch them."

There were roses round the door. I hadn't noticed the wandering stems because they merged with the stone, and the flowers had all gone, but roses there

were to make the honeymoon dream real. In the glove
compartment of the Morgan I found the large box of
matches and behind them, my small bottle of tablets.
I sat still for a while, staring at them, and my mind
was blank like black paper, with no thought wanting
to color it. On the box I read over and over *Olivers
Matches*. Sarah called my name.

"Coming!"

I swallowed two tablets, choking on their dry bitterness, and went to the kitchen. It was already warm
from the fire and spicy from dinner ingredients. Sarah
took the matches and lit the stove, flinching as the gas
popped. "Don't walk too far," she said. "You look
tired."

"The fresh air will be intoxicating."

"I hope it will put some color in your face. You're
very pale."

"Gazing upon your beauty reduces me to ashes, my
Lady of Shallot."

She laughed and kissed my chin. "Go and sing 'tirra
lirra' by the river, Sir Lancelot."

"Tirra lirra, tirra lirra, call me when it's time for
dinna."

"And abandon poetry at all costs," my loving bride
enjoined me as she shooed me out the door.

I did not walk far. There was no path beside the
stream and the hummocks of tough grass made the
going rough. Accustomed to being fit and able to walk
for miles, this blasted tiredness made me angry. Even
more frustrating was knowing it would never be
better; each day I would lose a little more. I sat and
smoked with my back against a skinny ash tree,
watching the river flow to the sea. The sun calls up
the water, the clouds surrender it to the mountains,

the rivers carry it back to the sea and the sun, and so on, round and round. The river has no consciousness, only direction and constancy. It always flows, it is always a river. I wished I were a river, unaware of beginning, unafraid of ending.

I crushed out my cigarette under my shoe and smoke rolled up my jeans like mist up a mountainside. Bernard Ford had advised me to give up smoking, but only halfheartedly, so we both knew it didn't matter too much.

As I listened to the quiet babble of the water and the distant repetitive gossip of sheep on the cold hillside, a sense of urgency filled me. I suppose it had been present all the time submerged in the dark tank of thoughts, but it popped out now, a big fat salmon of a feeling begging to be caught. I wanted it, needed it, but the bait was wrong, the hook barbless. I must find out what I was going to do before it was too late, but just now dinner would be ready and Sarah would be waiting.

In scrambling to my feet I caught my palm on a broken twig. It made a tiny ragged cut just below my thumb. I stared at it, memory creeping over my skull. What had Joan seen in my hand? Surely she couldn't have . . . Yet she had told only half my fortune, had Gypsy Rose Joan, and Alan had offered life insurance in almost the same breath. And my Sarah had heard it all with her crisscross frown on. Is there a pattern then, a way of things like the way of the sea, the rain and the river? I didn't know. There is so much I don't know and will never learn now. All the books never read, places unseen, people lost to me, wisdom never to be mine. That was the worst discovery. An intelligent man, I'm told, yet I could think of nothing of importance that I knew. Of philosophy, nothing. Of religion, an ill-defined little overlaid with the suspicion that in the end we are all destructible entities composed of indestructible atoms and that may be the only eternity. Of politics, nothing of the intricacies, only an observation of the results. Of love, nothing, because it may be different for all of us, or it may be self-interest after all. Of Joshua Steel, nothing, but I keep looking.

I wanted to see Sarah and talk nonsense with her and watch her smile, so I plodded toward the cottage that already said "home" in my mind, and the first star was prodding through the dusk as I arrived. It looked good up there, undimmed by yellow street lamps, brave and lonely and constant like the river.

I may have slept that night but I don't remember sleep, only a dazed half-awareness with my heart thudding fast, and being too hot, the pillow lumpy and the bed hard. A vague pain in my chest would not go and my thoughts raged uncontrolled, a good, leaping forest fire. The unfamiliar room grew strange shadows and the net curtain trembled in the draft as if a hand shook it. The silence was full and ominous after London's permanent animal purr; even Sarah's breathing was inaudible above my own rapid gasping. It has been my experience that thinking of old, tried pleasures can bring sleep. Ordinary things like stroking old Sur's yellow head and his floppy ears. Like cycling in Wellard woods above the village of Somerfield where I was brought up, with a tribe of shouting, excited children. Like drinking cold beer in the club in Benin, Nigeria, and swimming in the pool, half drunk, while the day hit ninety-eight. Like talking with my father in front of a good fire when he spoke of things I did not understand. He knew I didn't, but he knew I would, so he spoke.

Tonight, though, the pleasures kept backing away, refusing to be held and relived. Old Sur was a ghost and his coat was the wrong yellow, my father sat mute, the pool was ice cold. At five-thirty by the luminous travel clock beside the bed I sat up and shivered.

There was a small light above the hole for the stairs and I put it on, rather than blunder in the dark in search of my clothes. Sarah was asleep, I think, her mouth pouting into a smile. There is a rhyme about smiling in your sleep, something about having secrets locked in boxes in your head. That's my Sarah. She stirred as I finished dressing and her lashes fluttered.

"Are you all right, Josh?" She kept her nutshells closed.

"Yes, I'm okay; just can't sleep in a strange bed."

"Mmm. I can."

She turned over and fell fast asleep again. I'm sure she's half cat. I turned out the light and felt my way down to the kitchen where my old sheepskin jacket hung against the door. I found the torch we had brought, put on my jacket, and let myself out into the cold Welsh morning.

In the clean air I felt better, but I didn't know where to go. In one's own city or town one can walk familiar routes and see them differently because one is alone and it is night, but here everything was new. I set out along the lane by which we had come, feeling much as Christopher Columbus might have. He did not know if he would sail off the edge of the earth and I did not know if I would step off the edge of the world. It was that kind of night and I liked it.

My footsteps did not echo as they do in town, they fell sharp and died away immediately, absorbed by the low hedges. For a mile or so there was nothing to see in the long torch beam but the gray surface of the path and the dull green of the bordering grass. It was an ideal space into which to pour thoughts, a soft black uterus where embryonic decisions might form and grow and present themselves whole. Nothing was born though, only an idea that it was futile to make plans. I am not ready yet to decide; that was all I could think. The machinery that normally functions smoothly in a crisis had seized solid because it had never before been faced with a problem with no solution. I don't want to die. I don't want to die.

I turned from the lane into a rough track, just two ruts of bare earth with a strip of grass in the middle, and stopped in surprise. An animal with a rust brown coat and a long bushy tail stood a couple of yards from me, full in the torch beam. We stared at each other and he was plainly not frightened. For a moment the fox's eyes shone red above his elegant nose, then he slunk slowly through the hedge, continuing his predawn business. I have been told that my eyes shine red and perhaps because of it I felt I was the fox as he loped away; I could smell the night smells and feel the wet ground beneath my feet. "Good morning, Mr. Fox. Have you slain a rabbit with your teeth tonight, or sneaked a squawking bag of feathers from Farmer Davies' with the blood running over your paws, or preyed on the mice of the field? Good morning, Mr. Carnivore, who has to kill to live. Who has to kill to live, and that's the way of things."

The colors of dawn are quite different from those of sunset, and a Welsh dawn is as distinctive and separate from all other dawns as the Snowdonia hills are from the Swiss Alps or toffee is from bacon. As I fol-

lowed the cart track up a hillside, the sky ahead grew
pewter and the stars receded. When I put out the
torch there was almost enough light to walk by,
though it came from no fixed point and was as if an
opal lamp had come on behind the black cloth of the
sky. The path faded beside the remains of a dry
stone wall in whose shelter I sat out of a springing
breeze to light a cigarette and watch the sun come
up. Birds heralded its approach, sparrows with brash
fighting talk, blackbirds and thrushes with sweet,
mature reveilles. The stars went out, Romeo disap-
pearing for another day, then a broad yellow-white
band the color of Dad's roses lifted the clouds from
the horizon. The peace was unearthly and but for the
bird song to remind me of reality I could have been
anywhere in the universe, watching any star. I felt
big and clever and privileged. The clouds had pale
violet feet and blue-gray hair as they hurried back
over my head, fleeing the beetle and his burden, and
quite suddenly there was the sun, the first rays blinding my eyes.

I shrugged my coat round to get comfortable and
felt something hard and flat press against my hip. At
first I couldn't remember what the small green book
was, nor how it had gotten there, and I stared at it
stupidly. Then it came back. Sarah's borrowed poems
of John Donne which for some reason she had decided
to bring along at the last moment. I had put it in my
pocket and forgotten it. I flipped through the pages.

Somehow, reading love poetry at dawn on the top
of an obscure Welsh hill seemed an incredibly romantic thing to do, so, unabashed and even a little
proud, I did. I had never done so before, nor would
I again, so here was a new last chance opened. Telling

myself it was a last chance did not make me believe that, though I knew it was true. All of which sounds quite crazy . . .

I laughed aloud and quoted "The Sun Rising," and thought of Sarah at the end, then turned a page and my eyes caught the vaguely familiar words:

> Sweetest love, I do not go,
> For weariness of thee,
> Nor in hope the world can show
> A fitter love for me;
> But since that I
> Must die at last, 'tis best,
> To use myself in jest
> Thus by feign'd deaths to die.

I had to stop and put the book aside to light a cigarette. Once closed, it stayed closed, but it had already given an answer. Only glimpsed, but perfect in outline, was the solution for which I had been searching. The big fish had surfaced and the bait had been waiting—from Sarah's own hand. There must be a pattern, a system of patterns. It could not be that she had brought the book on a whim, that she had asked Joan and Alan round on a whim, that I had taken her to Gale's and discovered the Cottage Hospital job on a whim. There can't be that many coincidences. The plan was growing already, forming a solid house of bricks and mortar, and I knew it had been there all along. Sarah would be safe and happy. I would not leave a gaping hole in her life. Nothing could go wrong because the chain of circumstance had been set in motion and its own inertia would carry it along, and me with it, like the river.

I picked up the small green book and stroked its

cover as I walked down the hill in bright sunshine. I did not even wonder whether I would get the job. I knew I would.

The week was as blissful as such weeks can be. The fine weather held, I caught some fish, and Sarah lazed and wore a self-satisfied grin rather more often than usual. Although I enjoyed it all and we did the conventional things people are supposed to do on holiday, I was more than half occupied with my scheme and so eager to get it into action that the time spent in idleness seemed an interruption. Curious, when I knew there would never be such a week again.

On our last morning I lay awake beside Sarah, gazing at the trembling lace curtain as it brightened to gray and finally to white, thinking about Dad. He had died; we all die. He had died of a totally unexpected coronary thrombosis when he was sixty-two. There had never been a sign of illness in him before, he was tough and broad and not given to fat. We had no painful extended parting; one morning when I was home on leave from Nigeria he had gone off to the hospital where he was a consultant and he had not come back. By the time Gale and I reached his bedside he was already dead. I guess he would have preferred it that way. "Say good-bye and have done with it," he had said when I left for my year abroad. "I can see you much more closely when you've gone." He was right. I could see his face now, with the wide grin that was like mine, his long fingers spread behind a book. He looked across at me. "I shall have to cheat a little," I told him. "And I shall have to cause some pain to avoid causing a lot." He stared and said nothing, silent when I most wanted advice. "It's for Sarah," I said. "So she'll be secure and happy." For the first time I remember I could not make him speak.

Sarah woke up slowly. "Oh, how divine," she murmured. "Apollo leaning on his elbow and grinning at me, me, me! I love you, Joshua Steel. What's the time?"

"The year of our Lord, nineteen hundred and seventy-seven, maiden. Don't you think Pan would be more appropriate?"

"Yes, you have got funny feet and an impish air. What is the time?"

"Fast approaching the year of the Pig, oh, oriental blossom, and I'm going to leap out onto these funny feet and fetch your breakfast."

She pulled her eyes up at the corners. "Honolable gentreman velly kind, but betta I get it myserf. That cooker is a bugger of the first order."

"Then have cornflakes. Please, darling, I'll manage."

"I want toast." She watched me get out of bed. "Josh, you look thinner. Have you weighed yourself recently?"

"Yes, my daffodil. You see, I'm desperately ill and pining away with an unrequited desire to get your breakfast. Toast?"

"Fool. Put your robe on before you catch cold."

I laid a tray with cups and coffee pot, cereal and toast, and took two of my pills while I waited for the kettle to boil. On the deep windowsill was a small glass pot which I filled with water, then looked around outside the door for a flower to go in it. There was nothing but grass and a few uninspiring weeds and a lot of cold air. Under the sink I spotted a pile of old gardening catalogues. They had sweet peas and dahlias in glorious color inside; a few quick snips with Sarah's manicure sissors and my wife had a bowl of flowers to go with her breakfast.

She took the tray and looked first to see if the toast

was burned, which it wasn't because I had watched every second of its browning and my eyeballs were still hot from the eye-level grill. Then she took the bunch of cutout blooms in her hands, sniffed deeply and said, "Ah! Such delicate perfume, such exquisite colors! Compliment the gardener, Steel. Give him a trowel." She giggled. "Oh, Josh, you are a fool." She covered her breasts with the edge of the sheet and began to eat. "Put the fire on, please. It's cold."

We drank coffee in silence. After a while, I said, "We have to go home today."

"Now you've spoiled it."

"But you knew."

"Yes, but I wasn't thinking about it. What will you do when we get back?"

"I thought you didn't want to think about it."

"A change has come, Josh. I don't know how or why, but it has. I somehow can't imagine going back to the same old routine in the same old places. We've broken the cycle and we can't get back in. Now isn't that illogical?"

There must be a magic in mornings, a cleanness in the air between two people. Sarah's intuition had caught me out. How could she know things when I had no clear idea yet? I think she has feelings outside her skin, just feelings, not thoughts. When she thinks, it is of practical matters. "I must get up, Josh, there's packing to be done. Take the tray." I did so, and turned back from the table to hug her as she got out of bed. "You're trembling," she said. I nodded, her brown curls against my face. "What is it, my darling?" Her voice was gentle as an angel's. "Are you cold and afraid?"

"I guess so and I don't know why." I don't want to

die, Sarah, and I don't want to lose you, not even then, not before then. But I must, I must.

She kissed me once, but I was haunting the future. And old enigmatic headlamps knew it. At least, I think she did.

CHAPTER
FIVE

It is hard not to count the days between symptoms. It is hard to ignore pains, put them down to the little illnesses most people get occasionally. It is hard to hide anything from a wife who is a second nature. Or from a specialist. Bernard Ford looked at me and was wearing his stern compassionate face. "Feel bad?" he said.

"Chest pain, mostly. Jock McCleary frowned over my blood films, so I guess the remission is over, yes?"

It was the cold, forsaken week after Christmas. Parties over, Easter eggs in the shops, broken plastic toys in the trash. An appropriate time. Outside the warm office, sleet flew horizontally and the wind howled lonely round the canyons of the university and hospital buildings. A time to go inside oneself. Even Ford had lost some of his quiet extroversion. "Transfusion and cytotoxics will do the trick," he said. "We'll increase the dosages. I think you'll be able to tolerate it. But I wish you'd get more rest, you should be in bed." I stared at him.. "Have you told your wife yet?" he tried.

"No. It helps not to. When I could give in, I don't."

"You should. It would help."

"What difference does it make? Did you hear I have a new job?"

He passed me a cigarette from his pack. "I didn't believe it. It's true?" I nodded. "Are you sure that's wise?"

"Thank you, Mr. Ford," I smiled.

He frowned at his fingers, then pushed his mane of hair untidy. "It must be the day, the weather, the bloody awful time of year. We should be radiant with the remembered birth of Christ, but look, he's dead again already. A consultant should never be tactless. I'm sorry, Joshua."

It was the first time he'd used my Christian name. "Everyone is allowed to give in once in a while. Honesty does no harm."

"You'd be surprised. A man in my position spends a lot of time denying his integrity; that's amazing, isn't it? Eminent men, having attained that eminence because of ability and unimpeachable conduct, spend half their time, if not lying, at least molding the truth so as to avoid causing pain and worry. But you must know this. Doesn't pay to think about it, I know, just some days when it's cold and depressing . . . What's the new job?"

"Do you see a lot of children with blood disorders? Leukemias?"

"It's my subject. Yes, I see a lot at Great Ormond Street. That doesn't mean it's a common disease, of course, just that most of them come to us. We've developed some pretty successful methods of treatment."

"But they die in the end."

"Yes." He sighed and the sound held the moan of the wind outside. "Yes, yes. I have never cured one. I have had years and years extension of life, but contrary to statistical assessment, I don't call ten years a cure. Why do you want so much of the truth? The parents of my patients long to be lied to. Sometimes they even bring themselves to believe it will be all right in the end. Underneath though, they know. You can hear it in their voices."

We sat and smoked in silence for a moment or two. "I shall be working with children," I said. "Registrar at Somerfield Cottage Hospital. They have three departments: children's, general, and GP. It's very small."

"Your treatment?"

"I wanted to ask about that. Do you know anyone in the North Somerset area who could do it?"

"I do," he said immediately. "But must you?"

"I must. For my integrity, I think."

He shook his head, though I think he understood. "There's a man called Madison. I'll see to it."

"Privately, please. The Hospital Board might think twice about my appointment if I turned up in their best infirmary as a confirmed case of A.M.L."

"Don't you think this . . . this deviousness is going to be difficult to maintain?"

"Yes, Mr. Ford. Madison?"

We stared at each other but his eyes were sadly defeated. If he wanted to protest further, his innate diplomacy and professional acceptance of the inevitable prevented him. "He has a private clinic, Berkeley House, several miles from Taunton. It's a very elite establishment, all the latest equipment."

"My superannuation repayment should cover it. It won't be for long."

97

The telephone on the desk rang twice and stopped, an external call. Ford answered it. "For you," he said.

Alan Slater wanted to confirm our lunch appointment. He'd brought all the papers and sounded eager for a sale. "I'll be at the Blue Bowl at one," I said. His call reminded me that I wanted to phone Aunt Gale.

"I'll be at your morning clinic tomorrow," I told Ford. "As promised, at nine on the dot. I'd be grateful if you contacted Madison for me."

"Anything I can do will be done," he said quietly. "Good luck, Joshua, with whatever it is you need to do."

As I left I wished I had time to know him better. It was just one other experience I'd have to miss. But things were flowing into place, gently along like the river. There could be no other way of it.

Sarah had taken the news of my job in Somerset quite calmly. I think she realizes and accepts the inevitable far more readily than I, or Bernard Ford. "I told you things had changed," she said. "Somehow we couldn't get back into this particular rut. You've changed too, Josh." It was impossible for her not to notice, but she seemed pleased with the change, so my secret was safe. I was careful not to appear too relieved; soon I would change more, and further.

Alan Slater drank his whisky and soda in a businesslike manner, hiding the glass between gulps in his square, doormat fist. He was expansive of word and economical of gesture, but for all that his hands said more than his tongue. After putting away a pork pie and a ham salad, and ordering up two more drinks on his expense account, he produced four life insurance brochures by sleight of hand, laying them attractively across our table.

"Choose a card, any card," I said.

"Eh? Oh, I see. Very good that. Now—" and his grin vanished as if it had never been. Not for Mr. Slater the agonies of maintaining a twitching smile, no sir. Done with the pleasantries and on with the job. I bet Bernard Ford wouldn't have minded that technique, but then, he had integrity. I wondered whether Alan had. He would have said so, I'm sure, even though he spent most of his time inducing people to part with their money for a service they did not want.

Privately, I agree with Sarah, the whole idea annoys me. "We've four policies that would interest you, Joshua, for very reasonable premiums and covering every eventuality. As I mentioned before, the Anyman is our newest, realizing fifteen thousand in event of death from any cause but suicide or murder, obviously. Should you lose a limb or an eye in an accident you'd be well compensated. Do you know it's possible to obtain a mortgage with such a policy?" There was a lot more but I couldn't concentrate. I was on the other side of the mirror in another conversation, asking Alan what he'd do if he knew I was dying already, wondering how much he might be prepared to accept to keep it quiet. Not for the first time I watched myself die and tried to imagine what it would be like.

"You'll have to have a medical," said Alan, hunting through the heavy brown leather briefcase at his side. "But you'd know if you were fit enough, wouldn't you, being a doctor, eh?" He chuckled. "Ah, here we are. One of our doctors lives quite close to you in Kensington. Chap called Barry Bates; know him?" I shook my head. "Well, make an appointment and take this along. He'll let us know." He handed me a slip with an address on it and a folded official form.

Old Bates, old Barry Bates, the peril of Guys. I had to smile. We'd been at Medical School together, though he was a year ahead of me, and his reputation had been rather less than spotless. Casanova Bates, the darling of the nurses, from first-years to stiff-lipped sisters, and the best wing three-quarter the hospital had produced in years. That he had gone into general practice wasn't surprising; Barry had always loved variety, in everything.

I rang him and made an appointment for that evening after the surgery closed. "Great to hear from you," he said. "We'll slip out for a pint afterward."

Barry had changed very little. His hair was longer, his clothes more expensive and less flamboyant but his blue eyes still held the old enthusiasm and his smile was just as white. I gave him my form and he smiled. "Every little helps. How are you?"

"Well, thanks, Barry."

"Look a bit washed-out. I suppose being patient with eager students is as wearying as catering to the whims of the great British public who pour through my doors." He stared at himself in the glass above the wash basin. "I look worse than you. I think we can cut the cackle, don't you?" I shrugged. "Good, we'll just answer the questions on the form. Feeling fit?"

"I had a chest X-ray a few weeks back."

"Okay, was it? Just let me listen to your heart, test your reflexes . . . now where the hell's my stethoscope?"

We strolled round to his local ten minutes later. He had had only one comment to make. "Your pulse is high, been hurrying?" I had nodded. It was the briefest, scantiest medical I had ever undergone, though Barry wasn't to blame. One tends to trust members of one's own profession. Integrity again.

* * *

100

Spring came early to Somerset and particularly to Somerfield in its sheltered valley, protected from the north winds by the shoulders of the Mendips and shielded by the furry tongue of Wellard woods from the winter westerlies. By the middle of March the snowdrops and crocuses had disappeared beneath the soil for another year, and the daffodils bullied for sun space in Gale's garden though she cut and filled the house with armfuls of them. I have always felt good in spring, coming alive with the new leaves of that special green that seems to hold distilled sunlight, finding new reasons for living like every other growing thing. I had always felt good in spring. Even this one, though it was run through with the stains of autumn already, and was sad like autumn is, was good. The treatment had worked once more. I was as healthy as I could be. My plan was started, we had been living with Gale for two weeks, I was due to start my new job in two days, and Sarah . . . I didn't know about Sarah. An odd thing had happened before we left London.

"Joan was round today," my wife told me in her most abrupt tone one Friday evening.

"Cherub, Joan is round all the time. We call it obesity, a pertinent term at which most obese people gasp in horror. They prefer plump, or well-covered, or even fat. Joan is obese."

Sarah glowered. It must be serious; she can usually raise a smile at my idiocies. The gray of her eyes had gone charcoal, but hard. "Joshua, I asked you not to bother with insurance."

"Yes, my love, but I did. Does Alan usually discuss his clients' business with his wife, I wonder? That's most unethical."

"That doesn't matter."

"But it does, Sarah sweet, it does. I would have told you anyway."

"I'll believe that, oh yes, I'll believe that! Why should you think Alan ought to be trustworthy when you're not? You'd have told me—huh!" My darling was rattled. I think she has the idea that guarding against death in a monetary way will encourage fate to step in, but I doubt that she'd define fate or why she believes in it.

"Yes, I would," I said.

She clattered plates. "I asked you not to. I didn't want it. I don't want it. You deceived me, Joshua Steel!"

"No. I was going to tell you. I have to make my own decisions, Sarah, for my own reasons. I was going to tell you. I would have had to." I found Alan's envelope in my pocket and dropped it on the table in front of her. She made a small movement away like a startled bird. "You have to sign it because the payments are made in your name. You insure me, Sarah."

She stared through my soul for a while. "Why, Josh? Why are you so determined?"

"Will you sign it to please me?"

"No! Why?"

"So you will never be cold and afraid and lonely like the sea." She turned to me intently and to avoid her eyes I picked up and opened the envelope.

"But Josh, that's silly . . ."

I flattened the pages. "Will you sign, my rosebud, will you sign?"

"Oh . . . take that expression off your face! I never could resist the appealing look. See what trouble it's led me to. Changing our life, our home, our—our tidiness. All because of a man's silly grin. Shut up, Josh. Shut up!"

I hadn't spoken but we knew what she meant. "Will you sign, Sarah?"

Silently, she took my pen and signed her name on the dotted lines. Then she kissed me and went away to cook dinner without another word or look.

Gale had shown far less reaction to the suggestion that we live temporarily with her than I had been prepared for. In fact she seemed quietly pleased, though she did mention in a letter that there were some new bungalows being built in Westerleigh Lane near the school. I was glad to find the prices way above our range. I wanted Sarah to have someone with her and I wanted old comforts about her, not the smell of unfamiliar paint and the noiseless uncreaking of new furniture which would be all that was left to her of a home. I felt very remote thinking all that. I was shaving a stranger's face in the bathroom mirror at the time, and I wondered where the occupant of this long-haired head had gone. Sarah was in the bath. I prefer to be alone when I shave, but Sarah likes bathroom company.

"I'm putting on a bit of weight," she said vaguely. "Think I should diet?"

"What color?"

"Every one a gem. This'll be my last bath here." She rubbed her toe over the aged blue stain the immersion heater overflow had made in the white enamel. "I've liked it here, Josh. I know it's been bloody awful sometimes, with the cold and the condensation in the kitchen and everything, but it's seen a lot of happiness, hasn't it?"

I borrowed her bath towel to wipe my face. "We'll

leave some behind, shall we, for the next tenants. In the wallpaper and the condensation."

"Do you think it has a presence, then? Like a kind of ghost?"

"Maybe. Rosebud, will you please take yourself off now? I wish to indulge in some private contemplation."

"But I'm wet!"

I threw her my toweling robe and she dropped the tie in the bath water. "Did I tell you," she said, with her bottom sticking out, "that the removal men are taking the stuff we don't need into storage tomorrow? And Aunt Gale phoned to say she—ow! Joshua!"

Sarah has a neat, round, eminently smackable backside. "Tell me later, child of nature. Nature is calling. Out! I'll clean the bath."

She went, but not without finishing, "To say she has the big spare bedroom ready and she insists we have the small sitting room as our own, and the Matron of Somerfield Hospital is dying to meet you again because she knew you when you were at school, and now I'm going."

I sat and wondered how the hell I was going to do it to her. Perhaps there would be no one suitable. Perhaps.

Somerfield Cottage Hospital is a small building of local stone with additions in anachronistic glass and plastic, rather like an old lady with cheap new earrings. It has a GP ward of five beds, a children's ward of six, and a general ward, mostly geriatric, of fourteen. The new wings hold a minute pharmacy, the kitchen and catering offices, staff rooms, and consultants' clinics. As Matron explained, "We thought we'd give the important ones a nice new place to encourage them along." The poor registrar shared a Dickensian boxroom with the resident house surgeon, in the oldest section. Curiously, it suited me. On my first day I walked into it and felt at home. The heavy Victorian desk with bloated legs belonged there, indeed it was so large it must have been built in because it surely never came through the door, and the dark green filing cabinet predictably screeched as I opened its drawers. "Now, now, young lady," I told it. "This is the modern era. Queen Victoria is dead, long live the Queen, and girls no longer scream when a man touches their knickers. Sometimes they don't even wear them. What do you think of that? Still, a few drops of Three-in-One should silence your protests and then I can rape you with the notes of a short, unremarkable career and some old copies of the *Lancet.*"

There was little room in the glass-fronted bookcase for the nutritional journals so I left them tied in bundles and put up my small collection of books on pediatrics. Thumbling through a few as I did so, I suddenly realized the enormity of what I was aiming to do. Just a few lines reminded me of how much I missed and had forgotten about practicing medicine on real people, and that in turn brought pictures from Nigeria with its patient little patients suffering from kwashiorkor and God knows what else; those poor little bastards . . . I mean, who was I fooling? A new job, the insurance, Sarah, Madison—it wasn't real, I was dreaming. They were real, those pot-bellied, licorice-legged smilers back in my doctoring past. Soon there would be pale moonlight across the bed, and Sarah curled in the shadows with the dreams flowing from her nostrils, and me, Joshua Steel, fit and well and knowing he was not going to die for years and uncountable years. All flowing along in a different river. I put the books up and wished someone would come in.

The other desk in the room was larger than mine and shabbier, a wreck of its former self bearing the scars of many a coffee cup, and cigarettes left to expire along its edges. I hadn't met the resident house surgeon but I knew his name because he wrote it everywhere. *James Picton* or just *J. Picton* was inscribed on all the reprints in the neat tray, Dymotaped *J. Pictons* stuck to his pot of glue, his desk diary, his half of the bookshelf, and even the back of his wooden chair. James Picton seemed to be precise—all his books and pencils lay square—and I wondered, self-important?

The door opened and a man of about my age and height came in. Sarah says I am an eye person because I always look at eyes first and trust them more than I do tongues. I know they can lie, I know they aren't necessarily windows of the soul, but they do speak. A man with his eyes closed is like an empty house to me. It looks like there's no one home. All that to say that I noticed James Picton's eyes. They were the same blue as the cover I used to have on my bed when I was a kid. A grayish navy, sometimes dark, sometimes light blue. When the sun fell on that bedspread it changed shade and texture completely, and so I felt would Doctor Picton's eyes. They were wide apart coming down at the corners like a sailor's eyes should be, with several deep wrinkles as if he stared often into the distance, scanning the horizon for sight of land. He proved to be a farmer's son from Yeovil and suffered nausea in a rowboat on the river. When I told Sarah about it she laughed and added, "You are an idiot. I bet you were disappointed." She always says something provocative, then disappears to contend with the Hoover so she can't hear.

The rest of Doctor Picton was squarish, calmish, and pale yellow-haired. "Doctor Picton," I said, nodding to his labels. "Glad to know you, to know you, to know you." We shook hands and he chuckled immediately. When he spoke there was still a trace of Somerset under the smooth tones. "I had to," he said. "Your predecessor had a terrible habit of appropriating, you know what I mean? If I didn't stick things down or label them clearly they kind of drifted his way, and he was so untidy neither of us could ever find them again. There's still a set of X-rays missing. R.H.B. Medical Records played hell about it. Borrowed them from the Infirmary, you see. Still, he was a nice chap, very nice chap." He sat down on his labeled chair and waited.

"Uh, I'm Joshua Steel," I said.

He nodded and waited. He betrayed neither shyness nor animosity, he seemed quite bland and confident. "I've used some of the shelves," I said randomly. "But I didn't stray into your area." He watched me as I stowed things in drawers and laid out my pen tray with Sarah's pen in pride of place, but he stared neither rudely nor shiftily.

"I put a stack of headed notepaper and various hospital stationery in the bottom of the filing cabinet for you," he said suddenly. "Enough for a while. I'll show you where to get more when you need it."

"Thanks. That was thoughtful."

He looked away then, toying with the Dymo label-maker. I said, "Can I have one of those too, or is it unlabeled and common property?"

"It's all right," he smiled. "You won't need one. I love this gadget. I'll do anyone a label any time. Your predecessor took it once and lost it. Nearly broke my heart." He paused and his smile widened. "You mustn't take me too seriously, Doctor Steel."

"I wasn't sure if I was."

"You looked as if you were." He waited some more as I finished taking ownership of the desk. "I find people very entertaining," he said.

"You do?"

"Uh huh. Don't you? We're all so different yet so similar. Your predecessor, for instance; now he was untidy, haphazard when he spoke, you know what I mean? With ends of sentences and trailing words so you had to pick the meaning out for yourself; he was too lazy to be explicit. But he was also a brilliant surgeon. He's gone on to greater things on that talent alone." He spread his hands as if he had made a magnificent revelation. I felt inadequate at having missed it. "Coming to coffee?" He stood and opened the door for me.

We filed along the narrow gloss-painted corridor in silence. The shades were cream and waist-high brown, almost too typical to be true. Could the interior decorators have been pulling a subcommittee leg? Anywhere but Somerfield I would have suspected that to be the truth, but the tradesmen of the locality have always followed the code laid down through the ages by respected antecedents, usually fathers and grandfathers. Hospitals and institutions had always been cream and brown, were synonymous with cream and brown, could be nothing but cream and brown. I wondered how the architects of the new wings had persuaded any village firm to decorate the airy rooms in lilac or lizard green. Either they had lied about the purpose of the extensions, or compromised by allowing the old standards to be repeated within the old hospital block just to satisfy outraged dignity. Or, perish the thought, smuggled labor in from the permissive metropolises of Wells or Bridgwater.

The passage wound and wandered round storerooms with rusted keys in rusted locks, through unmarked doors I'd never be able to find again, up a couple of steps, down three, left, right, past one door marked in red *Danger! Drop other side!* which raised all manner of interesting and immaterial conjectures. "Is there a prize for finishing the course?" I asked.

James glanced round. "S'pose it would seem a bit of a maze to a newcomer," he said. "These Victorian places, you see. In the old days a patient might get out of a ward, but he'd never get out of the hospital."

"It used to be a workhouse," I volunteered. "Part of it; like *Oliver Twist.*" Surely that lumpy shadow ahead could be Mr. Bumble on his nasty rounds.

"Really? How do you know that?" We wound up a spiral metal staircase and our voices filtered through the treads.

"I lived round here for quite a while."

"Well, I never!" He seemed amazed. "No one told me that. I wonder why no one told me that?"

In a strange way I felt proud to have entertained him with a novel snippet.

We slipped through a heavy swinging door, one of those with a bedeviled personality that refuses to open without dislocating a shoulder, then catches you in the back no matter how fast you move. Opposite was the second of the two small operating theaters. "I see where I am now," I said. "This was the way that Mr. Bell-Withers brought me when I was shown round." Mr. B-W, James told me, attends the hospital for two sessions a week. I found him an abrupt man with an abrupt chin and a loud Yorkshire laugh, and that is all I gleaned from our brief and formal meeting. I guessed I'd never get to know Mr. B-W because he was a man who would take years to know. The surface of him gave nothing away; he could beat his wife or be kind to stray dogs, enjoy a pint with the boys or play the bagpipes. Even James seemed unsure of the man behind the consultant. "He drives a Mercedes and he's Church of England," he said.

Matron presided over the coffee room like an aseptic madam, and the sisters in their navy and white stood around hygienically, aware of her presence like hens under a fox's eye. I remembered Matron Dixon from twenty years ago simply because she has not changed. Her face has inevitably succumbed to time; what had been pleasing plumpness sagged beneath the eyes and dropped at each side of the chin, and her hair has paled from black to gray, but Miss Dixon has not changed. Her hairstyle was precisely the same, swept up with a curly bang across her forehead, and her wide blue eyes blinked coquettishly. Her mouth was dark red and smudged on her teeth when she spoke.

"Joshua Steel, I do declare! I'd have known you anywhere. I told your aunt I'd know you anywhere." The sisters parted as she came toward James and me. Matron Dixon has that effect. Her ample breasts, solid as the pyramids, lead the rest of her ample self on a straight course like a whaler in a choppy sea. "Sister Andrews, give our new registrar a cup of coffee. Come and sit here, Doctor Steel. My, you were only eleven or twelve when I first came to Somerfield and then of course I went to Glasgow so I missed seeing you all this time. Isn't that amazing!"

"Amazing," said James, before I could. He winked slyly at me.

Sister Andrews brought my coffee and it had both milk and sugar. I took one sip and put it aside. "It's nice to meet you again, Miss Dixon," I said. "You've hardly changed at all."

She giggled. On a fifty-odd-year-old woman a girlish giggle makes my scalp prickle, but for all her apparent empty-headedness I knew Matron was no fool. Her job was difficult and demanding and from my information she did it well. The nurses admired and respected her, but then, the nurses were not male and privileged.

"Oh, you're just saying that," she said. "Now I'd better introduce you all round, though I expect it'll take a little time for you to get all our names straight."

The sisters, and there were only four present, were Andrews, Kenny, McCarthy, and Knowles, and I learned their names right off. Only Kenny was remarkable in that she was young, attractive, and cool. The other ladies had tolerant, tired eyes and capable handshakes and were in Matron's age group.

"Your aunt tells me you're married," said Matron.

"Yes."

"Have you any family?"

"Well, there's Aunt Gale and Uncle—"

"No, no. I mean children."

I shook my head. There was a little hum of silence. Kenny broke it with a chuckle; she has a smile that alters a face so completely it might belong to someone else. "Don't stare at the poor man as if he'd committed a crime," she said. "Pediatricians don't have to be fathers, do they, Doctor Picton?"

James smiled slowly. "Not officially," he said, and the ladies giggled, Matron loudest of all.

"I must be getting back to my unpacking," I said, moving toward the door.

"Righty-ho!" beamed Matron. "Come and see me in my office later. Doctor Picton will show you. B-W does his little rounds this afternoon and you'll want to be up-to-date on the cases."

Outside, I said, "Can we have coffee anywhere else?" Jimmy Picton laughed so hard his face reddened. "It wasn't that funny."

"That's precisely what your predecessor said," he explained. "We always had coffee in our own room."

I never found out the name of my predecessor, but I sympathize with him, wherever he is.

James was due in theater at eleven-thirty for a prostatectomy, "If that bloody anesthetist turns up," and much as I thought I would like him, I was happy to be alone for a while. First days are murder for me. Too many impressions to collect and make, and the wrong one can color the job as long as it lasts. The reminder of passing time snagged my memory. I had promised to phone Madison for my first appointment. I borrowed James's labeled telephone directory. Bernard Ford had passed on all the details but Madison would have to see me anyway. I found the number of Berkeley House. The great man himself was busy but his receptionist gave me an appointment.

I sat back and looked round for the old friends I had often shared my thoughts with in London. The army had deserted. Only a very small loyal corps stood unevenly shoulder-to-shoulder behind the glass doors of the bookcase. "Welcome," I said. "Though I'm not sure what we've gotten ourselves into. What do you think of James Picton, Esquire, eh? Too soon to tell, I guess, but he'll be worth bearing in mind. He's probably married; I hadn't thought of that." The army was deaf behind the glass. I opened the bookcase and told them I was going to see Matron. It is strange that in these days my feelings have become contradictory and unpredictable. When I am alone I want to be with people and when I'm with people I can't wait to get away from their chatter. I don't think it's the sickness, I think it's the loneliness it causes.

Matron welcomed me all over again. "Do you know, I can remember you vividly in your school cap and tie," she said, offering a bowl of barley sugar sweets. "You were a bit of a terror, but I always thought you'd go a long way."

I unwrapped a sweet. "I must have been at grammar school. We had no uniform for Somerfield."

"Still haven't, my dear Doctor. Untidy little wretches, mostly."

"Some of them were very poor. They didn't pay dinner money."

"Oh, I know that. The Council house people still have the same problems. Too many mouths to feed and bodies to clothe. You know, the other day one of the fathers stopped me in the village to thank me for organizing the last church jumble sale. He got all four of his children outfits for school for a grand total of one pound ninety pence. I was a little embarrassed, I must say. I'm no snob, goodness knows, but he's hardly the sort of man one likes to be seen talking to in the street. Shirt sleeves and braces."

"But he thanked you."

She blinked brightly and offered the barley sugar again. I refused. "I do a lot of work for the church," she said. "Shall we be seeing you and your wife on Sunday?"

"Where?"

"In church, of course. Morning service is at eleven o'clock and evening at six. The vicar is Mr. Kingsley, Oliver Kingsley, such a nice man."

"Oh, no. I doubt it."

Matron was disappointed in me. "Your aunt comes every week. And helps out with church functions."

I nodded and smiled. "We each choose our ways," I said.

"It would be nice to have you," she said, patting her hair into place. "After all, you are a prominent member of our community in Somerfield. None of the consultants live locally."

I think my smile widened. If you can't grab a consultant for your Christian buttonhole, display the next best thing; Joshua Steel, the clip-on status symbol. "I don't go to church," I said. "Matron Dixon, when I die, will I go to heaven?"

She giggled uncertainly. "You're joking."

"Not at all. I have no reason whatsoever to joke."

She fumbled at a drawer of her desk and pulled out a pile of case notes, each in a brown clinical envelope. "Well, we'll be pleased to see you any time . . . Now. These are Mr. B-W's cases. If you'd like to study them first, we'll go up to the ward just before lunch." I was dismissed. I knew Matron Dixon would choose not to come to terms with the Joshua Steel I had presented, nor could she quite return to her preconceived notion of me, so from now on she would be confused and I, cause of confusion, would be faintly disliked and mistrusted because of it. I did not mind too much, but it certainly proved that first impressions are like indelible dye. And on my first day too. I went back to my room humming "Onward Christian Soldiers."

Sister Kenny was on duty on the children's ward

when Matron and I arrived. Miss Dixon reintroduced us and sailed away immediately. "What have you done to Matron?" said the sister. "She always stops to say hello to the kids."

"I suspect I may be a black sheep strayed from the fold."

As she looked up, interested, I noticed her eyes were rich hazel with curious gold flecks around the pupils. Very penetrating eyes, secret as deep wells. "I can't quite visualize Matron as a shepherdess," she said. "Have you been upsetting her on your very first day?"

"Not intentionally, Sister. A slight personality clash, I guess. I refused her Holy Orders, you might say."

"So. They're a very conventional lot round here, Doctor. The previous registrar was a keen member of the Church. But I wouldn't get on the wrong side of Matron. She has a lot of influence."

"I'll bear it in mind. Now, would you show me our patients?"

Five of the six beds were occupied, in the loosest sense of the word. Two children were actually in bed and the other three sat on the tiled floor in a square of sunlight from the windows and played with toy cars and coloring books. Kenny checked them off.

"Angela; adenoids and tonsils. She's going home tomorrow. Derek; tonsils. He's out tomorrow, too. And Fiona; tonsils. She's on tomorrow's list." The children did not look up. We went to the beds. "This is Veronica. She's seven and she's had broncho-pneumonia, but she's much better now, aren't you, pet?"

Veronica cuddled her teddy-bear and stared suspiciously at me. "Who's he?" she asked Sister Kenny.

"This is Doctor Steel. He's a new doctor."

The child coughed and her chest sounded congested. I sat on her bed. "Hello, Veronica."

"'Lo."

"What's teddy's name?"

"Teddy, stupid."

Sister Kenny did not laugh, bless her. "Can I listen to your chest with my stethoscope?" I said.

"No. The other doctor does it."

"Doctor Picton?"

"Jimmy."

"I bet he hasn't let you listen to his chest."

Veronica straightened up against her pillow and relaxed her grip on Teddy. "No. There's nothing wrong with his chest."

"How do you know if you haven't listened?" I took the stethoscope from my pocket. "Do you want to hear my heart beating?"

"Yes."

I put the earpieces to her ears and let her listen. "It's loud and there are other funny noises. Bump-rumble, bump-rumble."

"May I listen to yours now?"

"All right."

Sister tried to help with pajama buttons but Veronica was an independent young lady. "Hold Teddy," she instructed. "I'll do it."

There was still slight pleural rub and dull percussion at the base of the left lobe. "Is she having physio?" I asked Kenny.

"Oh, yes, and she's very good, too. Doesn't mind the thumping one bit."

"Thank you, Veronica," I said.

"Thank you. I like your tie."

"Good."

The last patient was asleep. "John," said Sister. "He had a simple fracture of the left femur and was first treated in Wells. He could be at home now but both parents are working so we're keeping him until he's properly mobile. Look, Staff Smith has written nursery rhymes on his plaster."

She had, too, Humpty Dumpty and Little Jack Horner, with illustrations. "Can't anyone stay home with him?"

Sister Kenny frowned. "The family has five children and they all go to school. He's the youngest. A very nice family," she insisted. "Very nice indeed. It takes some of the load off if we have John here."

"I believe you, Sister. No need for defenses. If we have the bed available, why not? I'm sure our wealthy sponsors can stand the strain on their bank accounts."

"You bet they can," she said sharply, then blushed. "I'm sorry. I always tend to think of people who give to charities as being eager to salve their own consciences for one reason or another. Doctor Picton has other ideas, I know."

"Does it matter?" I said. I seemed to be saying that rather often lately. "If we get the money does it matter why or how?"

"Not when the money and what it can buy are the sole objectives, no, I suppose it doesn't. But . . . " She moved away between the beds toward the ward office.

"I know the 'but,'" I said, following. "The point is, standing on the principle of that 'but' would harm not us, but the patients. Compromise, Sister, even if it kills us."

When I got home that night the air in the kitchen was full of questions, but both women waited for me to speak first. I kissed Sarah, hugged Gale, and went to change before dinner. They watched me go mutely.

The big bedroom is decorated with rose-patterned wallpaper, white paint, and yellow curtains at the window. Sarah had already made her mark with a picture and one or two posters for the walls, and her perfume and bottles on the dressing table, but I had laid no hand on it at all. I wondered whether I should. Small things like hairbrushes or cuff links can be so agonizing after their owner is gone. I kept all such trifles in the top drawer of the bureau.

I went up to the top floor, avoiding the squeaking stairs, to my old room. I didn't want to disturb it too much. The childhood books belonged there and must stay to preserve whatever joys and pains the room held, and nothing much else was portable. I moved to look out of the window at the back garden—funny how I call it a garden after years of Dad's unchanging "yard." He had a lot of influence on me, there is much of him in me that I recognize, but the language I speak is far more English. I guess language doesn't matter too much anyway. Dad thought it didn't, he had a liberal mind. "When a man shows you his heart it doesn't matter about the color of his skin or the tricks of his tongue," he said. "Look for his heart always."

My fingers played among stones, the pebbles from long-lost beaches. I was pleased to have found a token. I wet one or two with spit and watched their hidden color bloom. After all the years they still had their magic. A shard of gray malachite became emerald and an egg of pink granite shone like a gravestone. They should be polished. Polished granite must be one of the most beautiful rocks in the world. I piled the collection into one hand and took them downstairs. I put them on the bedroom windowsill with the promise that one day I'd get out the carborundum and aloxite and make them live again. Even then I knew it was an empty promise. They'd collect another batch of dust, and another, until the time ran out.

"How was it?" Sarah demanded when we all had dinner plates.

"Agony," I said. "I'm leaving tomorrow."

"You're not!" Gale's eyes widened.

"Of course he isn't. He liked it. Look at his face. Are they nice people?"

"Pass the rice, rosebud. Fairly nice, I'd say. Matron has her doubts about me, I'm afraid."

"Why should she?" Gale sounded indignant.

"Clerical doubts. I'm not religious enough. Sweet and sour sauce, please."

Sarah glowered on my behalf. "Huh! I bet she's the sort who preaches about it and never practices it."

"She does the jumble sales and the flowers," said Gale doubtfully. "And old people's outings. She's good at organizing. Don't you like her, Josh?"

I had to think about that. One's normal tendency is to think of others as they think of you, without reasoning the thing out. "Let's see. I admire the work she does; why she does it shouldn't be my concern. But . . . " I broke off and smiled at myself. "But I don't care for hypocrisy, not even when I find it in myself."

After a week at the hospital I felt I might have been there half my life. I'm not usually quick to settle into a job, but here I knew the place and its surroundings, and many of the faces. Most Somerfield families have lived in the area for years and have facial character-istics repeated through the generations. The Toveys, for instance, are fair-haired and coarse pink-skinned with a distinctive beaky nose. It is possible to recog-nize a junior Tovey, even when he or she has opted out of the family business of chicken farming. I knew without having to check that there were two Tovey sisters employed as nurses in our wards. They didn't remember me, but curiously enough, remembered my father. "He helped our Dad out with a loan once," one of them told me. "He still mentions it now." Oh, how are parents secrets to their sons.

Although Matron was distantly polite to me, presumably because I still spent my Sundays in relaxation rather than devout prayer, the rest of the staff went out of their way to be helpful. I felt I was cheating them; they made such provision for my future comfort. I was invited to be a member of the Joint Staff Consultative Committee, given membership of the Social Club, and asked to bring my wife along to coffee so the staff could meet her and show her the good works we all hoped we were doing. This last tied in well with the germination of my plan. So far, James Picton was still the most suitable candidate. I'd discovered that he wasn't married or heavily entangled with a woman, and as he lodged in Somerfield and seldom went home to Yeovil, he was often at a loss for company.

I took Sarah with me one Saturday morning when I knew things would be quiet. Jimmy should have been there but I overestimated my cleverness. He'd gone early. Sarah grumbled when I rushed her through coffee and away. "But I didn't meet anyone," she complained.

"You'd better come again during the week, my petal. There weren't enough people to show you off to."

"Silly man," she said.

The first days of April were unexpectedly glorious. March went out on a long windy squall and left a vacuum behind to be filled with blue skies and weak sunshine. The air still had a knife in its teeth, but one Sunday morning spent weeding in the back garden gave me a light tan, enough to cover the paleness and make me look healthy.

"I could do with a month of this," said Sarah, watching me from the back step. She has a fair skin that objects to oversunning quite violently, but she was sitting there bare-armed and going red. "How about the south of France, Josh?"

"You've just had a holiday."

"What? Before Christmas? That was years ago."

"You don't say. A month of sun would kill you, my magnolia. You're going to be sorry tonight. I'll have to get the calomine out."

"Mmm. It's such a pity to waste it, though."

"We've got plenty of calomine."

She threw her sunglasses at me. "Are we going on holiday this year, Josh?"

I pulled out a dandelion and left a long tap root behind; they go through to Australia. "The way they work me at the hospital I'll be spending any holiday I get in a wheelchair, peach feet."

"All the more reason to take one, then."

"It wouldn't fit into the car."

"Oh, stop it, idiot! Listen, Gale picked up some brochures for me in Bridgwater. I'll get them." She was gone before I could stop her.

I didn't want to plan a holiday because I knew I wouldn't take it unless it was very soon. It went against any integrity I had to discuss air fares and channel crossings when I knew they would never take place. But you'll have to change all that, said this man inside me whom I knew so little about as yet. You've got to be sneaky, you've got to compromise. Why not? Life's a compromise anyway. And it won't be for long.

121

"They have villas near St. Tropez." Sarah was back on the step with a handful of garish literature. "Look through these. I'll get some beer."

I hadn't touched them when she came back with a cold lager in each hand. "You read them to me," I suggested. I lay on my stomach in the grass and a forest appeared before my eyes. An ant struggled through the tall green fronds, an explorer in an unknown jungle. It came toward me, oblivious of any other world but its own.

"They're very cheap," said my wife. "Only twenty-one pounds a week. Look." She opened out the pages for me to see a white, Spanish-style house with a large patio overlooking the impossibly blue Mediterranean.

"How much would it cost to get there, sweet Sarah?" The ant came on after a temporary halt to inspect a buttercup leaf.

"Taking the car, not too much. Ferry from Dover to Calais, then petrol from there. We'd be late booking even now. Should we go in early September, do you think?"

"We could, bump. Do you want to make a provisional booking? Put down a deposit? Make out a check from our joint account for me to sign. When you've decided what you want you can put in the amount." I let some cold beer trickle round my tongue. It tasted good. Why hadn't I noticed before how good beer tastes on a hot day? Sarah's eyes were halfway out of her head. "You mean it?"

"Did I not say it, crackpot?"

"But it's not like you!"

Death descended on the ant from a world he did not know existed. I crushed it under my thumb for no other reason than that it seemed the symbolic thing to do. "Don't put people in boxes," I said.

"You're not interested, somehow," she reasoned unhappily. "You can't just say, 'Okay, you choose, spend my money any way you like.' It makes me feel guilty and uncomfortable."

I studied her face. How I do love my Sarah. "Women," I said, "are unfathomable."

"Don't put people in boxes," she retorted. "You mean it?"

"I've never fathomed them."

"You're maddening! Can I really do it, just like that? No arguments, no complaints; you don't even want to look through the books for a better place?"

"Sarah, I'm a reasonable man. How often do I argue or complain, or even disagree with you?"

"Oh, shut up!" she said.

always called the Main Road. "Mind the
say parents to children. Aunt Gale live
Road" in one of a short row of detach
due to a curve in the road and the
line, lie at least twenty yards b
is lawn and shrubs and "alto
old lady like me." She ke
complaints.

Somerfield village c
narrow roads and la
web from the cen
ware, and butch
shop which s
bakery used
in big ove
The s
mea

overnight—I had
say I had chosen not to notice.
along with the new, so I remember the one and
ignore the other.

A B-class road bypasses the village proper half a
mile to the east. It winds a little and bends more
sharply where the school and playing field gaze across
at the Church of St. John. Two children were knocked
down on that bend before the authorities employed a
lollipop lady. One of the victims was in my class, a
boy called Darrol Mays who had red hair and a snotty
nose and always got the cane for being, poor child,
stupid. When he was not there to be caned any more
we missed his trembling lip and his big red hand
flinching away from the stroke. The road has a name,
Bridgwater Road, for that is where it goes, but it is

Main Road,"

s "on the Main

ed houses which,

prescribed building

ck. Her front garden

gether too much for an

eps it beautiful with her

n be reached by a variety of

nes which spread like a spider's

er, where the Co-op grocery, hard-

ery stand. There is also a bakery and a

lls everything. When I was a child the

to make its own bread and confectionery

ns that opened right into the area at the back.

ell saturated the village each morning and

t more to me than any other smell of childhood. I

ess those are memories I shan't recall again for the

scent of them is gone. For many years now the shop has
had a big glass window full of wrapped, sliced,
bleached bread and sawdust cakes delivered by van
from the factory. For many years too, Mr. Arnold, the
bald and bespectacled baker who was stern and a little
deaf, has been gone, but I still remember riding my bike
with one of his cream buns, the biggest in the world,
crammed in my mouth. The shop that sells everything
now bears the impressive title Somerfield Grocery and
Off License instead of Evans' as it used to be, and
it now has ordered shelves and big cold cabinets. It
used to be exciting to visit; fat Mrs. Evans laughed all
the time and knocked things off the crowded counter
with her bulging bosom. It was an adventure, first to
find what was wanted, then to ascertain the price, then
to have the bill totaled on the corner of a sheet of

waxed paper that the bacon was wrapped in. It had been a warm, happy, grubby little place.

In between the village houses and cottages where people whose names I knew lived, have grown modern villas and glassy chalets with names like *Dunroamin* and *Chez Nous*. Their owners come from the towns and cities. I know no countryman who calls his house by name; even the Grange, a tree-huddled, dilapidated, eighteenth century place of great beauty and freezing bedrooms, has no sign on its gate. It was not until the summer of my twentieth year when a friend from Medical School stayed with me that I discovered it had a name at all. The friend had a passing interest in antiquities and found reference to Somerfield Grange in a book of Gale's. Rows of identical "semis" have blossomed along the Main Road, filling the unsightly gaps that had been left for fields and trees and hideaway bushes. Some were built on Mr. Muskett's bog and very shortly afterward gaping cracks appeared in the walls; eventually a garage fell clean away from a house and severe complaints were made. Muskett was heard to comment, "I told 'em it were unsuitable, but they 'udn't 'ave it," but by that time Mr. Muskett was several thousand better off. While I sympathize with the unfortunate householder, I do have a strong desire to smile with Mr. Muskett, though his motives might not have sprung from a preservationist's resolve.

My journey to the Cottage Hospital every day bypasses the village but threads along the Main Road past Doctor Gordon's surgery and past Somerfield Garage, which has undergone a metamorphosis from two wooden doors and a petrol pump, to a large edifice of yellow, green, and white concrete, a row of computers, and innumerable trading stamps. Next on the left is Hill Lane and at its end Vivian's shop and a housing estate, then the school, mostly untouched, and up beside it, the Wellington Inn. When I first entered its doors at eighteen—and there was no point in trying to get in before when the publican knew everyone's age from the newborn to Farmer Watts, then ninety-two—it had been a local pub. Brown paint, brown ceiling, brown beer, and accents thick as brown bread. Games of darts with the rubber mat below, packets of crisps with the salt in a blue twist, towel-draped wooden casks, and no piped music. The newcomers have brought perhaps what they did not seek to bring, perhaps what they had been trying to leave behind: pastel walls, plastic chairs, fairy lights, and artificial oak beams. A jukebox in the bar, infra-red steak pies, green chartreuse, and a new publican.

The church on the right has more slabs now in its overgrown graveyard and people who stare from the bus that stops outside can see the lilies-of-the-valley lying sweet under the slow yew trees. There is a new church hall behind, but the vicarage lawn where the annual garden party is held (inevitably on the wettest day of the season) still has its old horse chestnuts and its pond that one child is bound to fall into every year. Between here and the left turn into Glaston Road where the hospital lies, it is possible to glimpse countryside over and around the houses that have been, like Gale's, part of the scenery since the mid-thirties. I know most of the lanes that run illogically away to the hills and fields and woods of the distance. They lead to other villages and on to towns. I have known that all my life, but it was better to believe when I was young that their destinations were a mys-

tery, to go only part way long them and come back
circuitously, to leave intact the dream of a distant
wonderland where boys could fly and everything was
the Big Rock Candy Mountain.

Despite the changes I was glad I had come back.
Since I had known about myself the feeling had
grown, not to explore and examine and break new
ground as I had imagined it might, but to revisit good,
warm times. I stared hard about me for beauty, and
even a muddy gutter was beautiful because I might
once have lost a marble in it. I was hanging on to
things.

Most of all I wanted to hang on to the place where
I had met Sarah—a seedy, monotonous part of West
London. She'd lived with a girlfriend in a crowded
little bedsitter overlooking a stream of day and night
traffic. In my mind even that has a stark beauty in
its multitude of grays and blacks. They are colored
with the glowing of myself, the coming to life of
Joshua who had thought himself flowered and discovered he was scarcely a bud. Sarah had been a quiet
patch of sadness at first. Her parents had been killed
not long before in a multiple auto pile-up; and a
couple of years before that disaster the man she had
been going to marry had left her. She was scared to
love anybody in case they disappeared. It had been
my delight to watch her emerge, inch by careful inch,
out of the darkness.

I could not go back there though. Without her there
would be no color, and to ask her to come would need
a reason I could not give. So I clung to days and
places where I had been happy alone. I was going to
be alone anyway, I supposed. There seemed no sense
in attempting to see the world now. There is too much

of it and my eyes would always be turned toward my center, to the people I love. Travel is for the young or those who are lonely. I felt like an old man must feel, knowing the sand is running out.

By arrangement Sarah called in at the hospital one Tuesday morning to take coffee in the Staff Common Room. She found my office on her first try, which I still failed to do after nearly four weeks in the place, and threw her shopping angrily on the floor. "Those bloody travel agents!" she said. "After all the instructions I gave them they booked the villa for the wrong two weeks."

"Blossom, cool down. You've probably broken the eggs."

"Oh God." She fumbled through the carrier bag and came up red-faced. "They're okay, just a bit shaken."

"Who said you can't make omelettes without breaking eggs? He should have met my wife. And talking of meetings, come along. We're late already."

She followed me out. "Listen, Josh. They say the two weeks we want are booked." We wound and twisted through the dungeons.

"Keep a look out for a door marked *Drop other side*," I said.

"Don't you know where you're going yet?"

"Since you ask, Miss Needles, no. I'm following my nose."

"We have to go upstairs then, do we?"

"Such wit! Such repartee! Ah, here it is. Come on." We clattered up the metal staircase.

"Those shoes need heeling already," said my wife thoughtfully.

I introduced Sarah to various members of the staff, Matron included, and because my wife was occupied with holiday problems she was a little vague. Poor Miss Dixon took this as a personal affront and left us to fetch our own coffee. We talked awhile with Sister McCarthy and Staff Nurse Taylor, who sympathized with Sarah's views on travel agents.

"Where's Doctor Picton?" I interrupted.

"Theater," said McCarthy. "He ought to be finished by now though. There were only two cases. I expect the anesthetist was late again."

We'd finished coffee and James still hadn't arrived. "I must go, Josh," said Sarah. "I'll have to call British Rail to see if we can get passage on another boat." She pulled me toward the door, smiling good-byes.

"What's the panic, sweetheart? I thought you had all morning free."

"Oh, Josh, you don't listen. I'd booked our passage to coincide with the villa booking. Now I'll have to change it all round; if it can be changed. Aren't you worried?"

"You're doing enough for both of us. Are you sure you can't stay?"

She hesitated, then shook her head firmly. "I'm sorry, but I have some things here Gale wants for lunch. See you this evening, lover." We were in the corridor by now and Jimmy was coming toward us in his shirt sleeves with his white coat over his arm. Jimmy walks peculiarly; his toes turn out and he takes short steps and looks a bit like a penguin. Sarah kissed my cheek and turned to go.

"Wait a moment. Meet James Picton, our house surgeon. Jimmy, this is my wife."

"Hello," said Sarah, shaking hands briefly. "Excuse me, I must hurry." She trotted away, her hair making curls behind her.

"Sarah?" said Jimmy.

"Sarah. You must come to dinner soon and meet her properly."

Knowing one is to die soon imposes many restrictions. For instance, I was wary of allowing new friends to become close friends, of starting out on relationships that would only lead in the end to pain for someone. I admit I had my own feelings in mind, too. Aside from my one purpose for Jimmy I had laid no plans to involve myself with anybody else. It certainly had not been my intention to bring another woman on to the scene. Quite literally, the idea had never entered my head, nor would it have but for a bit of banter between Staff Nurse Taylor and James Picton at my expense. Staff Taylor is a bird, a gossipy brown hen who scratches and pecks at the surface of people and ideas, then moves on having picked a tasty morsel or two right out of context. She has rather more brain than a hen and does her job adequately, if untidily, but her outlook is strictly superficial. I often wondered whether she thought under that yellow-eyed, pert manner, and concluded she did not. She is probably happier that way. She talks of the Christian religion as if she owns it, but makes no attempt to live by it; not that she is in any way evil, but her twittering tongue often lays a path for unkindness and suspicion. She laid an egg of temptation right in my path and I remember with how few words she changed my attitude toward Sister Kenny. Taylor shares duty on the children's ward with Staff Smith and both come under the supervision of Sister Isobel Kenny, though when James and I stopped for a cup of tea in the ward office, Staff Taylor was alone and longing for conversation.

"Looking for Sister?" she said innocently to James.

"Heaven forbid," he grinned. "Frightens me to death. I never know what to make of her."

"Does she frighten you too, Doctor Steel?"

I hadn't been paying close attention because I'd burned my tongue on the brown tea. "Um? Sister Kenny?" Taylor nodded, folding her hands together and waiting for something exciting to happen, like a child. "Why should she frighten me? She's a pleasant young woman and always very helpful."

"Well, she would be to you," said Taylor knowingly.

"Why?" James glanced sideways at me.

"She finds Doctor Steel very attractive." She giggled and I was amazed all over again by woman, just woman.

"Did she say so?" Jim loves the scent of gossip. He finds it entertaining.

"Not outright, she's not the sort. But when she mentions the name she has a sort of look; and she puts on makeup for the ward round." She nodded confidently. A look and lipstick must have worlds of meaning.

Jimmy nudged me in the ribs. "You'd be all right there then, eh?" He chuckled lecherously.

The conversation dropped out of my mind until two days later when I had to check on a proposed appendectomy, a ten-year-old who had been admitted in acute pain and been treated with antibiotics to such good effect that he thought chasing a tonsillectomy around the ward under the beds an excellent pastime. Sister Kenny was busy in her office. I had noticed her before because I like to notice people, but I had not summed up what I knew simply because I had no cause to. Staff Taylor had pushed me on to a new road. I gathered facts together. Isobel was about twenty-seven, slim of build—Yeats's gazelle, neither pretty nor plain. She had an icy wit above her years which she hid behind, and that devastating smile one waited for and still did not believe. She used it rarely, and then for a morning, for a blue sky, for a passing song thrush or a fractious child, for the wind through the old beech tree outside her window. They always smiled back.

I put my head around her door. "Hi! Are you busy, Sister?"

She looked up sternly, tucking a curl of hair under her white bird of a cap. "No more than usual," she said. "I presume you want to see the current scourge?"

I checked the notes. "Master Wayne Ollis. He's on tomorrow's list."

"Wayne, indeed," she said. "When he grows up he should go into films; as a stunt man. He's fallen out of bed three times already, with the cot sides up. Perhaps the operation will subdue him for an hour or so. Oh, and watch he doesn't fall off the table, Doctor. He's that kind of child."

I laughed, hoping to encourage the smile. It came gradually and was quickly shut off, as if a portion of her mind poured cold water on flames. "You should do that more often," I said.

"What's that, Doctor?" She wouldn't look at me.

"Smile."

Her cheeks pinked a little, not a blush, an echo. "There's not much to smile about," she said.

"Oh, but there is, Sister. I've seen you. Every morning this week you've walked under that flowering cherry out there by the main gate and every morning you've given your smile to the blossoms."

She turned away with a handful of papers and

began to file them, her back to me. Her back was embarrassed but pleased, her straight brown legs with the calf muscles tense, going into good brown shoes. "That's different," she said, matter-of-factly. "That's things, not people." The filing cabinet drawer slammed.

"Don't people deserve it? Don't you think they might need it?"

"Some. The children and—and some others. I hadn't properly realized, Doctor. You've made me conscious of a perfectly natural, unnoticeable action. Now I shall be trying to control my face all the time." She grinned quickly.

"I'm sorry, but it's like having too much bread for yourself and not noticing others are starving."

"Is all your life so dramatic, Doctor Steel?" She looked at me with one eyebrow arched.

"Invariably. What better opportunity than life for drama, Sister? May I see Wayne now?"

"You may see Mr. Madison now." The cool receptionist was dressed in flattering pink, as was the waiting room. I guess I ought to call it a foyer. Berkeley House is that kind of place. It is the shell of a fine Somerset dwelling, damn nearly a castle, in stones weathered so long and well that they have no color yet have absorbed every living color. The gardens have orange blossom and roses, lilac and chaotic clematis bordering the curving driveway, and beside the front door, a magnolia. I had never seen such a beautiful tree, not even in the exotic bush of West Africa. It climbed the wall right up to the second story, so it was old, older than me, I think, and later in the year would bear creamy flowers big as

135

cupped hands and delicate as pearls. All the old things are on the outside of the clinic. The interior has been torn out completely and redesigned for medical needs and nowhere, except in the high ornate ceilings, is there a trace of its former character. The waiting area is rose-walled and carpeted, with chairs, telephones, and receptionist to match, the doors leading off are wide and the lifts spacious enough for a couple of hospital beds.

Madison had his suite of offices on the ground floor. The cool lady led me along a short passageway of blended blues into a room full of windows. The scheme here was tawny to complement the sunlight. The office was very warm, but Colin Madison wore a thick three-piece suit with carnationed buttonhole and looked glacial behind his desk. Even before he opened his mouth I felt I wanted to be cheeky to him. A very childish impulse.

"Good afternoon, Doctor Steel. Are you well?"

I put my thumbs firmly into the palms of my hands and clenched my fingers over them. "Quite well at the moment, thank you. My last treatment was on March second, before I left London."

He had my notes in front of him and idly turned the pages with a manicured, many-ringed hand. He had a long, severe face with colorless eyes and lips. The lid of his left eye twitched spasmodically. "So I see. On maintenance dosage? Yes, I see. And due for a check-up, overdue in fact. Yes."

"Yes."

"Yes. Well, we can give you a sternal marrow and peripheral blood today. My receptionist will send you an appointment when we get the results. Unfortunately we don't have the facilities for cytology here, but the slides will be through in two days. I shall study them personally."

"Thank you, sir. I see you are an F.R.C. Path." Bernard Ford had told me.

"Oh, yes, yes." A triangular smile lit his face for a moment and his twitch slowed. "Mmm. You see, we don't really need a surgeon here, though my Senior Registrar is well qualified. We treat mainly blood disorders, occasionally a case of Hodgkin's. We have excellent medical and radiotherapy facilities. Excellent. Patients come from all over the country, you realize."

"Is that so?" I did not whistle but a little breath escaped my pursed lips.

"Indeed it is. With our advanced methods of treatment we've been able to help a great number of cases with previously very poor prognoses."

I wanted to believe the fairy tale. Could he really have the power of a magician, wave a wand? Could he give me a year, maybe? "Acute monocytic?" I said quietly and it sounded so loud in my ears.

"Mmm. Each case is totally different, Doctor Steel. Have faith. Have faith."

"Thank you," I said. Mr. Madison, I sensed, would be a tough nut. His cold, faithful efficiency pervaded the clinic and hot, self-willed Joshua would not be looked upon kindly when he sought to get his own way.

Before any kind of celebration at which we are hosts, Sarah acts in a special, predictable, and peculiar way, and though I know what will happen and swear each time that she will not do it again, she does. I am sure my wife is not alone in this, but I am married to

Sarah and that is sufficient. A dinner party for four is
no challenge to her culinary skill, but she must make
it so; nor are the preparations of the table, the dining
room, the bathroom ("Because people notice people's
bathrooms even if it is Aunt Gale's"), but she must
worry and polish and point out faults. In the early
afternoon she is pert, vital, and untidy, working with
her hair tied up in a ridiculous pair of what she calls
bunches. By four o'clock everything that can be done
is done and she is nudging me to get ready even
though we have three hours before dinner. At six she
is dressed, adorned, and radiant and at half past she
is depressed, uncertain, about to change the menu,
her shoes, her dress, my hairstyle, the bathroom decor;
at six forty-five she is insisting I ring our guests and
put them off. When the guests arrive in the middle of
our flaming row she becomes gracious, relaxed, and
charming. We have not held a bad party yet, but I
still cannot understand the preliminary ritual. I
asked Gale but she just nodded sympathetically and
took refuge in astrology. "Cancer people are like
that," she said knowingly.

"You're escaping."

"Of course, Joshua. I'm going over to Mrs. Corbey's
to play bridge. Have a lovely evening."

This was the first time I had invited anyone from
the Cottage Hospital to our temporary home; the first
step in the plan. It had been easy to select a suitable
guest in Jimmy Picton, but the choice of a companion
had been harder. He had no steady girl and didn't
mind who I chose. Quite a few pretty young women
populated our wards, sweet clean faces under white
caps and neat round breasts in gray cotton uniforms,
all the same, all different. Some with freckles on noses,

some without; gray, blue, green eyes, all compassionate, all without passion. Sexy ones who wriggled starched bottoms, quiet ones who walked straight and avoided one's look, young flighty ones whose hair straggled and annoyed Matron, secretive, sly ones who were well groomed and never got found out. They were all very young, or so it seemed to me. I felt I had lived forever.

My first thought had been of Isobel Kenny, not unnaturally, but knowing how James felt about her made me hesitate. Finally I decided to ask him for suggestions. "I don't think it's good policy to socialize with the nurses," he said.

"What about the Sisters—or Matron?"

He looked up sharply from yet another label he was clicking out. "They're all rather old." I nodded. "Except Kenny," he added.

"I thought you didn't like her."

"She's formidable, but I don't dislike her. Do you want her to come?"

"It doesn't matter to me. You're the one to please."

"Suit yourself," he said eventually. "I really don't mind."

Sister Kenny accepted my invitation, not eagerly, but not hesitantly.

"They're here!" Sarah turned away from the curtains. "Josh, they're here. Oh dear, do I look all right? Is the room okay? I wish they hadn't come."

"Pour the drinks, dear birdbrain. I'll let them in."

I watched the evening like a voyeur through a lady's bedroom window. Somewhere outside myself I smiled and chatted and obviously did so sensibly and with good impact, but it was like viewing a play, not from the stalls but from the wings. I was a director, stage manager, and actor, and all these folks were carrying out my every wish, including myself.

"You've met James Picton, Sarah," I said. "And this is Isobel Kenny. My wife, Sarah." Taking Isobel's coat I saw Jimmy smile at my wife Sarah. They were both impressed. I wondered how it would have been if they had hated one another on sight, but that could not have happened. This game of consequences had to be played to its rules, and I a player too. It had momentum now, volition, purpose. It had come alive and was running the show. Something in me shouted faintly, "I want to stop it now before it's too late. I want to stop it. I only have to say a few words and it will be gone forever." And replaced by what? I hung up Isobel's coat and followed the three others into the living room.

Jimmy grinned at everyone, accepted a drink, and grinned some more, expecting in the curious way he has to be entertained. Sarah smiled back and asked where he lived, had he far to come? Isobel looked very attractive in something soft and yellow, but her aspect of calm self-assurance was firmly in place. I suspected she was shy and I wanted her to smile.

"Who's on duty tonight?" I asked, sitting beside her on the sofa.

"On children's? Staff Smith. They all like her, all our little horrors, but they get her running in circles sometimes."

"I've never seen Staff Smith as an Aphrodite, have you?"

"God, no! She's round and cuddly and sweet as hell, but hardly a sex symbol. Why?"

"That's what you think, my girl. You know the

mastoid called Adam something, the older lad who's due out tomorrow? He told me, in strictest confidence, that he experienced an overwhelming attraction to Staff Smith. His actual words were, if I remember rightly, 'I don't half fancy that bit of stuff in blue. Cor, when she bends over you she's got this lovely smell of talcum coming from her boobs.' Then he nudged me rather hard in the ribs."

I got my smile. "He's only thirteen," said Isobel. "I shall have to start watching the babes in arms next."

"I told Staff Smith about it, so she bought him some talc to take home to his mum."

Isobel nodded. "She's like that. She restores your faith in human nature for a while. I only hope the boy won't develop an Oedipus complex now."

I must have said more because Isobel was nodding over her drink and smiling quite often, but I was really concentrating on Sarah and Jim. They were sorting through our moderate collection of LPs and James was looking thoughtfully at my wife every time she spoke. Sarah rarely speaks directly to a person; do any of us, I don't know. But when she talks she talks sideways on so that you can look at her. When she wants to flatter, or is drunk, or good and mad, she may suddenly lift her eyes and fix you with them, but right now she was chattering and giving Jimmy every opportunity to look. He liked what he saw. I was satisfied. Far from happy, but satisfied.

After dinner, which was splendid but of which I ate little and tasted less, the talk came round unexpectedly to pollution. James and I share a hobby in fishing, though I hadn't been out since I'd come back to Somerfield. We'd promised ourselves a day on the river Tepe

soon, but so far our dates hadn't been able to coincide
and he'd gone alone the week before. "Nothing there,"
he said. "Nothing at all. I saw four dead perch. That
stretch has always been good before. You might remember it, Josh. Place near Wellard village on the
other side of the woods. You have to go through a
farm to get to the bank and there's a small weir.
Lovely pool top and bottom."

I remember it. I fell in the top one. We used to
walk across the edge of the weir as kids, bravely leaping from stone to slippery stone, sure of ourselves to
the point of folly. I'm still convinced I actually saw
minnows darting before my eyes until some kind hand
rescued me by the collar. Gale bawled me out for
shrinking my new trousers and nearly catching pneumonia, which I didn't, not even a cold, and Dad sent
me to swimming lessons. I was far more concerned at
having lost a brand new rod. It must have come out
well in the telling because they all laughed a lot, but
I was still in the wings, watching. Even the concerns
for dying fish in what had been pure water seemed,
not false, but remote. "What do you think is causing
it?" I asked Jimmy.

He shrugged. "There's a small factory quite a way
upstream. One of these 'bring light industry to the
countryside' concerns. It makes plastic toys or some
such nonsense and takes all the labor from the sur-
rounding farms with its high wages. Dad's always
losing hands to the same sort of places. I shouldn't
wonder if they're chucking out some untreated ef-
fluent."

Sarah's glance went from James to me and back.
"Don't get Josh started," she smiled. "You've found an
ally, but a verbose one."

"If people don't talk about it nothing gets done," I said shortly.

"What good will talking do?" said Isobel suddenly. "No one listens. It's too much bother. Tell a man he's being antisocial by fouling his neighbor's backyard and what does he say? What harm does it do, what difference does it make? I won't be here in seventy years' time. And who knows, he may be right."

"Do you really think that?" I asked her.

She shrugged, folding her fingers round her drink one by one. "Well, I won't be. I'm maybe one of the last Homo sapiens. We'll either disappear from the face of the earth like the dinosaur, or somewhere from all the mess we've made will appear Homo superior. Either way, I won't exist, individually or corporately."

"What if Homo superior already exists, raising his thinking little head out of the rubbish heap and deciding to do something about it?"

"It'll take too long for me to see."

Yes. Of course. But one has to try. If I'm in a position of responsibility I need to preserve that for which I am responsible, so all the world is mine and yours. That's what I thought on two or three brandies.

"Jim has just suggested you pay the place a visit," said Sarah.

"Uh?"

"The plastics factory, dearest. That you were so concerned about a moment ago."

"We could collect water samples up and down river from it. I've a young technician friend who works for a public analyst. He'd supply the stuff, I'm sure," added James.

We fixed a date. That is me all over; glorious on

principle but needing a Jimmy Picton to suggest the
spade work. Still, Sarah obviously admired his practical attitude and that was all to the good. Jimmy said,
"I'd like to shake those old dodderers on the Council
with a bit of solid evidence like that. Been getting
away with it for far too long, what with refusing
planning permission to those who can't afford the
backhander and so forth. Stopped my father putting
up a new garage, they did, because it was agricultural
land. But they allowed four new houses to be built on
the same spot a few years later by a very wealthy man.
Yes, a bit of pollution scandal might shift 'em."

When I laughed I hope it was to myself. I wish I
could discover whether any man anywhere ever does
anything for any other reason than self-interest. I
don't think I would find him, but I wish I had time.

The evening glowed to a late close. Conversation
idled and the records selected became softer and
older, the dreamy, seductive kind. James watched my
wife from under his fair eyelashes. He has freckles all
over his face, even on his eyelids, and a sheen of gold
on the forearms that protrude from his cuffs. Curious,
I thought, that I should notice more of Jimmy than
I did of Isobel, though she sat close beside me and I
could smell her perfume, and I talked with her to
exclude the other two. It was around one-thirty when
our guests left and we went to bed.

Sarah staggered a little before the dressing table.
"You had a bloody good evening, didn't you?" she
said, light but acid. "I thought you were going to end
up with Sister Isobelnecessary on your lap."

"Whom?"

She brushed her hair with the heavy silver-backed
brush I gave her on our anniversary. Our first anni-

versary. "When I was at school there was a girl called Isobel, and everyone called her Isobelnecessaryona-bike. See?"

"Sounds silly to me."

"Really? You usually like that kind of nonsense. And kids are silly. What do you expect from a group of seven-year-olds—Oscar Wilde? Just because you've been enchantingly witty all evening doesn't give you the right to be disgustingly superior about my child-hood jokes. Perhaps Sister Kenny didn't have a child-hood, perhaps she was born intellectual as well as pretty." She slammed the brush down and waited for me to get mad, as I normally will when she is entirely unreasonable. I was mad, but I turned away from her reflection with a shrug.

"Don't sulk!" she said.

"Peach bloom, nothing was further from my mind. I just feel tired and a little drunk." I undressed and was in bed before her, lying on my back and staring at the ceiling where vicious pictures of Sarah and James Picton exchanging smiles and glances flashed to taunt me. Was it all going to be like this? Would it get more tolerable, easier . . . or less?

"Did you really have an enjoyable evening?" said Sarah. "You seemed to."

"So did—yes. Yes, thank you, my love. I did. Hurry up and put that light out."

She stared a long time at me before she clicked the switch. I looked up at the ceiling. There were several hairline cracks like wandering rivers. Somerfield long ago had a coal mine of small proportions. It had soon run out and filled with water from the limestone tunnels under the Mendips, but it left a small re-minder of its passing in the subsidence. Gale's house has hardly been affected at all, but for the hairline river cracks in the ceilings. Sarah put the light out and got in beside me.

"Good night, Josh," she said, curving half her body over mine and finding my mouth with hers. I kissed her without putting my arms around her. "Are you really too tired?" she murmured, smelling of brandy and toothpaste, her tongue tip tracing my lips.

"I am a bit," I said. "Good night, Sarah. Sweet dreams." And slowly and deliberately I turned on my side with my back to her. She didn't say another word, but I was sure I heard her sniffling. She's not crying, I told myself. She is not crying. And if she is, they are only brandy tears.

I woke early the next day, Saturday, with the impression of a weight on my forehead and a tightening hand at my throat. I struggled up against the pillows, trying to breathe. The back of my throat was sore and dry and my sinuses ached dully. The air around me sang like someone was blowing over guitar strings. I kept wiping my hands on the bedspread to dry them. The light was faint in the room but I had to squint against it to count the roses on the wallpaper. I had got to twenty along and five down before I realized. Ever since I can remember I have had a compulsion to count things when I have a high temperature. Usually it signifies approaching influenza or just a bad cold. I pictured very clearly a chair we had had in the living room of our Los Angeles house. I was six, maybe. I was lying on the couch in this same dizzy state counting with my eyes the row of round-headed brass nails around the back of that chair. They were very close together and difficult to count because they jiggled up and down and I couldn't count much past twenty anyway. But I could not stop. Even when I screwed my eyes tight and turned my head into the cushions those nails wiggled and wobbled before my inner eye and demanded to be counted. Thirty-five, thirty-six, thirty-seven . . .

Sarah stirred uneasily. Although she seems so far away in sleep, she leaves the pieces of her that sense the unusual. If I sit up in bed or even get out and am quite healthy, she will not move, but if the pattern of me or other things around is suddenly abnormal some chord in her is plucked and quivers her awake. She can sleep through thunderstorms but not the quiet closing of a door that should not be closing. She can sleep through my occasional snores, but not through my entirely silent counting.

She opened her eyes and her baby face became a lady face. "What is it?"

It hurt my throat to reply and even though I was looking at her those bloody wallpaper roses marched across my vision. "Got a temperature. Don't worry, it's probably a cold."

She sat up and peered at me through the gloom, fuzzy thick gloom it seemed to me. "You look bad," she said. "Lie down."

"I'd rather get up. It's so airless in here."

"Lie down, Josh. I'll open the window wider. Now, do you want some tea?" She grabbed her robe and went before I could reply. In five minutes she was back with the tea, soluble aspirin, and several bottles of pills from the medicine cabinet. "Aspirin first," she instructed, pouring the tea. "Now, which of these is tetracycline?"

"Orange ones." The aspirin soothed my throat as it went down.

"Are your glands swollen?"

I felt under my jawbone with damp, shaky fingertips. "Yes, doctor. It's probably just pharyngitis."

"You look sick." She put two capsules in my hand. "Every six hours. Don't forget."

I grinned at her. She made me feel better just to look at her and her clean morning skin. "Bully. May I have some sloppy porridge for breakfast, Miss Flashman?"

"Good, you're hungry. It can't be too bad."

"I'm more afraid I might throw up all this medication taken on an empty stomach."

"Don't! I'm going, right now. Oh, Josh, what is that unlabeled bottle of tablets in the cabinet? I'd hate to take the wrong thing by mistake."

"I meant to dispose of them. They're old." I broke out in sweat, but she'd gone and couldn't see my guilt. Now I'd have to find another hiding place.

Even a slight cold can be dangerous as smallpox to a body with much-weakened resistance. Pneumonia can set in fast and once you're down you keep right on down. I lay in bed and fought with it. I remembered how once in Medical School I had been suffering from a disgusting cold; nose dripping, voice croaking, head throbbing, all the classic symptoms. Tom Donaldson, one of our lecturers, had finally tired of my constant sniffling. "For God's sake go out and lie in the rain for a few hours and get pneumonia," he'd said. "We can bloody well cure that!"

It may have been prompt medication or Sarah's attention or my determination, or a combination of all three, but by Monday morning I was well enough to go to work. Sarah fussed but I went anyway. Two days in bed are plenty for me; being incapable gets me mad. You're going to go out angry then, aren't you, said a voice I was beginning to know, and I wondered whether the illness and quick recovery had been a reminder, a payment in advance.

CHAPTER SEVEN

The river Tepe is a graceful old lady, meandering like an old lady's mind, bordered by corsages of willows and the lace of white cow parsley. Scarcely an inch of its banks had been unknown to me as a child. I had crawled eye-deep along them as an Indian and found cover, bunched like a caterpillar, among the bushes as a gold-laden outlaw. I knew where the bluebells hid and where the yellow buttercups lived among the emerald grass, the marsh buttercups with their roots deep in river mud. I knew where to find Aunt Gale the first primroses because she asked that I find them, and I carried them home inside my jacket. I knew where there was frog spawn to take to school in jars, and dragonflies, and where the mayflies cavorted on their one and only day of love, if the trout didn't catch them. There had been wild strawberries too, in Wellard woods, and plump fish to curl in the frying pan and the river water still upon them. There must have been drawbacks, there must have been hours when nothing took the bait, there must have been arguments with stinging nettles and with Dad for being late at meals, that is the way of boys; but I couldn't remember them.

This day was like the days of memory, yellow as corn with sunshine, green and fresh as new lettuce with last night's rain. We strolled the Tepe's banks, James, Sarah, and I, carrying plastic sterile pots and long poles with loops at the ends. Each for our own reason had come to take water from the river; James to confound the Council, Sarah because I asked her, myself to watch and encourage and monitor. Of the three, James was the happiest. Sarah looked uncertain. I was mostly silent.

I hadn't really believed James would turn up; he wasn't on duty at the hospital but his father's farm had been keeping him busy most weekends lately, and since the dinner party we'd exchanged very few words about the pollution of our local river. He'd talked about my wife several times, though.

"Tell Sarah how much I enjoyed the evening," he said. "She's a marvelous cook. Lucky man, aren't you." And, "Delightful person, your wife. Wish I could find one like her." I could have wrung his neck but it was all going my way. You started it, Joshua, I heard my thoughts say in the voice of my father. Never start what you don't want to finish. But how do you know? How does anyone know?

One morning I drove out of Somerfield to collect James from his cottage lodgings and take him to work after he'd called to say that his car had broken down. As we drove back I guess I was showing off Auntie Morgan a little; the Somerset roads are winding and hilly, just the thing for fast motoring and quick gear changes. I came out of a left turn rather wide and in front was a stationary truck. A car was coming toward

us and that road is only wide enough for two. It oc-
curred to me that my whole plan would be futile, can-
celled, if James and I hit the truck at fifty miles per
hour, and for a moment I admit I considered it. There
were advantages, but mostly for me and my conscience,
and my hands had already swung the wheel, my feet
had already hit brake and clutch. We stopped behind
the truck with inches to spare.

"You all right, old chap?" said Jimmy.

I wiped away the beads from my top lip and
grinned at him. "Trying to get us all killed. Sorry."

I let them get ahead of me along the river bank but
Sarah, sweet child, kept looking back for me. Each
time she turned I looked away, staring at the fast
water, and watched them intently as soon as they
walked on. We were about half a mile downstream
from the factory when I saw Jim stop and attach a
sample bottle to his rod. He slithered down the bank
in his short rubber boots and leaned out over the
water. As the bottle dipped into the stream he slipped
and wobbled and Sarah caught his straining left hand,
holding him steady until the jar was full. It took an
awfully long time. She pulled him up the bank and
he picked a wild flower and gave it to her. "For my
savior," he said. I heard him say it as I came up. "And
a very pretty one, too."

They exchanged a brief glance, then Sarah noticed
me. A little defiantly, she threaded the gaudy dandelion through the buttonhole of her coat and it lay
against her breast like a medallion. The milk of the
broken stalk stained her fingers and she sniffed them.
Do you remember the smell of dandelions? She smiled
at me. I could smell dandelion clear in my memory as
she rubbed her fingertips together. "Why are you so
slow?" she said. "You keep falling behind, Josh."

"I'm exhausted with all these samples Jim keeps giving me to carry."

"Aw, you poor little soul." She sounded snappy and her mouth had that top-lip-down expression, but she took the bag of bottles from me and walked with her arm through mine for a while. James strode ahead, but not so far I could talk without him hearing.

"You remember me telling you about the little girl we had in, Sarah? The one we sent to Taunton with osteosarcoma."

"The one with the widower father?"

"Um. I heard she died two days ago. Lung secondaries. She was a lovely kid, you know. Only twelve."

Sarah frowned to herself. "I should feel sorrier than I do," she said suddenly. "But I didn't know her. What about her poor dad, though? He'll have nothing left; that makes me sad."

"Yes. He has nowhere to turn, my rosebud, nowhere for his love to go. It's a bad thing."

We strolled for a while, Jimmy in front with his square, healthy frame in sports jacket and cavalry twill, his head brazen as a crown. "We're being morbid, aren't we?" said my wife. "What a subject to choose on such a lovely day."

"What difference does the weather make? Caroline died on a day like this. Lots of people do. I think I shall choose a sunny day, exit thus in a blaze of glory, go down with the sun, fade into the dusk."

Sarah penetrated my skull with her eyes, but I smiled. The wall I was beginning to build gave a small degree of immunity. "Don't say such things," she said. "You make me cold. Hey, Jimmy!"

He turned so sharply he must have been listening.

"Yes, Sarah, my dear?" He treated her to his open, honest smile.

"Josh is depressing me, and on a day like this. Don't you think misery should be reserved for cold rain and foggy Novembers?"

James checked my face. "That depends," he said diplomatically. "Shall we cross the Main Road to pass the factory and come back to the river at Turner's Lane?"

"Good idea." Sarah let go of my arm and followed him.

The small factory that we glimpsed behind its new fencing and row of neat fir trees, all fresh and the same height, looked innocuous enough. One chimney breathed a plume of steam. An attempt had been made to disguise its presence from the roadside, half an acre or so of grass and carefully arranged shrubs hid most of its gray utility, but it looked out of place, as if the Martians had landed and quietly set up home in the middle of Somerset.

"It could be the Martians," I said.

James stared at me. "What could?"

"Take no notice of my husband's foolery," said Sarah. "He gets these aberrations. He means the factory."

"Oh. Look, I may be dense, but how?"

"Just set down way out here," Sarah said. "A quiet invasion by aliens and we insular British would never question it. Josh would, but then he's a nosey, impressionable Yank, aren't you, love? That has its drawbacks too though, being credulous all the time. Remember *The War of the Worlds*?"

"A slight! A slight!" I clutched my chest and staggered. "Pierced to the heart! I die! I die! Sarah, run fetch a candle to illuminate the seven hundredth codicil; I've decided to leave it all to a cat's home. Gather round greedy eyes, feast yourselves upon one who breathes his last in defense of his noble homeland and its peoples. Bring the leeches and the star-spangled banner. I will shuffle off this mortal coil with my credulity round my ankles."

Sarah snorted a little, she is sometimes most inelegant. "Get up off your knees, you idiot," she giggled. "Those jeans have just been washed."

James watched with a smile round his mouth and total confusion in his eyes. I'm sure he thought I was insane, but he'd never have said so. Sarah was there and Sarah was laughing. "I thought you were Canadian," he said to me.

"I was."

Above the factory I let him take the samples. The day was resting on the couch of afternoon and the trees stretched their leaves like fingers at the ends of muscled limbs toward the sun. Across the river a man was driving a motor mower across the factory grass for the first time this year. You could tell it was the first time. There is a particularly keen evocative smell with the first cutting that is never so pungent afterward, and the care he was taking, the stylishness with which he clipped the edges would cease as the job became a summer chore.

Sarah came over to where I was standing, too lazy to move my back from an oak trunk. As she came I saw how she moved, always cat graceful, and how her hair was bronzed and how her head was down to pick her way between the thistles and the coarse, buttercupped grass. It was like watching a complete stranger because I saw her every day and yet had forgotten how she was. I hope I will never miss her.

I hope there is no heaven where I'll spend mean time just waiting for her.

She took a bottle from her pocket and handed it to me. "Jim wants another," she said, so I opened the small bag and gave her one. As she took it, she said, "Josh, are you all right?"

"Yes, thank you. Smell the grass over there."

She didn't. "Look, are you sure?"

"Of course. Why?"

"You're different somehow. Your attitudes have changed."

"Don't they always, flower feet? Go give James his bottle."

"That's part of it," she said unhappily. Her funny crisscross frown flickered on. "I would never have believed a couple of months ago that you would be so disinterested in a project to do with pollution. You'd have been pacing the banks like a madman and issuing orders and getting water over the tops of your waders. You'd have been bending everybody's ear with arguments, pounding a bench at the Council, driving me out of my kitchen . . . oh, everything. You know you would. Today you've hardly bothered to look at the river. It's not like you, Josh. What's wrong?"

"Priorities change," I said quietly. "Maybe I've decided mankind is already lost and I can do nothing about it."

My wife glared at me; she does not like me to change. It is a personal affront because it alters my reliability. "You've never believed that!" she said. "You always say that someone somewhere wants to know. You can't give up, Joshua!"

"Sometimes these things give one up, Sarah. You turn round and they've deserted you without a word. Self-interest motivates us all, my bird. A cause or a

157

fight may perch on your shoulder and take advantage of it for a while, but if a stronger self-interest comes along, away it flies. And it's always gone before you know it and it always leaves a sad little footprint behind."

"I don't believe it!" snapped Sarah, and walked away. I wondered how long it would be before she analyzed what I had said.

The letter arrived from Madison's clinic in a pristine white envelope, engraved in black with the great man's name and titles, typed on crisp, thick, unnecessarily large notepaper. Aunt Gale gave it the most cursory of glances before she handed it to me, but after she'd read her mail and shaken her head over the electricity bill, she said, "Have you got anything interesting?"

"Yes, dear Aunt." I put the letter in my inside pocket.

"Hospital business?"

"Yes, dear Aunt. Don't fish. A second opinion is wanted, that's all."

"Joshua! I never fish!"

"Come on, you're not that inhuman. What were your letters?"

She has a very straight back, my Aunt Gale. "None of your business, boy."

It was easy enough to obtain a few hours' leave from the hospital. I hadn't realized how pleasant it was to be rid of a superior like Desmond Marker. I recall one desperate day when Sarah was ill with 'flu and I was heading for it rapidly, when a pipe had burst and the ceiling had fallen in all over the bathroom, when a fuse had blown and we had no water and the car wouldn't start. Mercifully, those days are rare. Marker told me very formally that I had been

AWOL for four hours, a very serious matter, Joshua,
and no excuses. It was good to be able to say I had
important business to conduct and have no questions
asked. I trusted to luck that Sarah would not change
the habits of two years by calling me at work. Even
if she should, my absence would bring uncertainty.
Don't ring me, Sarah. Please don't need me today.

She gave me breakfast before I left and made a
tray to take to Aunt Gale while I ate my toast.
"Haven't you noticed?" she said, taking the marmalade
jar out of my hand just as I was about to use it. She
spooned some into a dish on the tray, then banged
the pot back on the table way out of reach.

I glanced up at her; it does not suit my Sarah to be
sour, her eyes and mouth go small. "You're feeling
mean," I said, standing for the marmalade. "Why so,
truffles? Did you sleep badly?"

"No." She hurried out with the tray. When she is
angry Sarah does things in neat, swift spurts. She
moves smoothly and fast. Really hurt and sad, she can
do nothing at all. Her hands won't coordinate and her
feet drag aimlessly. She was angry because I hadn't
noticed her new robe, a much-needed replacement for
the old woolly one. She was back soon; it would not
have been like her to stay and complain about me to
Gale. There is a weakness or a strength in her that
makes my plan easier. Sarah never shares her feelings
for sympathy. I think she prefers to suffer pain or joy
alone, and it's usually pain for joy has no endurance,
because talking and bemoaning soften it and change
it and make you feel better when you have no reason
to feel better. I knew a lot of the hurting I must cause
would be perpetuated and enlarged by my wife
herself.

There was a Joshua Steel sitting at the kitchen table

159

that day whom I hardly knew and disliked on sight. I tried to recall the mornings of twenty years ago, hurried bacon-smelling mornings with my school cap on the table between Dad's large fist around his coffee cup and my small one trying to be strong like his. Those childhood mornings would not come clear. My father's hand seemed to push me away with the palm outward. I couldn't remember him ever having pushed me away.

I looked and Sarah was there, scrubbing the roses off the breakfast dishes as she washed up. "I must go," I said, fetching my jacket from the hook behind the back door.

"Good-bye," she said.

I went out, then put my head back around the door. "By the way, petal, the new robe is most becoming."

She glared for a moment, then blew me a kiss on the soap bubbles. "Drive carefully," she said.

Some days come in frustrated. This day was one like I'd had before; a day demanding useful things to be done but suppressing action. A screaming day if you're near screaming. It was gray, cool, not wet, not dry, a day you couldn't grumble at because it was in all respects inoffensive. I drove toward Taunton two hours earlier than I needed to, two hours that could conceivably be spent in practical or intellectual pursuits. Glastonbury was only a few miles to the east and I hadn't seen the Tor for many years. Beautiful countryside, the most beautiful in Britain so people say, lay on either side of the road. I had only to stop and look. My eyes were wide open yet saw nothing. My mind had halted but said I ought to be doing.

I drove toward Taunton. The Morgan eased along more quietly than usual for no matter how I tried I could not concentrate on her throaty voice. It was a day for wide, staring eyes and not blinking, for vacancy underlined by confusion. We nosed into the town and wondered what we were doing there. After growling round in circles for an uncounted while, the Morgan found a car park and stopped. It was hard to believe that I had any control of events. My hand surprised me by taking the keys out of the ignition. The leather smell of the seats and the faint petrol fumes were attractive but I left them. Maybe some days take over. I did not know where I was going and my feet trod the roads according to no design of mine, in a placid, uneasy fog. In the shop windows I saw my own reflection and nothing behind the glass. My eyes saw people and places with great clarity; they must have, because I remember so well. But to my inner sight they were a pastel blur and over and over in my head ran a silly tune I'd heard on the radio, a song with half the words missing.

I wandered for hours but when I looked at my wristwatch only twenty minutes had passed. Some days are so slow. I don't know why we break them into twenty-four equal portions, and sixty and sixty again. Such divisions are emotionally irrelevant. Today had heavy feet whereas some days are golden-slippered and some barefoot. So it was very slowly that the idea came to find a cup of coffee somewhere. I knew Taunton quite well, but not today. I did not recognize the street nor the buildings, nor the small bakery cum coffee house into which I wandered. A waitress brought me black coffee and I couldn't remember having asked for it.

Sister Kenny spoke to me twice, she said, before I realized she was there.

"May I join you?" she said.

"Of course, Isobel. I'm afraid I'm not good company today. At your own risk."

She gave me an outline of a smile and sat down. "Would it be impertinent to ask what you're doing here?"

"No." I fully intended to give an explanation, but words were slow in forming.

"It's my day off," she said. Her eyes were very beautiful and mysterious in the dim interior light. "I'm shopping."

"You have beautiful eyes, Isobel." These days have no room for spoken trivia; I felt I wanted truth told and nothing else.

She looked away from me. "I wouldn't say you are bad company," she said. "Thank you for the compliment. How is Sarah?"

"Sarah is currently unhappy because she is uncertain."

We were silent for quite a while as Isobel's coffee came and she took a cigarette from her bag. I tried to find my lighter but she had lit up with a match before I could offer. "I liked your wife," she said. "The evening I came to dinner was one of the best I've had for years."

"Jimmy said so, too. You'll have to come again."

"Thank you. I would like that. How do you get along with James? I realize it's ridiculous, but he frightens me. All those silences. He never seems to use extraneous words and I'm no good at small talk either, so we communicate in short bursts with ages of nothing in between. I never know whether he has understood me, whether he's very clever or rather dumb."

I grinned. "How odd. He thinks almost the same about you."

"Really? Oh, he can't. Jimmy isn't the least bit shy."

"Are you?"

"Very. More with James than with you. You don't always seem ready to criticize."

"Neither is he, believe me. It's his way, that's all. He's very kind. I'm sure he'd be quite worried if he knew what you think of him."

"I've known him for four years," she mused. "And it takes a stranger to show me Jimmy. And myself. Do you do it purposely, Doctor Steel?"

"Josh. Want another coffee?"

The morning was becoming sharper, the silly song had gone from my head. Over the second coffee we talked shop and the silences were comfortable. Isobel seemed in no hurry to go and the time speeded to normal. At ten-thirty I called for our bill. "I'm sorry to leave," I said. "Thank you for keeping me company, Isobel."

She gave me a proper smile. "My pleasure."

As we emerged from the cafe, Staff Nurse Taylor passed us. She glanced first without recognition and then with a comprehensive stare that absorbed all the facts and came up with the wrong answer. "Hello, Taylor," said Isobel pleasantly, but the young lady had already hurried along the pavement with her buttocks bouncing indignantly.

"How rude!" said Isobel. "And she's usually so talkative."

"She'll be talking, never fear."

Colin Madison received me in his tawny office again and this time a very expensive Zeiss microscope stood on the table in the window. I think he had been waiting on cue because he put the last slide away as I entered, turned in his revolving chair, and smiled his triangular smile. "Good morning, Doctor Steel."

"Hi. Are those mine?"

He frowned. "Uh, yes, yes. Just been checking them."

"May I see?"

"Well, I think we should discuss your treatment." He moved to his desk and hid behind it, back in the power seat. He sighed in a chill, cosy way and his eyelid ticked like a clock.

"By all means. May I?" I sat in the chair he had left and pulled the tray of slides toward me.

"Well, all right. Are you familiar with that type of microscope?"

"No, Mr. Madison, but I'll touch no more than the eyepieces and the fine focus. Please, do expand about my treatment."

He waited in tense silence as I adjusted the Zeiss to my eyes and put the first smear under. I didn't have to look. Back to the same old picture, down the same old hill, only farther. Even though I had already known, the confirmation was depressing, sobering, infuriating.

"Uh, not too good," said Madison. "Eh?"

"Bloody awful," I agreed.

He stroked his face carefully, pinching a fold of skin above his twitching eye. "I think we must try blood transfusions and a different cytotoxin. You've had methotrexate, yes. Now, recently we have been trying a brand new drug, much less indiscriminate . . . " He trailed into thought. "Better come in soon."

I took a deep breath. "I'm afraid I can't be an inpatient, sir. I appreciate it makes things difficult for the clinic and the staff, but there are overriding reasons."

Madison was not the type to allow himself more than sketches of facial expressions. He raised one eyebrow slowly and let it sink again. "Difficult is an understatement," he said. "Are your reasons so pressing?"

"Yes, Mr. Madison. And private."

"Well, I don't see how it can be done as an out-patient. Either you must place yourself in our hands completely or not at all."

I spun the revolving chair to look at him. "No human being is another's property, Mr. Madison, nor should he be blackmailed into becoming such. I am willing to meet any extra fees the work might incur."

His mouth drew down at the corners as he turned the cards of medical inclination, profit motive and my temperament. Such was his inscrutability that I could not guess which was winning. "It is because of my wife that I ask," I said pleadingly. "She's a very sensitive, hysterical person. The shock, when it comes, will be enough without protracted agony beforehand." Integrity, where art thou?

"The fees could be considerably higher," said Madison.

"They will be met."

"An out-patient cannot receive the comprehensive treatment he would enjoy here at the clinic," Madison continued.

"All enjoyment is relative."

We had, it seemed, an agreement.

I was rediscovering loneliness and it had a bitter taste. I am fortunate in not having been often lonely;

it is a sad thing which people either endure or finalize in their own way. To some it becomes their only friend, a thing to be grasped and hugged and called "independence"; to others it is a mortal dread that sends them into the streets and crowded pubs on Saturday nights for fear of their own voice. That my loneliness was self-imposed made it worse, for I could not truly understand why it had come about.

Had it not been for my own loneliness I might not have noticed Jimmy's, so perhaps that means that no human sensation is totally bad. Jim's life was mainly work. He arrived at the hospital always before I did, worked through coffee and often lunch breaks and seldom left before seven in the evening. Weekends not spent at his father's farm saw him in and out of Somerfield Cottage Hospital. He was an institution, a rock, reliable and heavily relied upon. Desmond Marker would have mistaken his love of medicine and his loneliness for devotion to duty. I could hear the old devil say, "He's a sound man, Joshua, sound."

When I asked James to drop in any time for a drink I thought he would say, "Thanks, I might do that," and not bother, but it was a step I had to take anyway, a prelude. As it happened, he said, "Thanks, I might do that," and arrived on our doorstep that very evening. Sarah was pleased to see him and forgot to grumble at me for not giving her notice. This ball had momentum now; it was going so fast it was getting away from me.

It was the first of many visits. Jim took to coming home with me two or three times a week for dinner. Often he would arrive at nine or ten at night, just to sit and watch television with us. I watched Sarah. At first she treated Jimmy as she might any friend of mine, taking pains to include both of us in the conversation, but as I grew less and less responsive, she talked more and more to him alone. I would even excuse myself and go up to my old room at the top of the house where I would sit for half an hour or more on the hard little bed, trying to read or write, but it is futile to attempt to occupy a mind whose only awareness is downstairs in another room.

Sarah said, one evening after Jim had gone, "Don't you like Jimmy?"

"No, rosebud. Why else should I invite him to our home, as if it were his own? Why else would I share my food and wine with him?"

"Yes, why else?" she murmured. The television programs ended and the set began its wail. She got up to turn it off. "You're not very polite to him," she said.

"I don't have to be. He's a friend. People are so much more polite to strangers, or hadn't you noticed."

"Familiarity breeds contempt?"

"Or respect."

"Then why do you go off when he's here?" She came to sit on the arm of my chair and her fingers trailed on my hand. She likes to contact lightly, perhaps to feel a mental pulse. When she wants me she wants strong, warm drowning, but when she does not she eases away from all but the gentlest touch.

I patted her fingers and she took them away. "Jimmy understands that I have things to do whether he is here or not," I said. "He just wants a little company. Besides, I see him all day." She looked down uneasily. "Sarah, my sweet, don't you like him? Shall I tell him not to come again?"

"Don't be silly," she said. "I think he's very nice."

"Good. I happen to know he's very fond of you and he keeps telling me how grateful he is for the delicious meals you cook."

"I know. He said." And Sarah's eyes had small, quietly pleased sparkles in them.

"I rang the Cottage Hospital today and they said you weren't there." Aunt Gale was doing things with dishes and saucepans and her words were barely audible. I sat at the table drinking tea and feeling dizzy. Madison's registrar had dropped me at the front gate but the twenty yards walk up the path had damn near killed me. Even the tea tasted dry and disgusting. "Sister McCarthy said you'd not been in all day." Now that was more ominous.

"No. I . . . uh, I had to go to Taunton unexpectedly."

"I see." She poured herself a cup of tea and sat opposite me. For all the world she could have been Samson watching a mouse. I felt naked. "Are you sure that's all it was?"

Gale can spot a lie in most people before it's thought. I can remember wishing often that I had that ability; even Sarah says I'm too trusting. After all, why should people lie to me? But they do, like me. So I shrugged.

"You look unwell, Joshua. Are you working too hard or is it personal?"

"Personal?"

"I'm not stupid, boy!" She still calls me "boy" sometimes, when I deserve it. "I live in this house, you know, and I have poor eyesight, but not that poor. That Jimmy Picton who keeps visiting—you know who he comes to see, don't you? And you keep talking about Isobel Kenny as a person will when he's fond of someone. I thought you had a good, happy marriage." There must have been a quality in my look that I did not mean to put there because she suddenly blushed and hid behind her teacup. "I'm sorry, Joshua. It's none of my business, you have your own affairs to manage. But be careful."

I patted her hand and smiled at her. "Charmer," she said, and I thought I'd won, but like a bloody idiot, as I got up and went to the door my knees sagged and my head spun and I wasn't prepared for it. Our combined efforts got me back into the chair and I sat there feeling sick and very, very foolish. Gale felt my forehead and pulse, looked worried and said, "I'll call Doctor Gordon. I knew there was something wrong with you."

I held on to her arm for a while. "No, don't call him. It's nothing."

She made a disbelieving noise. "You don't almost pass out for nothing," she said. "I'm calling Doctor Gordon. You look dreadful."

The way I felt it was easier to be honest. I said, "I know what's wrong with me and it's being treated. That's why I'm so groggy, why I was at Taunton. It's all right Gale, really."

First she didn't believe me, then she looked again and came round to it, then she poured two more cups of tea, checked my pulse again and seemed happier. Then she spoke. "What is it? What have you got?"

I'd wondered when someone would ask, so it was all ready. "Bronchiectasis and an odd kind of anemia. The two together make things worse, of course, but don't worry. Although these diseases are distressing they're chronic and not major disasters." I had said it so many times in my head I wondered whether this time had been out loud, but Gale nodded.

I think even so well-polished a lie did not go entirely undetected. Maybe I was a little too glib. Gale certainly had doubts, but where illness is concerned doubts like that are easily pushed away. I watched her push them away with her teacup. "You should have told me before," she said reproachfully. "I would have looked after you better."

"Than what, dear Aunt Gale, pearl of my life? I could ask for nothing more than I have already. I'm all right. Fine as a day in May."

"Your father used to say that. Fine as a day in May." Her eyes looked back at a spot in the past and she smiled. Sometimes when she smiles she looks like Dad. "Does Sarah know about this, Josh?"

"No. Don't tell her."

"You're being stupid."

"Perhaps, but don't tell her. I don't want her worrying over nothing. Please, my sweet?"

"Charmer," she said again.

That's another thing about dear Aunt Gale; she respects your wishes most of the time. Not like my darling Sarah who does exactly what she thinks is good for me, most of the time.

When our holiday plans fell through my wife was both upset and angry. I heard about it on the day after my treatment. It was a windy evening, too warm in our sitting room to light a full-blown fire and too cold to sit comfortably without heat. Sarah came in with a one-bar electric fire she'd unearthed from the toolshed.

"Gale says it works. Put a plug on it," she said, dropping the plug and a screwdriver on my stomach.

"Hey, Sarah! Sarah, come back!"

"What?" I had grown to dread my wife's face. In a month it had changed so that too often it was rumpled with a frustration of spirit, too often her mouth shut tight with small vertical lines on her top lip. And too often her eyes relaxed and daydreamed while secret thoughts furrowed her forehead. Now she glowered at me, and at all things.

"Why are you so disgruntled, Miss Muffet?"

She hesitated. My wife is not very big and when she hesitates she shrinks. "Oh, it's all gone wrong!" she said. I wanted to pick her up and cuddle her.

I breathed in and out very slowly. "What has?"

"Our holiday. Josh, I'm sorry. It was going to be so wonderful. I tried so hard but it didn't work out. That was a lovely villa, big enough for six, we could have taken a couple of friends. It would have been such fun."

"Oh," I said.

Sarah came to kneel on the rug, staring at the soot patterns at the back of the empty grate. She began to poke at them with the coal tongs and bits fell on the hearth. I took the plug apart and began fitting in the wires. "Are you disappointed?" said Sarah.

"Yes, of course. What happened?"

"I couldn't get places on the ferry, not any ferry. They're booked solid all season. I even inquired about air fares but it was too late and too expensive anyway. I'm sorry, Josh."

"It wasn't your fault. I realize it's academic now, but who had you in mind as a couple of friends?"

She checked me over for sarcasm. "Jimmy would have liked to come if he could have found a friend to bring."

"I see. You discussed our holiday with Jimmy."

"Yes, I did. You left it all to me, you weren't in the least interested. Why shouldn't I?"

"No reason. I'm glad he's such a good friend."

"Yes, he is!" she shouted, leaving me to finish with the fire.

Gale came in shortly afterwards. "What's the matter with Sarah?" she said. "Doesn't the fire work?"

I plugged it in and switched it on and the bar began to tick and sparkle as specks of sawdust burned on the element. Whiskers of wood smoke reminded me of garden bonfires and their good smells. "Our proposed holiday had fallen through. She is annoyed."

Gale sat down. "I think she's worried, too; about you. She asked me yesterday if I thought you were looking unwell. I had to say yes."

"I hope that's all you said. I don't ask you to lie for me, Gale, but please don't tell her the whole truth. Make her ask me herself if she mentions it again."

"I did. If she hasn't asked, I presume she has her reasons. You're being very silly, you know. I wish your father were alive. He'd make you see sense."

"I wish he were, too, but he wouldn't change my mind on this point."

"I don't understand, why be so secretive? Sarah's an intelligent girl. She's not going to panic or run away. She'd come to terms with it."

The fire glowed red in the darkening room, warming my toes. "My dear Aunt Gale, you are an intelligent person, too, but already you've changed your attitude toward me. From now on you'll watch over me like over a glass animal. You'll make excuses for me if I'm unreasonable, you'll forgive all sorts of things you'd never have forgiven before, you'll keep an eagle eye out for any sign or symptom and read terrible meanings into a cough or a headache. You will pity me, Gale, even if you're determined not to."

My aunt frowned severely. "Aren't you overstating

just a bit? You always had a fanciful imagination. I shall worry about you, naturally, but I always did."

"Knowing changes a person. You can't be the Aunt Gale who did not know again. You are stained with the knowledge and it has made you different already. And because I asked you to keep it to yourself you'll find it hard to rationalize. It will gnaw at you. That's why Sarah mustn't know. If she pitied me, and she would because she's made that way, I'd pity myself and all of us would suffer."

"It could cut two ways," said Gale. "She could jolly you out of self-pity. Remember, you must have changed too, because *you* know."

"That's different," I said, but was it true? "I'm the one who is sick."

Gale wasn't convinced. She squared her shoulders and pulled down her sleeves. "I still think you're being ridiculous. People are much tougher than you seem to imagine. Sarah certainly is. She is very much mistress of her own soul, and don't you forget it. Now, I must put some fresh flowers in here, that lot are almost dead." Blood-red petals drifted to the floor as she moved the vase.

"What do you mean?"

She groaned down to her knees and gathered the broken flowers. "Sarah? If you haven't got eyes in your head that's your fault. I sometimes think you were spoiled, Josh, or too much by yourself when you were a child. You spend so much time inside your own little world. You're generous and thoughtful, but that's not the same thing. Pass me the paper bin."

I did. "Isn't Sarah what I think she is?"

"How do I know? What you think has always been a mystery to me. Open the door, please."

I mulled over what Gale had said when I was in

bed that night. My body was tired but I couldn't sleep. My brain had discovered an idea and wanted to reason it out. Once I read a book in which it was said that the human ego is by its very nature vain; it expects all other egos to be the same as itself. When they are not, it allows for but cannot understand the difference. So we each inhabit the universe inside our own head and it is never exactly the same as any other. There is a word for the philosophy but it fluttered at the back of my mind like a gray moth and would not come out. In chemical analysis it is permissible to extrapolate, so I followed the notion. I wondered whether Gale's Sarah was totally different from my Sarah, and Jim's Sarah different again. If that was so, only Sarah could guess at her real nature, just as my real self is often a stranger to me. After that it all became too perplexing. I could only think that I knew probably more of the important things about Sarah than any other human being and if I am selective in what I know, I am less selective about her than anyone else. I am grateful to have learned so much of a woman. I have seen the shades of Sarah's soul, and sometimes when the emptiness has been on me, when all the world has been terrible and wrong and wasted, only those unchanging colors have lighted me. I wished that I had told her because now I never would, but I hoped that she had sensed it, I hoped.

Aunt Gale is right, I think. I think I think I think too much. Why analyze loving people? I heard once that when a bell is cast it is possible to locate the actual surface points where the harmonizing notes are made, but the true sound of the bell, the ding-dong note that calls across the fields, that can never be pinned down. Maybe loving is like that; pulled apart it is unformed bits of melody, but whole it is a symphony, not just a tune.

It was raining outside, a steady soft roar. I tried to visualize Dad. Surely there had been nights when the rain sounded the same, pleasant nights; but all that came was a fleeting glimpse of Matthew senior with a cold gleam in his eye and the one word, *Liar!* I remembered what it was about. He had left a potted hydrangea standing on the path below the kitchen window, and Sur had done what any self-respecting dog would have done. He sniffed this intrusive object thoroughly and decided to incorporate it into his territory. I knew Dad was hoping to put the prize bloom in a local flower show, but after Sur had finished there was nothing prize about it. I arrived on the scene after the damage was done and, panic-stricken, took the pot inside to wash the flower. Horticulture was not my strong point then. In my haste I scalded the heavy, pungent bloom under the hot tap, tried to shake off the water and broke the flower stem. Sur and I looked at it, me horrified, him with reproachful longing. The prospect of what Dad would say was not to be brooded upon, so I mended the broken stalk with a matchstick and cellotape splint and pulled the leaves up to cover the join. Unfortunately my plant surgery was not good enough to withstand the journey to the show. As Dad, beaming, placed the pot before the judges, the flower fell off.

I tried to explain about Sur, but the sly cellotape had really got to him. "Lies!" he cried. "Deceit! How dare you blame a defenseless animal. Joshua Steel, you are no son of mine!" And the soft rain had been roaring outside.

It's for the good, I reasoned to his clenched fists,

those long clever hands all bunched up. It must be done. I am not changed, really I am not changed.

On Saturday mornings Sarah sleeps late, gets up to a prolonged bath, washes her hair, and does all sorts of nonsenses that seem to give her pleasure and take hours. While this process goes on I am often sent to the village for the Sunday joint or milk checks or some oddment. Saturday lunch is cold, so Gale doesn't grumble if I drop in at the Fire Engine, which is Somerfield's second pub, and don't get back until midafternoon. A particularly well-dressed Saturday called me out early to catch the shine in the air. It was so good to walk in sunlight under pale sky and I was feeling so much better after the last treatment that I strode along the footpath and the fields that hold back Wellard woods. I did not go right into the wood where the trees link arms and close the sun out with their hair, but I scuffed along the edge through pine needles and last year's unrotted oak leaves with the dapples in the air around me. The yellow fell so heavily through the branches I could almost hear it. The breeze blew my hair over my eyes and usually that annoys me, but today it did not. I enjoyed the light touch on my scalp.

A narrow road skirts Wellard woods, leading to Somerfield one way and Wellard the other. A few scattered properties line it but they are well concealed behind high hedges and banks full of wild garlic. Very little traffic comes this way, the Main Road is straighter and quicker, so I walked along the middle of the lane breathing in the fresh air and swinging my arms. A walleyed old dog joined me for a spell, wagging his tail like a pup, but as the village came in sight he stopped, sat down and stared at me.

I went back to scratch his head. "Thanks for your company, Mr. Dog. Beautiful day, isn't it?" He huffed at me and then turned back the way we had come, his pink tongue lolling out.

The figure coming toward me as I turned into the village street was very familiar, but I didn't properly recognize Isobel Kenny until she came closer. She wore her uniform and was looking tired, but she said hello nicely and gave me a smile.

"I'm just going home," she said. "Night duty. And where are you off to this lovely morning, Doctor Joshua?"

"Nowhere special. I have time on my hands."

She looked at me nervously. "Uh, would you care for a cup of coffee? Mum will be out shopping but she always leaves me a flask to come home to."

"I'd like that. Thank you, Isobel."

She relaxed and walked beside me easily. I had often passed her house but hadn't paid it special attention. There had been a Kenny there long ago, an aunt who had died and left the place to Isobel and her mother, and apart from repairs and a coat or two of paint, the small villa was as it always had been. The front door had a leaded pane with pieces of colored glass in the form of a sailing ship.

Inside, the house was neat, precise, and polished. I had a landlady once who moved and cleaned under and behind every piece of furniture in the place at least once a week. Even the grand piano did not escape. I never saw a speck of fluff under a bed, nor one tiny spider annexing a corner of the ceiling. Far from being the harridan one might expect, she was a pleasant, talkative lady who did not mind muddles and dusty footprints on carpets. She was, she said, a compulsive cleaner who would scrub and vacuum anything that did not move. I wondered whether Isobel's mother was the same; she certainly used the same brand of polish. Everywhere was lavender.

"Come through to the kitchen, it's more comfortable there," said Isobel.

The kitchen had been two rooms at one time. The cooker stood in front of the blocked door. At one end was a solid fuel boiler flanked by two easy chairs. I saw Isobel and her mum sitting either side of the glowing doors on cold winter nights, sewing on their laps and radio tuned to a concert. I grinned to myself. The picture sprang from a combination of old movies, books about the Second World War, and plain fantasy.

"Something amusing you?" said Isobel. She had taken off her cape and was pouring black coffee from a thermos into bright, cheap mugs.

"Only my silly imagination. Any problems last night?"

She sat at the table and kicked off her shoes, wriggling her toes. "Only my feet. Two children are going home today and so far there are no admissions for Monday, which is a blessing. James looked in this morning just as I was coming off duty. He had the results of your antipollution expedition."

"Good. What were they?"

"I'm not sure, but he did say they weren't what he'd expected. I gather that the factory is in the clear."

"Poor Jim, he was going to blast the Council with a fait accompli. Now he'll have to look elsewhere."

"Aren't you interested any more? I thought it was one of your hobbyhorses."

I stared at her across the room. "I have more important things on my mind right now."

The atmosphere took on a charge. It had been innocuous but now it carried a dozen unsaid meanings. Isobel brought my coffee over and her hand was unsteady. I took the mug from her and smiled. "You look a bit weary, Isobel," I said and touched the shadow lines under her eyes. "But it suits your fascinating eyes." She said nothing, just stood there with her hands by her sides and her fingers trembling, so I put my coffee down, folded my arms, and studied her.

"I'm not in the least fascinating?" she said.

"Yes." She did not move as I looked at her. She is thin and straight, with narrow hands and short, almond nails. Her hips are narrow too and I caught myself wondering whether they had ever widened to a man. I put my hands on her shoulders and pulled her to me and her skin was burning through the cotton. She would not look at me so I had to take her face in my hand to kiss her.

There must have been an age of passion locked up in Isobel; it seemed Staff Nurse Taylor had been right. She kissed me and left me feeling guilty. I had not wanted to be given so much. I had not wanted to take anything from her but an excuse to be more friendly with her in front of James and Sarah. She clung on. I kissed her again and pushed her gently away. Her face was pale, pleased.

"Cigarette?" I offered.

"Please. More coffee?"

"I haven't drunk this yet."

There was quite a silence while we lit cigarettes and Isobel went to fetch her mug from the table.

"Where's all your conversation gone?" she said brightly. "You're usually so talkative."

"I'm dumbfounded," I said honestly.

"You couldn't be." But she thought I could.

"No one ever believes me. I must go now. Sarah wants her shopping."

"Your wife sends you shopping?" She was more surprised than scathing.

"Why not?"

"It's a woman's job."

I smiled at her and led the way to the front door. "I do it in a very manly way," I said. "I'm gruff and short-tempered with all the shop assistants."

Isobel shook her head. "I don't believe it."

"Then you should. It's true."

She let me out, still smiling. She glowed. "See you on Monday," she called as I left.

The Fire Engine lounge bar is a small room with five corners, a fireplace for logs in winter and a profusion of horse brasses. In the evening the pub is far too crowded, but Saturday lunchtimes it caters mainly to the locals and most of them use the larger public bar. The clunk and whirr of the one-armed bandit never stops. There were two men in the lounge when I arrived whom I knew by sight from my youth. They stared briefly and without recognition. One was Thomas Crisp, the coal merchant, whose Daimler was occupying most of the car park, the other Ronald Bassie the news agent, who had taken over his father's country business and made it thrive. Both had rosy cheeks, middle-aged spread and Harris tweed jackets. I got my pint and took it to the corner seat behind the bar, out of sight of the two men. They were talking

football with all the assertion of addicts who haven't
played the game in years.

I sat and thought about Isobel. I didn't want to
think about her, it made me feel uncomfortable. Her
hot mouth and willing little body were not for a
casual relationship. I had better not see her alone
again. Poor Isobel. Poor, lucky Jim.

"Hello, Jim. You're quite a stranger. What are you
drinking?"

I thought I was dreaming, but the voice that answered Thomas Crisp was none other than that of
Doctor Picton.

"Pint of bitter, please, Tom," he said. "How are
you?"

"Splendid. Haven't seen you in the village lately.
Been doing a spot of courting?"

There was quite a pause. "Not particularly," said
Jim. "We're busy at the hospital."

"Not that busy, eh? Ron here saw you the other
evening with a young lady in Bridgwater."

"Smashing bit of stuff," added Ron.

My scalp contracted. I didn't hear Jim's reply because I was trying to remember which night last week
Sarah had gone to the movies in Bridgwater. She was
going alone, she said. I hadn't offered to accompany
her because I'd seen the film before and anyway she
was still in a bad mood about her thwarted holiday
plans.

"She's not a local girl, is she?" Ron was saying. "I
don't think I've seen her before."

Jim sounded quite embarrassed, or did I hope he
did? "Uh, no, she's not local," he muttered. "Same
again?"

I felt sorry for him. I took my empty glass to the bar. Jim's eyes widened and his forehead wrinkled under the freckles. "Why, James, I didn't know you were here. Nice to see you. Have a drink?" He looked relieved.

"Josh, uh, I called in because I thought I might find you here. Do you know Ron and Tom?"

"I do, but they don't remember me." We introduced ourselves and I paid for a round.

"I've heard the name," said Tom Crisp. "Mavis Dixon mentioned you at church. I'm a warden." I nodded. "She said you've just come from London." I wondered what else she had said, but didn't ask. Mr. Crisp was not keen to add more. He downed his half pint quickly. "Excuse us," he said, gesturing at Ron to finish his drink. "We have a lunch appointment." They filed out.

"Why did you want to see me, Jim?" I said, taking my drink back to the corner.

He followed. "It's not important. I felt like a beer and I knew you came here most Saturdays so I thought I'd drop in on the off chance."

He sat down and tore open a bag of peanuts. "I've had the results of our pollution sampling."

"Ah yes. Isobel told me."

"Isobel?"

"I met her in the street. She gave me coffee."

"That was nice."

"Surely was. She's a very sweet girl when you know her. What were the results?"

He ate the peanuts one at a time, chewing each one thoroughly with his front teeth. "It wasn't the factory. There were constituents in the water consistent with its having been polluted with untreated sewage. Bloody nuisance. There's a plant about a mile upstream from that factory. I rang them up. They were very apologetic. A processor had broken down and been out of action for about a week. The Council and the Water Board had been informed. Apparently it's all working properly now. I checked up on the dates and they tie in with when I saw the dead fish. We can't do a damned thing."

I smiled. "You were looking forward to demolishing the Council?"

"It's about time somebody did." He sounded rueful.

"And what about all that muck that's flowed in the river right down to the sea?"

"I can't do anything about that now, can I?"

I shrugged. He was probably right.

The door opened and Sarah came into view round the bar. She was wearing new slacks and her hair was different. She looked excited and nice. "I thought I'd surprise you," she said. "Why, hello, Jimmy. What brings you here?"

It was very plain in his eyes what had brought him. He is nothing like so good an actor as Sarah. I stood up and my wife took my seat next to him. "Lager, Sarah?" I asked.

"No, I'll have a dry sherry, please, Josh. I've discovered I like it." She grinned at James. While I waited to be served I tried to listen to their conversation, but the bar was filling up and other louder voices drowned them out; their faces glowed secretively and Sarah laid a hand on Jim's sleeve as they laughed.

"There you are, honey," I said.

"Don't call me that!"

Jim stared at her. "What's wrong with honey?" he said. "I think it's rather charming."

Careful, James. Sarah is unreasonable when crossed. "He knows I don't like it," she said. "He does it on

purpose. He used to call me sweet names." There was
a bitterness that James heard and pretended he
hadn't.

"Honey is sweet," I said.

Sarah flashed me a tartaric look and turned away.
Jim began telling her about his sewage-ridden river.
She interrupted to give me a pound note from her
purse. "Get another drink, please, Josh," she said coolly.
I did as I was told.

After four sherries I suggested to her that we go
home for lunch. She ignored me. Later I tried again.
"I haven't finished my drink," she said.

"Gale will be waiting."

"She won't. It's only salad. Did you get my shopping?"

I pointed to the handful of paper bags beside me
on the seat. "I think we'd better go. It's quarter past
two."

"I can see the time. Jim, would you like to have
lunch with us? There's plenty."

He looked at both of us. "No, I'd better not. Mrs.
Bird always get a meal for me and she takes it as a
personal offense if I don't eat it."

"Poor you," laughed Sarah. "Well, you know you're
very welcome any time." I nodded agreement.

He gave us a lift in his Mini. "Don't forget,"
called my wife as he drove away. "You're welcome
any time."

As we walked up the path I said, "I'm glad you
don't mind Jim coming so often. He's a good friend to
me."

"Don't be so bloody reasonable!" said Sarah, strid-
ing away in front.

CHAPTER
EIGHT
***

"Josh, can I talk to you, are you busy?"

I looked up and tried not to be surprised. My wife rarely asks to talk; she talks and I listen, or don't listen. I worried for a second or two while my eyes read a few more lines of a paper on the nutritional value of legumes. It was written by Vernon and Creasey, two old colleagues from my London days who had been kind enough to use a reference of mine and send me a complimentary reprint. "I'm not very busy," I said.

"I don't know if you'll be interested," said Sarah. "What are you doing?"

I waved the paper at her. "I won't be interested," I said.

"Oh." We waited until she broke. "How do you know?"

"Because you haven't told me anything to be interested in yet, rosebud-bump."

She sat in the wing chair by the empty fireplace and clicked one thumbnail against the other monotonously. "I don't know," she said, "if you're fooling or not."

"You're slipping, Sarah. Is your concentration elsewhere?"

"You always had a certain look so I could tell, a sort of bend at the corner of your mouth. You don't have it now, and what you say when I hope you're fooling has a kind of savage truth behind it." Click, click, click, click, and her head bowed so that I could see the white of her scalp where her hair parted.

"Stop clicking, child! You know how it annoys."

"I'm not one of your patients!" she retorted, her eyes flaring up. "I'll click as much as I want." But she stopped anyway. "I wanted to talk about us," she said in a different voice. "About getting a home of our own."

I took a deep breath and concentrated. "Don't you like it here, then? Gale has given us half the house, isn't that enough?"

"Yes, yes, of course it is. Gale couldn't be kinder, but—but it's not ours, is it? Not a place of our own, not even so much as our flat was." Her eyes pleaded with me to understand, and I did. How I did.

"That bloody dump!" I said. "Surely you can't compare that favorably with this?"

"No. Yes, yes, I can. We were happy there, Josh. It made up for every deficiency. Since we've come here we've, oh, I don't know. I feel excluded somehow. I don't say you mean to shut me out, I'm sure you don't, but this house is a part of you I don't know, it's secret for you and it won't let me in. It has all your memories and none of mine. If we could just have our own home, start it all from scratch together, it might bring back the happiness."

The shiny paper of the reprint grew sticky under

my fingers and there was a burning at the back of my throat that I had to speak carefully around. Don't push too hard too soon, whispered a watery voice. Don't make her hate, that's too close. Indifference is what you want. Indifference. "Have you seen a place, Sarah smiles?"

She came over to the desk then, feeling my change of attitude. "You know that terrace by the Co-op," she said eagerly. "The four white houses? The end one has come up for sale. It has a garden and a garage and central heating and—"

"Okay, okay, honey. Leave the eulogies to the estate agents. Do you want to look at it?"

"Yes, please. Could we? Tomorrow evening?"

"Not tomorrow. I shan't finish until late. Jim is off all afternoon and I have to cover for him. Day after suit?"

Sarah's face dropped, and she can do it too, but her eyes were—how? Worried, I think. "All right," she said. "I'll arrange to collect the keys. And don't call me honey."

"I just hope Gale doesn't think us ungrateful," I said coldly.

"I thought you knew your aunt," said Sarah.

"Better than most." My wife gave me a shriveling stare before she left.

For reasons I've already explained I did not want a place of our own. Well, I did. I let my mind forget the grayness for a second to dream in the sunlight of a future. Sarah and myself in our own home with a garden for the roses and room for my books in a den, maybe, leathery and cigar-smelling like my father had once had; and a greenhouse for a vine, and vines take years to grow, and a dog or two to walk in Wellard woods on Sunday afternoons. The clouds returned. I couldn't decide whether they were selfish or magnanimous clouds, but they rolled over and were gray, bringing back the rain to my mind. I wanted to discuss the problem with someone, but there was no one. Gale would have been my choice, but to ask Gale to dissuade my wife from house-hunting would bring a question and Gale already half knew the answer. She had believed my story, I'm sure, but it was a story she realized, without realizing, needed also to be believed *in*. We all tie off parts of our lives with myths, little twistings of the truth. Some of us tie up our whole being in such a way and never live in the real world at all. Unadulterated truth is the last thing we want to know; there are a few exceptions, my cousin Geoff for one. He fought and struggled and cried out for truth and because he looked hard in the right places, he found it. He was not a great man, though he could have been. Perhaps it is not possible to be both great and realistic. Great men lead and those who follow need dreams to chase, and dreams are fiction, aren't they? If they become fact there must always be better and better dreams to replace them, and dream makers for you and me, all of us deceived. Geoff found truth and fell down into its gaping, bottomless black because there was nowhere else to go. In destroying all his illusions he destroyed himself, and even the lady who loved him had no truth to stop him.

And all that because I could not talk to Gale.

The afternoon I spent doing both Jimmy's work and my own was hectic, a blur of hours. I hadn't realized just how much the slow-moving James managed to cope with in his quiet way. Not surprisingly it left me feeling exhausted and depressed. As I walked to the car park at six o'clock in the blustery evening through a storm of petals, my knees shook and my briefcase dragged at my arm as if gravity had doubled. I could have gone to sleep in the driving seat of the Morgan. Her seats were hot from the sun and cosy as a bath. But I was anxious to get home for a real rest. Had I waited to stockpile a little energy before driving home, I would not have seen what I did.

I drove into the lane at the back of Gale's house, the lane which turns off the Main Road before the front of the house comes into view, and I thought I heard an engine start as the rumble of the Morgan faded. A car pulled away and out of a village interest which I had never known in London, I turned in my seat to watch it pass the end of the lane. It was a blue Mini. I saw neither the driver nor the number plate clearly, but a cool prickling of certainty ran up my forearms. I went into the house slowly, past the budding roses and under the acid-sweet tang of the flowering blackcurrant bush. Samson raised his head and grinned at me from his bed in the window box.

"That you, Joshua?" Gale had heard the gate squeal.

"No. Doctor Jekyll." I let the briefcase drop to the floor. I was afraid it might take two hands to lift it to the table.

"How are you, dear?" Gale stopped whisking something in a bowl to give me her full attention.

"Tired and ravenous, otherwise fine." I smiled at her but I don't think she was fooled.

"Dinner is almost ready."

"Doesn't Sarah usually get it?"

"Uh, she's been out. I thought I'd get on with it." She whisked rapidly, her gray head bowed.

"Where?" I said casually. "Spending all my money again?"

189

"I don't know, dear. She didn't say." She began to make the omelettes, the eggs spitting and sizzling in the pan. "Go and wash. This will be ready in five minutes." I glanced at her carefully as I went out but she was giving nothing away.

Sarah was in our bedroom, hanging a dress in the closet. She closed the door quickly and walked away from me to sit at her dressing table. "Hi," I said. "How's my wife today?"

"All right," she said calmly, inspecting her face in the mirror.

"Put some clothes on, woman. I've had a tiring day, don't make me more breathless."

She did not even smile. "You wouldn't have said that a month ago," she said. "In fact, I would have been invited to remove them, not put them on." She spun on the low stool and relaxed, her knees apart and her stomach rounded out. I gave her a quick smile and looked away. "You're tired, Josh," she said. "They keep you busy at the hospital, don't they? Jimmy says they do."

"I guess so, but I've never heard Jim complain."

"He didn't. He just said it was a busy little place." She caught her hair in her hands and twisted it up on top of her head, turning to see how it looked. The long muscle from ear to shoulder curved smoothly.

I took off my shoes. "When did he say that?"

"I don't remember. One evening when he came round. Is he lonely, do you suppose?" She turned this way and that and the sun whitened her skin with its low window light.

"I don't know. Do you?"

"Maybe. He comes here a lot. Gale says he comes too often."

"Does she?" I couldn't help but be surprised.

"Not exactly. The way she avoids saying it is far more obvious."

It was hot in the room. I threw off my jacket and shirt and opened the bureau drawer, looking for a T-shirt. "Where's my yellow thing?"

"In the wash. The blue one's there."

"I don't like the blue one."

"Then don't wear it." She came up behind me as I sorted through clothes, putting her arms round my chest. "Do you think," she said quietly, "that our marriage is getting a little stale, Joshua?" Her breath was hot on my back and I could feel her lips move against my skin as she spoke.

"You are a fanciful woman, Sarah fair. Been devouring the agony columns in the women's magazines again? 'Dear Miss Pinbottom: My 'usband comes 'ome knackered every evenin' and only makes love to me seventeen times a night. Am I losin' 'is affection? Starved, of Harrow. Dear Starved: How about keeping rabbits, it would give you an outside interest.' "

Sarah chuckled and kissed the spot between my shoulder blades. She knows where I am weak and I had to fight off a shiver. I found the blue T-shirt, turned and touched my lips to her forehead, then pushed her away. Her eyes hated me red for a second, then sorrow filled them, then she blinked and only gray coolness remained. "Gale's cooking omelettes," I said. "She loathes them to get spoiled."

"It doesn't matter," said my wife. "Not now." She dressed without another word and I followed her downstairs knowing I had won a small step in the plan. A pain grabbed inside my chest as if a giant hand squeezed my lungs to pulp. I had to hold the bannister rail until my fingers bruised against my wedding ring. It lasted so short a time that Sarah did not even notice

I'd faltered. I told myself it was the illness and maybe it was, but I felt it might not have happened if I had said, "I love you, my wife, and if I knew you had been out with James Picton in his car this afternoon I'd break his neck."

Dinner was quiet and eaten in the kitchen. The back door stood open and Samson slouched on the step watching our blackbirds eye the lawn for worms. They know each other, Samson and the birds, and play their own game. The cat will crouch for hours with his fat belly on the ground, tail scything away behind, gold eyes fixed, fondly imagining he is lean and hungry. Sometimes he crouches for so long he forgets why and falls asleep, but other times the birds flirt and tease and he wiggles his backside and makes darting little runs at them. Being large and ginger is not Samson's only disadvantage, he is pretty useless at pouncing, too. The blackbirds laugh at him from the hedge as he glares bewildered at the spot where one of them should be pinned down by a cruel set of claws. Samson is a clown and resigned to the role, though this year the early spring had encouraged the birds to build twice and they were too busy to provide much of an audience. The only time Samson ever killed anything in one of his games was when an old one-eyed mole emerged blind right under his nose. It didn't know the rules and Samson broke its back. He patted and prodded the sticky lump of fur for a while, then went away to sulk under the toolshed.

"Do you remember the blackbird with the white wing?" I said to Gale.

"Goodness me! That was years ago, when we had Smokey. You must have been about ten."

Smokey cat had preceded Samson by several cats

and Smokey had been knocked down on the Main Road by a passing motorist who did not stop. Dad had carried in his gray body and I was told to stay outside, but I remember clearly staring unnoticed through the kitchen window at the cat seated on an old wooden chair. He was not dead but one ear had gone and a foreleg was mashed and blood all over the dapple of his chest, such a lot of blood it seemed. And he sat so still and so upright while Dad and Aunt Gale watched. I suppose the vet, or maybe Dad, ended his agony. I never knew. I wonder whether I shall be as puzzled and resigned as Smokey, who moved like a shadow. I wonder whether I can be as brave and mute as Smokey, who chewed buttons off shirts and had one eye blue and the other green.

"Yes, I was ten," I said. "The blackbird used to come in here, right by your feet, and take bread and milk from a saucer. Seemed a strange thing to do with a young tearaway like me around, always bumping and banging into things."

"Did you?" said Sarah. "I've never seen you as clumsy. You are coordinated, not awkward."

Gale smiled at me, then Sarah. "His father reckoned he had some deep psychological need to be noticed," she said. "Matthew had these theories from time to time, when he wasn't too busy, you understand. In my opinion Josh was clumsy because Josh was always in a hurry. He'd lose himself in a book or some puzzle, then right at the last minute, away he'd go, through things instead of round them. The phase didn't last too long, I might tell you; he got fed up with bruises."

"Did Dad often get theories?" I asked. "I don't recall."

"That's because you only saw them in action. I had

193

to hear the rhymes and reasons your father elucidated for me. Women with kids to raise have been applying them since time began without conscious effort, but he didn't know that." Her face creased fondly and she caressed her pearls. "Poor dear Matthew. He did well, Josh. He missed your mother badly but he didn't complain and tried to help make up for her. Sometimes it pushed me out a little; but it wasn't meant. I know it wasn't meant. 'I'd just hate for him to grow up all wrong,' he used to say. 'I've seen rejection, real or imagined, and it makes a soul mean.'"

I pushed my plate away in the silence that fell. It wasn't my silence, it belonged to the women. Gale was lost in the quiet past and Sarah was lost in the words of a man she hadn't known. I thought I could see her thinking, "Am I to be a soul made mean?"

I saw not Smokey, but Sarah broken and bloody with stoic eyes. I lit a cigarette, blinking against the picture in the smoke. I coughed and couldn't stop coughing. Sarah poured a glass of water and handed it to me. Her expression was only vaguely concerned. I drank and the spasm stopped. My eyes watered.

"Are you all right?" said Gale anxiously, searching my face for a secret sign.

"Yes, thanks. Went the wrong way."

Sarah said, "I've got the keys to the house. We can go tomorrow at seven. Okay?"

I nodded. I don't know why I think I know my wife. I shape her thoughts to mine, but of course they are not mine. The image of Smokey faded like his name.

Later that night, it must have been about two A.M., I lay awake and stared into the dark. Insomnia was becoming the rule rather than the exception, a rule I somehow welcomed. I had Mogadon and could easily have reached for the big white pill and a glass of water, but hours asleep were hours I thought lost, so I stared at the darkness instead. Some people say the color of darkness is myriad, a blend of every color swimming in dots. Children have told me so, and also that it is the thick black cloak of a wizard, woolly and abrasive to the eyeballs, and that it is the breath of a dragon dozing, his fire smoldering and the smoke of his lungs as oppressive as a mine. Adults don't say much about the dark. In my room I could see nothing, and everything I knew was there. Quite clearly in the air hung the image of the Beardsley poster Sarah had pinned up, Salome's fat belly lurching in time with the unheard cacophony from the devil and his instrument at her feet. She danced more vividly then she ever did in daylight. I felt suddenly well and energetic. I stretched my arms up and my feet down and breathed out long and enjoyably.

Sarah ran her hand along the inside of my arm and I almost yelled out. I thought she was years away in sleep. She mumbled at me.

"Mm? Can't hear you."

She lifted her head and moved closer. "Still awake?" she said.

"I don't feel tired."

"Good." Her hand ran up my neck into my hair. "No omelettes now."

"No, but—" But no excuses and I wanted none. So what if it caused a setback, so what if the grand and kind-cruel plan was ruined. Too late now, too late when her soft mouth was asking for mine and I had reached out.

My head was washed clean by the little time of honesty. I slept immediately and woke late, but by then the burden was back and the night seemed not to have happened. I ignored Sarah's glowing across the breakfast table and rushed away without a smile.

"Don't forget we're to see the house tonight," she called after me.

It would feel good to say I didn't want the house anyway, but it would not be true. Sarah led me eagerly from the car to the brown front door of the little house. There were weeds which I longed to dig out between the fancy bricks of the path, and a honeysuckle about the porch that would smell sweet and attract the moths when it came into bloom. Honeysuckle would pervade the rooms all summer. I wondered how anyone could have left the place.

"Why is it for sale?" I asked Sarah as she turned the brass key.

"The owner died. A stroke. He was quite young. Mr. Aston who worked in the ironmongery."

"He died at the hospital."

"That's right. Oh, what a nice staircase! Look at that mahogany rail."

The place was bare, picked clean by magpie relatives or auction mongers. Whichever, Mr. Aston of the Co-op hardware store had left very little personality stamped behind him. The walls were uniformly neutral, gray, beige, cream, I don't remember—didn't as soon as I looked away—the floors were bald and unstained, the windows closed and misty with dust. It was the good, solid kind of house erected before the war when blue brindle bricks were standard material and skirtings were oak and built into the walls. Jerry-building had gone and was yet to come again. Places like these had been allowed to stand a year or two before occupation; they had matured like good cheeses and held a lasting fineness no march of time and elements could seriously damage. Fireplaces were plumb, doors did not droop or swell, wood-framed windows slid as well now as when new, and rising damp did not attack from under the suspended floors. It was an ideal home with bright possibilities.

Sarah was not slow to spot them. I listened to her cries of admiration and her chirpy pointings out where furniture might go, but did not hear them. I found in myself a feeling of jealousy, green and slimy, and tried to push it away; but it would not go so I studied it to see what stamp it had and where it had come from. I was envious of Sarah's pleasure, and her pleasure came from anticipation, the good things her future must hold. Feeling sorry for yourself, Joshua Steel, like the vandal who scratches the depth of his confusion along the body of a Rolls Royce simply because he's never likely to own one. I followed Sarah from room to room with slow feet and no comment. In the kitchen she allowed herself to notice my lack of response.

"We'd have to get rid of that china sink," she said. "Look, it's got curtains at the bottom. The original kitchen sink theater. Ta-ra!" She drew the faded cotton aside with a flourish to reveal the plumbing and a couple of empty soap flakes packets. "We could put in a new sink unit, one of those stainless steel ones. Josh?" I was looking at the ceiling. "Josh, don't you like it?"

"It's all right."

"But not really your style? I know it's a bit old-fashioned, but think how it could look with new paint and those old cupboards replaced and perhaps a back door with a glass panel to let in more light. And it does have a garage. You know how you hate leaving the car in Gale's lane."

As we went upstairs I panted silently and wondered who would have the Morgan. Sarah might like to keep it though it cost a lot to run, or she might sell it to a good home. Why should I worry? But it is hard to shuck off the materialistic notions that mean reality for most of us. I ought to make a will soon.

There were two bedrooms and a bathroom opening from the square landing. Sarah went into the largest bedroom first. A board squeaked under her feet. I stepped over it. The ghosts of furniture and pictures which had stood and hung against the walls were all around. Each had left its outline on the mottled wall and there was a yellowed greasy spot above where the narrow bed had been; Mr. Aston had left a ghost of himself behind in his hair cream.

"It's a good size," said Sarah. "Don't you think so?"

"Mmm. There's a damp patch up there in the corner."

"Oh, that's nothing. Probably a blocked gutter. This room would get sunshine nearly all day in the summer."

"Supposing it needs expensive roof repairs?"

"You're picking holes, Josh."

"From the look of that ceiling they are already picked. How much is this place anyway?"

She stared sullenly at me. "You don't like it."

"Can I afford it?"

"What's wrong with it? What's wrong with you? Why are you so turned away all the time? You know, Josh, you were always smiling. Now you hardly ever grin and when you do it's perfunctory, as if your mind was miles off. Is it me, have I done something?"

"You'd know better than I."

It was a stab in the dark with a mean blade, but it had an immediate effect. Sarah bit her lip and her crossed-up frown came on and she looked guilty. Then she changed and her annoyance was nudged along by the guilt. "If I have it's your fault!" she said, then stopped and the anger went out of her. "You are clever and unkind," she said quietly. "If you don't like the house you only need to say so."

"Sarah, how much is it?"

"Could we have it, could we?"

There was no need for fake exasperation. "How much, for Chrissake!"

"Nine thousand, nine hundred."

"Oh, Sarah!" It was a reasonable figure and one I could have afforded providing I could have raised the deposit. She must read what she would into my words.

She blinked furiously at me. "We could afford it," she said tightly. "I'm sure we could. I have some money saved and Uncle George, he'd always give us an advance." She faded into uncertainty and sniffed hard once or twice. Poor Sarah's case was lost now. We'd had Uncle George a few times before when matters of money arose. I'd always refused. If he were my Uncle George, things might have been different, but he was Sarah's nearest relative and, though a pleasant old man, the kind given to saying that the younger generation couldn't stand on its own feet, et cetera. My wife only throws him up as a last line of defense.

"I'm not going to borrow money, Sarah, particularly not from George, particularly when we have a good home to live in at a nominal rent. Are you ready?" I walked back to the landing.

"Josh! Aren't you even going to look at the rest of it?"

I started down the stairs and she stared at me over the handrail. "What's the point, my dear girl, when I haven't the bread? Come along, we're supposed to be meeting Jimmy and Isobel at the Wellington at eight-thirty and I want a shower first."

She said nothing as we drove the half a mile or so home. Her face was white and her eyes black and she was so tense it was like sitting next to a bomb, one of those with a short, sparky fuse on top.

"Don't get so mad," I said gently. "I'm sorry, Sarah, but there's no point in raising your hopes." She didn't seem to hear.

When I had showered and changed I went into our bedroom expecting her to be ready to go out. Instead of being pretty in the new long skirt she had made and smelling of lily-of-the-valley, she was curled on the bed with her face to the wall, still in her jeans.

"Hurry up," I said. "We'll be late."

"I'm not coming."

I didn't blame her at all. "Please?"

"No. I've got a headache. You go."

I sat on the bed and she curled away from me like a scared woodlouse. "If that's the way you want it." I kissed the top of her head and stood up.

"Josh?" One eye followed me, glinting among her tousled hair.

"Yes, love?" Bland, oh very bland. This person in me, was he becoming me? What a cold bastard he was, and how I hated, admired, congratulated, and despised him.

"Nothing," said my wife.

"I'll leave the car. You can come along later if you feel like it."

As I closed the door quietly I heard her say, "Oh, Josh, why don't you understand any more?"

And, "But I do, but I do, but I do," thumped with the rhythm of my feet down the sairs.

Sarah did not come to the Wellington and I watched Jim's evening flatten as it progressed. At first he glanced hopefully at the door whenever it opened, then he drank several shots in quick order and dropped disconsolately out of the conversation. I caught him gazing broodily at me and Isobel a few times, so I made our laughter gayer and our talk more intimate. He noted it all in his label mind. "You seem to be enjoying yourselves," he muttered, later in the evening. "Shouldn't you be getting home, Joshua? You know what I mean, if Sarah isn't well."

"She had a headache," I said mildly. "She'll probably be asleep by now. Don't look so morose, James. Have another drink."

"No, thanks, I have enough here. I must consider my reputation." He said it with a drunken ostentation that made Isobel smile. Her shoulder was close against mine.

Did you think of that when you took my wife out yesterday? It was such a loud and unexpected thought that I couldn't be sure if it had formed words in the air or not. I waited, but no expressions changed. I pushed my glass aside. That sort of mistake now could spoil everything.

The night was still and warm when we left the pub, the first night of the year to feel like summer. High clouds blurred the stars but did not hide them, and below, the windows of the cottages and houses stood open. Someone sang softly as he went to his car with the keys in his hand jingling in time, and a woman laughed. "Nice night," I said. "Can you drive

Isobel home, Jim? I walked." Isobel looked up at me but I didn't take the hint from her eyes.

"Yes, of course," said Jim. "Give my regards to Sarah. I hope she's better soon."

"It was only a headache."

We walked to the blue Mini and I squeezed Isobel's arm gently as she got in. Jim noticed. I smiled at him and waved as they drove away.

When I reached home the front of the house was in darkness. I let myself in and felt my way along the hall. A light sneaked out from under Gale's sitting room door. I could talk to her or not. I decided not. Liquor makes my tongue honest. The vein of light broadened and a voice whispered fearfully, "Is that you, Joshua?"

"I've come for the jewels and the thousand pounds you keep under the mattress," I whispered back.

"Can you never be serious!" There was an asperity in my aunt's voice as if to say she'd had her fill of evasive answers. "I thought you were a thief, moving about in the dark like that."

"It's eleven-thirty. I thought you'd be asleep, my guardian angel."

"Well, I'm not. Angels don't sleep, do they? Come in, Joshua, I have some coffee made."

I told you, long ago Aunt Gale had been a teacher. Right now I could have been in short pants, with sweaty palms and my heart thumping in my ears, outside the Headmaster's study. Gale left the door open and went back to the softly lit room. I dropped my coat casually into one chair and moved Samson from another to sit down. My aunt poured coffee from a porcelain pot and passed the dainty cup and saucer. A curtain breathed in and out with the late breeze and let in a smell of lilac. The coffee tasted good. In all her

English years Gale has not forgotten how to make real coffee. I began to relax, lit a cigarette. Samson poured himself on to my knees, hoping I wouldn't notice. He is doggedly sly. I pulled his ears and he grunted.

Gale was ready for bed. Her gray hair was twisted into several curlers and her long quilted robe hid her slippered feet. She leaned to take a cigarette from my pack and waited while I lit it for her. Through the smoke, like a prophet's voice, I heard, " 'Thou art thy mother's glass' " . . . and my aunt's eyes pierced the dispersing haze, hard as sapphires. The warmth of her tone confused me. An old feeling of panic fought its way through the whisky I had drunk.

"No, don't build a wall," said Gale, putting out a hand. "You are very like your mother, Joshua."

"I was always told I looked like Dad."

"Looked, maybe, though he was tough and red and you are slender and, oh, I don't know, a different texture. You have your mother's expression, her atmosphere. That's what I can't understand. I knew her well when we were young, we went through high school and college together. She had your caring and gentleness and a core of something bright and unalterable. It made you respect her even when she was wrong, even when you hated her for being right. She never lied to herself. That's what I can't understand."

I sighed. "Gale, when I was a small boy you talked round things to excite my interest, to encourage me to find an answer. You made me a searcher. I have been looking ever since. But tonight I'm tired. Is Sarah in bed?"

"Yes. Please . . . have some more coffee." She refilled my cup before I could reply. "Will you look at this with me?"

"I did not know my mother, Gale."

"But I did, and now I don't know you!" She colored up. "You were as she was, but now that bright core has gone. Why, Josh?"

"Has Sarah been talking to you?"

She glared and shamed me. "If she had I'd respect her confidence just as I respect yours. And that's a question I never thought to hear you ask." We were silent for quite a while and Samson, oblivious, purred. It was like the little buzzing of anger in Gale. "Forgive me," she said suddenly. "I've always believed I am my brother's keeper, and that includes my nephew. Is it your illness, Josh? Does it give you pain?"

I shrugged. "Sometimes. Tell me, how often has Sarah been out with Jimmy Picton?" The question burst from me and I'd no idea it was coming. It rose from my aquarium mind and splashed out between us, ugly and sluglike, in the open.

She stared me in the eyes and said slowly, "You must ask questions of those who can answer. And if you want to know why, look to yourself. I'll always love you, Joshua, but I could easily despise you right now. Because you're letting your brightness go out."

"I'm going to bed. Good night, Gale." I eased Samson off and went to kiss my aunt's cheek. She turned away. I wanted to turn her back to me, I wanted to say all that was in me and get her approval, but I said nothing and stumbled up the stairs in the dark.

In the bathroom, I looked in the mirror for the man Gale had seen. All that looked back was an ordinary male face with beads of sweat on his upper lip. He looked tired and the muscles of his jaw bulged where the pain showed, and there was a lopsided frown, as always. I could see no more; the room slid sideways suddenly and I had to run to the lavatory to vomit.

Shortly after Sarah had shown me the house of her dreams, which I had reduced to metaphorical rubble, it was brought to me that I too was dreaming. I had not thought about dying. That sounds senseless; plans were laid, schemes already in operation concerned with it, but I had not thought about dying.

Gale asked me one morning if I could drive into Taunton during the day to collect a parcel of dress material she'd been waiting for for months. It would mean an extended lunch break but I agreed, and it worked out well because I remembered when I got there that the pathologist at the Royal Hospital owed me a report. I collected Gale's stuff and drove to the hospital.

"Doctor Ash is in the P.M. room," one of his technicians told me. "With the students. Do you want to go down?"

"Sure. I've corresponded with him but we've never met."

Like most hospital mortuaries this one was well concealed from the public eye. It was in a basement annex, corridors away from the live patients. I followed the technician's directions, and when I got near, my nose. P.M. rooms, especially old, ill-ventilated ones, have a particularly revolting smell. From behind a door marked sternly *Keep Out. No Admittance. Ring for attention* a faint sound of singing came, overlaid by the noise of running water. I rang the bell. After several seconds the door opened to reveal an oldish, smallish man in a white cap, long red

rubber apron, and short green boots. He frowned at
me.

"I'm Doctor Steel from Somerfield Cottage Hospital.
Pathology said Doctor Ash would be here."

The small man relaxed. "He's almost finished," he
said. "We've been busy today. Five cases. I still
haven't had my lunch. Come on in."

He led me through the first room, the mortuary
proper where the bodies lay awaiting collection in
cold drawers. A stack of empty formalin bottles stood
on a trolley in one corner. The cloying stench of blood
and intestines brought back student memories. I have
been in many P.M. rooms but always with the idea
that their grisly duties would never concern me personally. I was alive, wasn't I? Now, it made me
nervous. The running water stopped as a hose was
turned off and a skinny young man emerged from the
inner room, pulling off wet rubber gloves. "God, he's
taking his time," he muttered as he passed us. "Oh,
Phil, did you put that piece of carcinoma breast aside
for Doctor Blackwood?"

Phil nodded. "And some rib. Was that what she
wanted?"

"Mm. Her technician's coming down for it." He
padded away, his boots thudding wetly.

"Hang on a bit," said Phil to me. "I'll tell his nibs
you're here. Might hurry him up." He left me by the
door. There were six tables in white enamel, each
with a groove round its edge to drain the blood away.
There may have been marble slabs in Rembrandt's
day, but I have never seen one. Five tables were
occupied and one surrounded by a small group in
white coats paying close attention to their leader who
was holding a brain in his hand and slicing through
it at one-inch intervals with a knife sharp enough to

sever his arm if he faltered. "No sign of tumor," he was saying. "Now, who's got the thyroid?" Doctor Ash, I guessed.

Standing there, still on my own two feet despite the malignant cells trying to take over my bones, I shuddered. These carcasses around me, these objects with liver sausage skin slit from larynx to pubis, had they ever been real? That one with scanty cotton wool hair, male or female? Its ribs, cleaned of skin and muscle, stuck out jaggedly like the shell of an upturned boat whose wood was red. Its liver, lungs, and spleen lay on a tray across its knees and its plastic yellow toes stuck up in the distance. There is nothing dignified in a P.M. room, no TV-style white sheets to peek under sorrowfully, no quiet, clean obsequiousness. The dead names are written in chalk upon a board and rubbed out each day, and underneath, white pots hold bits of the names. The benches, not yet washed down, were blood-smeared and so were the scales on which an attendant might weigh a heart or a brain with as much flourish as a butcher would half a pound of sausages.

They won't do that to me, I thought; and that was what set it off. Keeping my illness from Sarah was all very well now, but what if the sickness got suddenly worse, overwhelming? She must be gone by then, she must. But would Madison have a P.M. done or let it go because I was a confirmed case already? I must speak to him about it before it was too late. Though I knew with my head that it would not matter one jot to me, I felt with my heart that I could not tolerate the final ignominy here. Illogical, I know, and more so coming from a surgeon, but not this, something said firmly, not this. I know they sew you up all neat again and even give you a "not dead, just sleeping" smile,

but that is for the benefit of the mourners, another
myth.

The group broke up, putting notebooks in pockets
and exchanging cute remarks, and Doctor Ash came
toward me. He was short and broad and beaming,
with round brown eyes like old coins. He looked
gentle, not a man to harm a fly, if he could help it.
"Doctor Steel?" he said, "pleased to meet you. Sorry I
can't shake hands. Come outside where I can wash."
As we left, Phil busied himself with water and disinfectant and whistled loudly in the echoing little room.

"I came for a report on the Fisher child," I said.

"Ah, yes, yes. Didn't they give it to you upstairs?"

"No. They didn't seem to know about it."

He clapped a hand to his forehead and left a brown
mark. "Bugger," he said mildly. "You know, that mob
upstairs couldn't run a piss up in a brewery. Of course
they've got the report. I signed it myself yesterday.
Fancy making you come all the way down here!"

And I thought, if they had found it at once, if I
hadn't come all the way down here . . .

When I got back to Somerfield Hospital Jim was
in our room, cleaning his fingernails with a scalpel
blade. He made scraping little sounds and dropped
the bits in the ashtray. A manicure should be a solitary
thing; it has a deadly fascination. I watched and
waited for him to cut himself.

"Matron wants you," he said. "She asked to see you
as soon as you got back."

"My dream come true. What about?"

"Didn't say. It sounded important."

I pulled on a clean white coat. The laundry starches
them so hard the sleeves seal up and have to be fought
into. "She'll have to wait for her desires," I said, prying
open pockets for my necessary bits and pieces. "B-W

is coming to the ward specially to see one of our little patients."

"He's still in clinic."

"He won't be by the time I get up there. If Matron calls again tell her I'll drop in when I can—and send my love." When I could was two hours later at half past four. I tapped at her door and waited for her to call "Come in."

"Hello, Matron. I got your message."

He mouth quivered and her eyes were offended behind her glasses. "I sent the message at lunchtime," she said.

"Yes, I know. I've been rushed off my feet. Now, what can I do for you, Matron?"

"Please sit down," she said. There was a tight barrel of air about her as if her corset were too tight or she'd eaten a stale pork pie. "This is very serious, Doctor Steel."

"Please go on." I sat and watched her. Her nose was just about to run, a tiny glitter showed. She took a tissue from her pocket and wiped it quickly. Then she sneezed twice. "Have you got a cold?" I asked.

"Hay fever. I get it every year though it's a bit early this time."

"Do you have some antihistamines? I'm sure we could—"

She interrupted quite violently. "My hay fever is not what I asked you here to talk about!"

I looked at my watch. "What was it about then, Matron?"

She sniffed, took a deep breath and said, "It was about the reputation of this hospital and its staff."

There was quite a pause. I had absolutely no idea what she meant. "Yes?"

"Yes. I think it is my duty to step in here and protect

the hospital and my girls. You may think it's none of my business, but if it's allowed to continue, this kind of thing can lead to trouble. Please understand, Doctor Steel, that I only approach you in this matter out of a sense of duty."

"So you said. Matron, would you care to tell me what is wrong?"

She stared at me disbelievingly. "You do not know to what I am referring?"

"Correct."

"Oh, you don't fool me for one moment!" she exclaimed, putting her elbows on the desk and thrusting her bust between them. "Oh that this too too solid flesh would melt . . . " ran through my mind. "You know precisely what I mean, Doctor, and I won't have that kind of thing in my hospital!" She pursed her lips and sat back.

I stood up. "I'm afraid I don't. Unless you can elucidate very quickly I shall have to go. Mr. B-W has left me a whole lot of work to finish."

"You are a married man," said Matron. "I think you should remember that, particularly when it comes to relationships with members of staff."

A light glimmered at the end of a long tunnel of insinuation. "Well, Matron?"

"It has come to my ears that you are rather too friendly with one of the sisters here."

Dawn broke. I smiled. "I wonder what little bird dropped that worm in your lap, Matron. Don't tell me; I know Staff Taylor's fine hand. Now, suppose I tell you there is nothing to hide. Whose word would you accept?"

"It's not a matter of whose word. It's a matter of rumor. A doctor in your position could have his reputation ruined by gossip alone and imagine what that would do to the hospital. We're a small community, Doctor Steel. We can't afford the slightest trace of scandal." Her blue eyes blinked fiercely.

"I sometimes think I agree with whoever it was that said ours should be called the Hypocritic oath," I said quietly. "What do you suggest I do? The sister to whom you refer is a friend to both me and my wife. She visits with us occasionally. We go out in a group. Am I to have no friends in case a rumor is started? Perhaps I should ask Doctor Picton to come to my house less often in case empty minds misconstrue his intentions toward my wife or, God help us, me."

She plainly overlooked my blasphemy. "Friendship is one thing. Seeing a young woman alone in her own home is another," snapped Miss Dixon. I noticed she has very small hands for her size, and they gripped the edge of the desk and whitened the knuckles. "I want these rumors stopped, at once!"

I smiled again, widely. "Did you tell your little bird that? Come on, Matron, you know as well as I do that silly little girls chatter among themselves, especially about a man who is older and in various ways attractive. Put any man in a good position and there is always competition to knock him down. He doesn't even have to do anything, and anything he does, however innocent, is bound to be a subject for gossip. Intelligent people hardly bother to notice it. They believe what they know of a person, not what they are told." That wasn't entirely true, but it stung. I have found that even when men and women are close as lovers there is always the sneaking suspicion that what is said to be bad is real, and what is good is assumed, or luck.

"What I think in this matter isn't important," said

Matron. "The local people might get to hear of it and from there our benefactors. You realize we are only fifty percent supported by the National Health? Where charity is involved one cannot be too careful."

"I agree, Matron. It begins at home, they say. Now I really must go." My hand was on the door knob.

"Are you going to do nothing about this?"

I shrugged. "What should I do? I didn't start the rumor so how can I stop it? I can't issue a denial without implying there is something to deny. You have control of the nursing staff, Matron."

She sighed angrily and tried a different angle. "What if your wife should hear this gossip?"

"I would certainly wonder who told her."

I went back to my room with my teeth clenched and my fists deep in my pockets. It had been a mistake to come home to my talkative village. I had forgotten just how hellish life can be made for a man who dares poke his nose over the strictly delineated social boundaries. In Somerfield, and I guess in plenty of other small communities, the moral code is quite clear and unbalanced and, of course, always applied to someone else. It is perfectly acceptable for a man to make a profit, even on the occasion when the Council had paid out thousands of taxpayer's pounds to a local builder for a plot of land to be developed and that land still stood vacant after ten years; even when it was no secret that various Council members had had new garages and patios added to their houses by the very same builder. But let a man be seen talking over the fence to his neighbor's wife, especially on the new housing estate, and immediately cries of disgust and relish go up and the village seethes with tales of wife-swapping and drugs. In a very short time half a dozen people can be found who have actually seen these orgies, and the unfortunate man who wished his neighbor's wife good morning is bewildered to find himself ostracized in every shop.

I was angry with Staff Taylor and Matron and the whole damned bunch of them, but the devil on my shoulder whispered in my ear, "Use it. Use it; it's what you need, it's heaven-sent. Let them mind your business, let them have their stories."

The anger rumbled away like thunder in the distance on the Mendips.

Jim had finished his manicure and was writing busily at a paper he was hoping to submit to the B.M.J. He'd given me a section to read and I had advised him to cut it down. Jim is as verbose on paper as he is laconic off it. I watched his square wrist and oblong fingers jerk along, and a sentence of Matron's came back . . . "a young woman alone in her home" . . . who knew that? Jim looked up. "Is there something wrong?"

"I don't know. Do you believe all you hear, Jim?"

"Of course not. Why?"

"All you see?"

He screwed up his eyes and the wrinkles at their corners were freckled leather. "That's different. The camera cannot lie, you know what I mean?"

"But you might misinterpret?"

"I suppose so. Why, Josh?"

"No reason. I'm going up to see Isobel." He frowned at me as I went. I hoped I hadn't overplayed it.

Isobel went off duty at four-thirty and wasn't due back until ten so I knew I'd find Staff Taylor alone. Actually she had two first-years with her when I arrived and while she gave them instructions I had time to compose my thoughts and my face. I walked in full of reproach. Sarah says it is one of my more

J. J. McKENNA

telling expressions, to be avoided if at all possible, though I've never seen it so I don't know.

"Oh! Hello, Doctor Steel. Are you looking for Sister?" said Taylor. She avoided me, her eyes sliding away. "I'm afraid she's gone."

"I'm not looking for Isobel," I said, sitting on the desk. "I'm looking for you."

"Me? Whatever for? Would you like some tea, the kettle's just boiled." She poured water in the teapot and forgot the tea, then had to do it all over again. She knocked a cup over and spilled milk on the floor, then put sugar in both and had to throw one away.

"Staff, why are you so flustered? Has Matron been on your tail?"

She set my tea down, spilling half in the saucer. I poured it back in. "No! No, Matron hasn't said anything to me."

"But you have said something to Matron."

"What? I don't know what you mean." She was fidgeting with a couple of galley pots on the bench, her back to me. I caught her arm and turned her round. "What do you mean?" she said defiantly.

I spoke soothingly. "My dear Taylor, you cannot tell tales about people and expect to get clean away with it. Matron has spoken to me. She left me in no doubt as to where her information came from." I squeezed her arm hard.

"Don't! Leave me alone. I'm entitled to tell the truth to anyone I please, so there!" Her face was red and puffy.

I smiled. "So you are, child. But what is the truth and where did you hear it?"

She pulled away and tidied the desk top which was tidy already. "Everyone knows about you and Isobel Kenny," she said bitterly. "It's no secret, you

214

haven't tried to hide it. You've been seen out together and you've been to her home. Tell me that's not true."

"As far as it goes, but you haven't seen it all yourself. Whose words have you taken, Staff? How do you know he isn't a liar?"

"Because he's a reliable, honest doc—it's none of your business, Doctor Steel. Now please go, I'm busy." She brushed past me and I could smell the dust from ruffled feathers.

I caught her shoulders and stared deep into her vacuous yellow eyes. "Staff, do you know what it's like to be lonely? Do you know how it feels to be an outcast, to be loved by no one, no one at all? Can it be so wrong to seek affection in a cold world, to be warm and needed instead of wanting and wasted?"

She stared back and took in every word. I almost added, "God, I can't stand it any more," but that might have been a bit too much to swallow. I shook her gently and let her go, closing my eyes.

"I'm sorry, Doctor," she said after a pause. "I didn't know you were unhappy. But still . . . you should be more careful."

"Yes, yes." I nodded sadly. "Bye, Staff." I went out with my shoulders drooping and my face set. Boy, would our little Staff Taylor have some talking to do.

CHAPTER
NINE

I could not mark the moment when Sarah made up her mind. I don't know if she marked it either, but it became clear that she had almost given up hope for me. She began to fill the gaps I left with new clothes, borrowed records whose singers were sentimental and sweet-sad, trips in the car alone, hours of silence while the TV blared unheard and unseen by her wide eyes. Gale marked the time more clearly, and to a lesser extent, Jimmy. Since our last tête-à-tête Gale had said nothing of importance to me. It seems strange that three people can live closely in a house, sharing meals and bathrooms, without saying something to one another. That was how it was, though. We chatted about friends, the news, politics, work; Sarah and I talked about what to buy Gale for her birthday. But no one said anything and there was such a lot breathing in the walls of every room, waiting to be said. It was on Gale's birthday that something got said, but it built more tension than it relieved. Sarah had gone in the car to the off-license for a bottle of wine to go with the celebration dinner and Gale was hanging the picture we'd got for her. Her sitting room was bright with cards.

"That is nice," she said, climbing down from the chair and surveying the effect. "I've always been fond of boats. Thank you, Joshua."

"You're welcome," I said, looking through her cards. They were signed by "Flora," "Fred and Janet," "Kate," names I did not know, but one I recognized: "Mavis Dixon" and a mention of God in the verse. "I see Matron sent you a card."

"Mm. I don't know if I appreciate it after what she told me and Sarah about you. Still, you've become such a stranger to us she could have been telling the truth. It's all over Somerfield, Josh." She looked at me sadly. "Then, I suppose I shouldn't interfere."

"What tales has that fat old bitch been putting around now?"

"Don't be rude! People who live in glass houses, Josh. I tried to help but you wouldn't listen. It's on your own head now. You're fast losing your wife, you realize that, don't you. She tells me you don't want her now, not in—in any way, you won't even talk to her properly. But I don't suppose you care, not with your head full of another woman." She was near to tears.

I put my arm round her shoulders. "Now, Gale, not on your birthday, eh? We're supposed to be full of merriment and feasting. Don't worry about us, it's just a bad patch. We all have them. We'll come through."

"I think you're mad, both of you," she sniffed.

"A plague on both your houses?"

"Josh, if you would only make the effort, give up Isobel completely, I'm sure Sarah would do the same."

"Forget it, please. Listen, that's the car. We'll have

a slap-up meal, get a little drunk, and I might even sing you a song if I can find my guitar."

"It's in the cupboard under the stairs," she said.

It is funny what a village can make of you, can do for you, and all you have to do is sow a seed. Since the night when Sarah and I had disagreed about the house I had seen Isobel Kenny twice, both times in the company of James and my wife. We all enjoyed the outings. I learned more of what Sarah was thinking then than in all our silent hours alone. Aside from those occasions, I saw Isobel at work quite frequently, but never alone. Her eyes spoke volumes and sometimes she tried to add her voice to them so I had to rush away busily. Staff Taylor latched onto clues like flypaper. I had thought I might need to do more, but the grapevine took over and exceeded my wildest dreams. Surely then, this plan must be right. A thing wrong or bad could never flow so easily without constant attention.

Jim still came to the house two or three times a week, but he was very quiet when I was in the room. Sarah chattered to him about all manner of things and he did not listen, he only watched. In one way I was glad and proud that he cared so much for my wife. It was a compliment and I certainly could not blame him for it. But I longed to see Sarah's eyes laugh for me just once again; selfishly, I wanted to be the only man in the world who could hurt her to death and enrapture her to paradise.

The afternoon after Gale's birthday I found her crying over a book. Sarah hates crying publicly, she has this built-in horror of betraying emotion before strangers and refuses to go to movies with animals dying in them, or Walt Disney, or any of what she calls "sentimental rubbish like that." The only time

219

I ever saw her bawl in front of the television screen was over Paul Gallico's *Snow Goose*, and I guess I wasn't seeing too well myself. That, I might add, was not sentimental but brilliant.

She blew her nose as I came into the sitting room and went out quickly, humming a broken tune, secret Sarah. The pages fell open in my hand where they had been folded back, so I read them. It was an historical novel full of "My lady" and "Brave sire, I beg you do not enter upon this mission," the kind of stuff my wife borrows from local libraries on occasion. She amazes me, as I may have said before. Poetry, classics, biographies ancient and modern, all of them she loves, really loves. Then she reads average moronic stuff like this. To be fair, she is a compulsive reader. Stand the cornflakes packet on the breakfast table and she will read every word including the price stamp over and over until you move it; or sauce bottles, every ingredient and sometimes aloud—and in French.

The only paragraph on the pages I could find that might have caused her tears was a brief dialogue between "My lady" and the sire, or squire, her lover.

" 'Madam, I must leave you. My horse awaits and the battle draws near.'

" 'Bartholomew, must you go? I know . . . I feel . . . I will not see you again.'

"He clutched her to his armored bosom. 'Be not afraid, fair Joannah. If I must die it will be in glorious victory with you in my heart. Farewell!'

" 'Would that I could die in your place, my love. You are too great and good to perish thus.' "

I sat where Sarah had been sitting and the warmth of her was still in the chair. I put the book aside and lit a cigarette. The sun fogged the room with dust motes and smoke thick in the corners and the shadow figure of Samson as he sat on the windowsill behind me was silhouetted on the far wall, huge and menacing. He rested, a silent black thought-panther between the potted azalea and the willow-patterned vase on Gale's sideboard. I half expected the glasses inside to tinkle as the shadow moved its head. Haunted you are, Joshua Steel. Haunted, by sentimental silly Sarah. It was just a cliché-ridden book; trivia. But I sat solemnly and wondered why, why those words, while the black panther looked on. We were all in the same river; had Sarah felt some of the currents and eddies, knowing without knowing? Maybe this had been her marked moment.

My will almost broke then. The hurt I do now I feel too. The hurt that is bound to come, the hurt that I won't feel at all, could that really be greater? I seemed to be punishing myself and everyone around, a sharing of the blame for dying. The hole got deeper. I could hear Bernard Ford say, "See a psychoanalyst, Doctor Steel. Problems of adjustment," though I could not recall his actually having said them. It almost broke. It seemed much too complicated to continue. Then I felt a heaviness on my leg and heard a warm feline whisper, and Samson came to curl up on my knee and sleep with his tongue sticking out.

I stared across at the wall between the potted azalea and the willow-patterned vase, and the panther shadow had gone.

He came back just once more, in the night. I had been restlessly asleep. When I woke the bedclothes were tangled round my feet and Sarah was half uncovered. I tried to place what had woken me. A noise? It came again, a keening wail as if from submerged sea caverns where shipwrecked sailors moan, and it

came from right beside me. Sarah was lying on her
stomach, her head turned away, and as I got used to
the dim moonlight I made out her hands grasping the
pillow. They relaxed and clung again, and again she
cried out, a brief, broken "No!" It is eerie when a
person you know well becomes a total stranger in
their dream hours. Before she could moan again I
shook her shoulder.

She woke up and began to cry. Her shivers shook
the bed. "Oh, that was dreadful," she mumbled. "Oh,
Josh, I had a terrible dream."

I cuddled her. "You scared me, too, making all that
noise. It's all right now, Sarah. Go back to sleep."

"I can't. I might dream it again." She was still sobbing. I could feel her tears on my neck. I smoothed
back her hair and kissed her wet eyes. I felt the hairs
of her eyelashes, each one on my lips. Right then I
was glad she could not see me. She sniffed a bit. "I'm
sorry I woke you up. I'll be okay now." She moved
away slightly.

"Tell me about it, then it can't come back."

"Can't it?"

"Of course not. What was it about?"

"It doesn't seem much now. Silly really."

"Tell me all the same."

She rolled away on her back. "I don't remember all
of it except it was sort of desperate, but the last bit
was horrible. I was standing alone on a tiny island in
the middle of a lake or sea or something. All around
there were boats, fishing boats and dinghies. You
were in one and Jim was in another and Uncle George,
and lots of faces I didn't know, too. Suddenly the
water began to rise and I couldn't move. It got over
my feet and I called out and waved but nobody
noticed, then it got higher and higher and I yelled

but it was lost in the water sound. The people just wouldn't notice. I was screaming when it got to my throat and there you all were, fishing and laughing and talking. Then it got to my mouth and I woke up. I've never been so relieved."

"There now, you've looked at it and it was only a dream."

"Not only," she said. "Dreams aren't only; they're important. They could be glimpses of a future or a past or even a parallel life, who knows? They could be the most vital things we have. People go mad when they don't dream. I think this was symbolic."

"You do?"

"Yes. I know you think I'm stupid, Josh. You've always scoffed when I've mentioned what I believe. I don't think you even know what I believe. Good night. I'm sorry I disturbed you."

"Good night." It was dawn before I slept again.

Sarah often went out alone in the evenings. At first she asked if I would come.

"Where?" I asked.

"Anywhere. Just out for a drive and maybe a drink."

"I'm tired, blossom-bump. I've been standing up all day. Why this sudden urge to shake the dust? You used to be happy at home."

"I'm bored, bored to tears. There's nothing for me to do all day but housework, nobody round here wants typing done. It's okay for you, out all day meeting people. What about me?"

"Why don't you write or paint?"

She snatched up the car keys. "I'm no good at painting and anything I wrote these days would be so full of frustration it would be unreadable. Are you going to take me out or not?"

"How about tomorrow?"

"No! Just forget I ever mentioned it, Joshua!" The door slammed behind her. I went to the window and stood behind the curtain to watch her drive away. The roses were coming into bloom along the back fence.

"Good-bye, my Sarah," I said, and turned to the liquor cabinet.

The liquor became a habit. I would not say I was an alcoholic, but when Sarah went out alone I drank to drive away the thoughts that crowded in. Most evenings spent this way became blurry at the edges and fogged with old memories. I found I could retire into the past and surround myself with familiar faces in the familiar room. Dad could be there among his books and we would talk of California, and sometimes he'd tell me about Canada, of which he'd seen a lot in his youth. We sailed into Vancouver Island together and marveled at the dark Douglas firs against the blue-white mountain tops. We traveled to the east coast on the Canadian-Pacific to watch the Nova Scotia fishermen haul in tunny and cod from the cold gray Atlantic. We tramped the lush green meadows and we explored with our boat every inlet round the Bay of Fundy.

He had missed the sea, living in Somerset, and given an opportunity to get away from work, he first tended his garden, then headed for the coast.

The memories only faded when stupor set in, then I could stagger to bed and not fear the blackness. Colin Madison might have had a word to say about my drinking, but it would have been a wasted word. What possible harm could it do now? That was a question which answered itself.

One night in May I asked Sarah where she had

been. It was eleven-thirty by the tiny round clock with gold hands that stands on the kitchen shelf beside the recipe books, and I had been staring at it on and off since ten. The kitchen after dinner has always been a good place to study in, warm and stuffy from the cooker and away from the radio and television noises, but the papers under my elbows were still as I had laid them out. Today I had woken up lonely. Days have a face, maybe, or maybe I'd been dreaming a solitary dream. Fancy trying to blame the day when I must color it myself. Otherwise all people would be depressed together, happy together. I drifted away into the possibilities of such a situation, imagination flying aimless. There would be a suicide season, a sillier than silly season, no-work days, and frenetic days, alarming opportunities for the entrepreneur, and forecasts . . . yes, the ubiquitous weatherman would have another string to his bow, assessing depression factors and psycho-meteorological data.

My mind was avoiding what it so obviously needed to think about, scurrying around and diving off after red herrings. Do it aloud, then. Pretend you have a willing listener. "Next week I see Colin Madison," I said, but quietly. Gale was upstairs in bed. "I know already what he will say and do and recommend to be done. I shall be lucky to see out another couple of months. Remission is still attainable and apart from this bloody nagging backache, I feel reasonably well, but the intervals are getting shorter. Less than four weeks this time. Doctor or not, I find it hard to believe the evidence of my own eyes when I see the blood films. I am a proper battleground, a proper bloody battleground." I think I laughed a little. "I had a word with James today, willing listener. He suspects I

225

know and I act as if I don't and we're both pretending and that's limiting. Honesty is so much easier, especially for him. I asked him if he had a girlfriend. It was a shabby trick, I guess. He muttered, 'Sort of.' He's changed and that's good. He doesn't dig at me any more about Isobel Kenny and he doesn't talk about Sarah at all. Never mentions her name, let alone chide me for neglecting her as he has done in the past. When I speak the magic word his poor open face and kind blue eyes collapse—he feels really guilty. I find I mention her purposely to make sure his attitude hasn't changed from day to day. I hope he doesn't get too guilty, he might 'do the right thing' and walk proudly out of her life clutching his self-righteousness to his chest like a dagger. Maybe not, though. I know my Sarah."

Words stopped coming there, or something stopped them, or there are no words for it. I went to the cupboard where the whisky is kept, brought out the bottle, and took a glass from the drainer.

At twelve o'clock my wife let herself in the front door. She must have seen the light from the kitchen because she came straight through. Her cheeks were pink and her coat unbuttoned.

"Where the hell have you been?" I said, realizing that I was on my fourth whisky.

"Is his Lordship interested or merely vicious?" she said with a pursed little grin. "Been at the booze again, Josh?"

"Yes. Did you have a good time?"

She narrowed her eyes. She uses the same expression for shopkeepers who try to overcharge, or door-to-door salesmen offering the world for next to nothing. "I've been out often recently," she said. "You haven't displayed the slightest interest in why, where, or with whom. You've been so indifferent I might as well be living on another planet. Now you ask did I have a good time. I could have been at a funeral, couldn't I?" She ended on a strained artificial pitch.

"At midnight? No . . . no, I'm sorry, Sarah. You're a grown woman and you make your own decisions."

"You make me sick!" she said. "Why can't you be angry? At least that's emotion, that's Joshua Steel with a face I know."

"I'm tired," I said. And I was, but I was scared, too. She was right. My anger with her was real and anger can turn so suddenly to desire. Sarah knows it; whether consciously or simply intuitively I am not sure, but she knows. Many times she has lit a fire in me just so she can join me in the flames. My stomach curled under my ribs as I thought of her doing it to Jimmy. After the first jealous contortion I found I could pity him. I thought he might miss out on a lot of Sarah.

I emptied my glass and shuddered. "Going to bed," I said, and stood up.

She watched me go. "Josh, are you ill or something? I mean, you've never been like this in all the time I've known you."

"Petal, I keep trying to convince all those about me that I am really very sick and suited only to the lightest of light work like pressing flowers or peeling a grape or two, but no one believes me." I grinned at her quickly. "Seriously, this is a strange time. The change of lifestyle, coming back here. I'm reminded of my childhood often."

"Will you come through it?" she said softly. "Or will it be too late to grow up again?"

I shrugged and went upstairs slowly, struggling for breath.

It is rare for Aunt Gale to demand a ride in my car, particularly on a wet Saturday morning, but she found me in the sitting room looking through the bookshelves for something to read, and requested I take her to Bridgwater. I had in my hand at that moment a copy of Tolstoy's *War and Peace* and was wondering whether to plow through it again when the old sickbed joke crossed my mind. "Don't give him that book, it's a serial." I smiled at Aunt Gale. "Is it urgent? Look at the weather."

"I'm not frightened of thunderstorms."

"I am."

"Rubbish, boy! You used to love watching the lightning and counting the seconds before the thunder. Where's your coat?"

Gale was ready in a pale trench coat and shiny red hat, her straw shopping basket over her arm. Outside it began to hail. The sky was bright gray and I couldn't see the backs of the houses less than fifty feet away. Mrs. Corbey's cottage loomed brown and ghostly. Lumps of ice hurtled down. "It's June," I said. "I hope your cold frame doesn't get broken."

"I'll put a sack over it on the way out. Come on, Josh."

"Is it very important?"

"I have things to do. I'm not waiting about for buses in this. Give me the keys, I'll drive myself."

Gale used to drive my father's automatic with rather more enthusiasm than skill, and though she'd kept her license up-to-date she hadn't touched a steering wheel in years. "Where's my coat?" I said. She bustled me through to the kitchen. "I'd better tell Sarah," I added.

"I've told her. Come on." She walked quickly to the car, covering the cold frame on the way.

The hail gave way to heavy rain that bounced noisily off the hood and slapped back against the windshield. I had to drive slowly because the wipers could hardly cope. Gale's fingers played scales on the handles of her shopping bag and she kept glancing at her watch.

"Do you have an appointment?" I said. She raised her eyebrows and shook her head.

For a couple of miles we were silent. I got stuck behind a truck that was doing twenty-five miles an hour and throwing a thick spray of black water from its rear tires. Finally the driver waved me past, then accelerated as I did. A car coming toward us left me nowhere to go. As I tucked back into the blinding wheel spray again, Gale asked me why I was swearing. "You're very temperamental," she said.

"Didn't you see what he did?"

"No." I decided I had been right not to let her drive. "What are you going to do next weekend?" she said.

I searched for special dates, anniversaries, birthdays, but nothing materialized. "Why next weekend?"

"I thought you might go fishing with Doctor Picton."

"Did he mention it?"

"No, but Sarah will be away and I thought it would be a good opportunity, especially if the weather improves. The long-range forecast was good." She spoke quite easily and her fingers were still and relaxed. I blasted past the lorry regardless.

"This may come as a surprise to you, Gale, or it

may not, but I don't recall being informed that my wife will be away next weekend."

"Oh, of course. I'm sorry. It wasn't arranged until yesterday evening and you were at the hospital on that emergency, weren't you?"

"Yes, I was."

She stared at me. "I don't doubt your word, there's no need to snap. A woman called Joan Slater rang to ask Sarah up to London next weekend."

I went through a set of traffic lights at amber. "Joan asked Sarah alone?"

"I don't know, dear. I think Sarah said you'd be busy."

"But I won't be."

Gale shrugged and played scales with her fingers.

She shopped briskly in two stores in Bridgwater while I drove around the block avoiding sodden, suicidal pedestrians who carried paper bags and tried to keep the contents from splitting out all over the road. When I picked her up again she said, "Now, take the next turning left and look for a place called Cumberland House." I did as instructed but my Aunt Gale does not know her right from her left. In a heavy stream of traffic we detoured a mile or two to get back where we started. The Morgan hates idling. Great choking clouds of blue followed us as the plugs oiled up. Gale was quite unapologetic; I think she did not realize the faintest need for apology. Some folks are just not transport-minded. She pointed out Cumberland House as we passed it. I kept going.

"Josh, it's there," she insisted, pointing backward.

I nodded. We were in a one-way system with vehicles parked on both sides and at least half a dozen frustrated motorists inhaling my fumes behind. On the third time round a parking space had become available opposite the building Gale was so intent upon visiting. The Morgan coughed to a stop and I dreaded having to start her up again. "Don't be too long," I said. "It's half an hour in any hour."

Gale glanced at her watch. "Will you come with me?" she said.

"Why?" I couldn't understand her mixture of apprehension and cajoling smile.

"Please."

I followed her across the street. Gale walked and traffic skidded to a halt. I closed my eyes but she was standing on the opposite pavement quite unscathed when I opened them. Cumberland House was one of the concrete shoe boxes with more office suites vacant than rented and a bleak entrance hall where the lifts and stairs began; large wooden boards told the names of the businesses contained on the various floors. Gale scanned a couple, apparently found what she wanted and pressed the call button for a lift. As we ascended, in the smell of stale cigarettes and new plastic, I asked where we were going. She did not reply.

On the fourth floor landing another wooden board with arrows left and right indicated insurance companies and a couple of government departments. Gale strode away to the right. I caught up with her outside a glass door. She turned to me. "Josh, listen to me. You may not think this is a good idea, but I did the same with Sarah last week and she was happy to go along with it. She realized that I acted out of concern for both of you." She stopped nervously.

"Gale, what are you talking about?"

"You might be angry with me, but now that you're here perhaps you might listen to what she has to say."

I began to suspect that either Gale or I was going insane. "Who is she?"

My aunt moved to allow me to see the gold lettering on the door behind her. *Marriage Guidance Counselor*, it read.

Already it had been a bad morning; now it was turning into a ridiculous one. I took one look and walked away. Gale called out behind me and I heard her feet trotting on the plastic floor. I did not want to stop. I always walk when I'm mad or scared or even elated. I cannot be held in a room, nor will my feet keep still. I started down the stairs. It was a long way and I think Gale was behind me but I can't be sure. My thoughts were, I suppose, predictable. First I was angry; at the deception, at the presumption, at the interference in my private affairs. Second, and by the second floor, I was already beginning to forgive the well-meant fumblings of Aunt Gale who loved me and wanted everything in our garden to be lovely. By the first floor my legs were aching and I was wondering what my poor sweet Sarah had said to the Marriage Guidance lady. When I reached the car and somehow Gale reappeared magically at my side I was wondering what the Marriage Guidance lady would have said to me, before and after I told her the truth. I thought I had probably done her a favor by missing the appointment.

Dear Gale seemed annoyed and confused. "Oh, Josh," she said as we sat in the car. I put back my head. "What the blazes are you laughing at?" she demanded. "You're ruining your marriage for no reason and that's funny? Or am I funny because I tried to help?"

Her face rumpled and her freckled knuckles bunched like extra handles on her shopping basket. I watched her and felt I had to help. "None of that is funny," I said gently. "It's just been such a hell of a morning, if I didn't laugh I'd weep. Gale, I think I've a right to a couple of questions. Do you think Sarah is really unhappy?"

"Of course she is!" She glinted at me.

"Now, think about it. You see our marriage breaking down, you say, and to you that means that both parties are bound to be unhappy. Am I unhappy, Gale?"

"You're good at hiding your feelings. So is Sarah."

I started the car and though the Morgan protested at first, we were soon moving northward to home.

"I don't think my wife is unhappy," I said later. "She is changed."

"Because of you," said Gale. Now she was feeling guilty. She pulled at a loose piece of straw on the basket. "You changed."

"Everyone changes. Sarah goes out often and enjoys herself. She buys clothes and stuff, anything she wants. She doesn't mope about or cry, does she?"

Gale shook her head grudgingly. "She seems all right," she conceded. "But you don't know what goes on underneath."

As we neared home a small worry was buzzing at the pane of my mind like an autumn wasp. Casually, I said, "What did Sarah have to say to the Marriage Guidance Counselor?"

Sullenly my aunt answered, "I don't know."

"Aw, come on, Gale."

She bit her lip. "It's none of my business." I laughed and made her smile, too. "All right," she said, "I suppose I can't be interested and disinterested in the same breath. She said it was a fascinating little exercise that revealed nothing that she didn't know already. She even laughed a bit, like you did. But at least she tried," she added darkly. "And she's a deep one. I couldn't tell if she'd discounted the whole thing or not."

I walked into the house feeling quite easy in my mind, but when I saw my wife at the kitchen table laying out lunch things, I remembered she was going to London next weekend, and any trace of gaiety was wiped clean off the slate by the damp cloth of loss. She smiled brightly at us. "Get your wet clothes off," she said. "Lunch is almost ready. Jim's coming, Josh. He rang to remind me you had asked him."

"Good." I helped Gale out of her coat and she gave me a look which indicated my intelligence was non-existent and there was nothing more she could do about it.

Before James arrived Sarah told me she was going to spend the next weekend with John and Alan. She did not mention me, so I did not complain at not being invited. "Give them my regards," I said.

"Of course. I'm going up on the Saturday morning train and I'll be back on Sunday night. Could you collect me from the station?"

"I expect so. Maybe I'll go fishing with Jim while you're away."

Sarah nodded her bronze head. "Good idea. You should relax more, both of you."

It sounded to me as if two comparative strangers were talking in a train compartment.

Most of the important events in my life have happened by accident, pure chance. It is only after they are done that I see where I should have stood and waited, where I should have said no instead of yes. I have always said yes too easily and that's not so self-opinionated as it sounds. If I have agreed so readily it is only because it was easier that way. I know of men who plan their lives, their wives, their hives of industry. Men who have an aim and strive toward it, cutting across people and sensitivities and district councils and loyalties, straight as canals. In my way now I was trying to carve, not a canal, just a small short cut from one bend of the river to the next; but this day, this particular day, the accident happened and I had not foreseen it. Before my illness most of what I had foreseen never came to be, as if foreseeing it prevented it. Only the unexpected happened to me. I thought I'd been clever enough this time, but clever reason is not all that rules a man. I'd forgotten about the emotion boiling away without a safety valve.

On the day before the London trip I lay beside Sarah in the early gray room, with the roses on the wallpaper just coming into focus. It must have been around six o'clock. Outside it rained, not June rain in petulant, childish handfuls, but more like October rain, tears of a sorrowing old man. I got out of bed shakily, sweating all over though the room was cool, and went to the window. The cold draft made me shiver worse than before. I was glad that my next appointment with Colin Madison was only four days away, glad now because the disease was becoming worse than the treatment. I looked out at the spongy garden, gripping the windowsill hard. It would be soon. A great wave of self-pity came down with the straight rain lines. When I cleaned my teeth last night a lot of blood came out with the toothpaste froth; there were tiny petechiae on my gums and buccal mucosa. The skin of my body was paler than ever, not just sallow and easy-to-tan like it was before, but a frightening, telltale white. I wanted Sarah to notice. I really wanted her to notice, though I deliberately turned her head away.

"What are you doing?" Her voice made me start, it sounded so sharp and unlike Sarah, especially against the gentle pattering of the rain.

"Nothing. Just looking at the day. It's raining."

"You don't normally go mooning out of windows at this hour." She heaved herself up, her hair flattened on one side and sticking out on the other. She looked quite beautiful and Sarah is not beautiful. "Can't you sleep?"

"No. I wanted to see the day before it got spoiled. I often moon at this hour."

"You don't!"

"I do, but you normally sleep through. Why did you wake up today?"

She turned away, thumping the pillow, muttering, "I suppose it's that Isobel woman. Why don't you say it, Josh? Why do you stay around being a different person all the time and making me want to hate you? I'd rather end it on a cool note before that happens. Let's split up if that's what you want." I had to listen hard to catch it all. Her face was half buried in the pillow as if she hadn't really wanted me to hear it at all, and hadn't wanted to say it.

So the moment had arrived, the center, the crux, the solution. I had set the plan in motion, watched it grow and blossom dreadfully, devoted my existence and sold my soul to it. There was no trumpet blowing, no flags waving; just a sinking chill. "What do you want, Sarah?"

She was sobbing dry little coughs, not real tears. "My Joshua," she said. "My old Joshua or nothing at all. I don't know you. I want to leave what you've become."

"Jimmy?" I forced out. The window was receding and attacking, receding and attacking though I held the sill so tight it hurt my nails.

"Why not?" she shouted suddenly. "He's kind to me. He doesn't exist in a cold, amusing cell where no one can reach him unless he wants them to. He's not clever-clever and living on the moon. Oh, Joshua Steel, I wish I'd never seen your smile!"

I was drawn to her tense back and shoulders as if I was on elastic. I should have stayed by the window clinging to my triumph with my fingernails, but I staggered round the bed to face her and took her clenched fists into my hands. They were cold like little hard snowballs. Her eyes felt the same as I began to say, "Sarah, sweet, it's all a lie, don't believe it," but I hardly got past "Sarah" when her expression changed from angry pain to bewilderment and I was slipping back and away, back and away, very slowly. Don't believe it, Sarah, I was saying to the darkness. Don't believe the lie I made.

CHAPTER
TEN

In an intimate, expensive restaurant of half a dozen tables two people watched each other over brandy and coffee, covert examinations alternately. The waiters, shadows with alert eyes, knew an illicit meeting when they saw one. They winked the most genteel of winks at one another and gave the subtlest of attention to the table in the corner, replacing old candles with new, bringing more coffee before it could be called for. The occupants stopped talking every time someone came near.

"Where are you supposed to be?" asked the man.

"You asked already. You always do. Why are you so worried? No one else is."

"Not you?"

"No. It's his fault as much as mine, isn't it?"

He smiled ruefully. "I don't know if that makes me a weapon of revenge. Which came first with you, his coldness or your, um, attraction to me?"

The woman blew gently on the candle flame and a

trail of smoke smut carried across the table. "Neither. Your attraction to me. It is flattering to have a good-looking man pay compliments. He used to." She fiddled with a knife, turning it so the blade reflected yellow light. "I might be using you. I don't know for sure yet."

"You're honest, at least. So many women aren't."

She smiled. "So many human beings aren't. It's a kind of self-protection. We don't like to look upon the damage we might do. I was testing, that's all. To you, I'm safe. You can pull out any time."

"I don't understand. You know how much I care about you."

She shook her head. "I don't and neither do you. Your reputation, you said, but you didn't mention mine." She laughed at him quietly.

There was a silence and a waiter rushed into it with the coffee pot. The couple nodded and he poured, then slid away. The man cleared his throat. "I wish you would leave him," he said. "I feel terrible having to sneak and hide, particularly when your husband is a friend of mine."

"They mostly are, aren't they?" She reached over and squeezed his hand. "You make me happy, you know. You are good and straight. I don't think you're clever, not the kind of clever that scares me. At home I feel tense all the time, I don't know what to do or say any more. It's nice to relax and laugh, though I must say you seem a bit depressed tonight."

"Not depressed. Serious, you know what I mean?"

"I will not permit seriousness. We've too short a time anyway."

"That's why I'm serious. It doesn't feel right."

"Change never does, I guess. It's exciting and a a little frightening."

"You shouldn't have come tonight, not with him being ill."

The woman's eyes fired like matches. "He told me to. He said he didn't want me there. The doctor's been and Gale collected the prescription. He's comfortable and drowsy and there's nothing I can do anyway."

"What's wrong? Did the doctor say?"

"It was a new man, Doctor Gordon's locum. Called March, I think. Do you know him?" The man shook his fair head. "He says it's a bronchial infection and there's a typical pleurisy pain." She drank some coffee and smiled.

He frowned back. "Look, you're very unconcerned, aren't you? Cold, hard even. It's not like you."

"Whatever gave you the idea that I'm soft? Are women supposed to be, even when their husbands have virtually ignored them for three or four months, and blatantly flirted with another woman right under their noses?"

"Are you really that fierce about it, my dear?"

She frowned a crossed-up frown and her mouth dropped sadly. "I don't know. I have to be. It makes no difference. At this moment I'm sorry he's ill and lying in bed because I hate to see anyone sick. Illness makes me cold and efficient, you know? The minute I allow myself to sympathize and get personally involved I can't function. So, I'm sorry, but it's not breaking my heart and it's certainly not breaking his. You don't hate me for that, do you?"

"I love you," said the man softly. "I can't blame you for defending yourself. I suppose your London trip is off?"

"I don't think so. I'll see how he is tomorrow but I'll probably still go. I want to see Joan very much."

241

"That much?"

"For all our sakes, really. I need to talk to someone outside it all."

The man sighed. "I just want it to be all right with us," he said.

"Then it's bound to be at someone's expense. Wait just a little. I think it won't be long."

At eight-thirty the front doorbell rang and Gale Steel hurried to answer it. "Now who can that be?" she said to herself as she left the kitchen, drying her hands on a tea cloth. Isobel Kenny stood on the doorstep, her deep eyes black with worry. She smiled quickly into Gale's unwelcoming face and said, "We heard at the hospital that Doctor Steel was ill. We thought someone ought to come and see him."

"So you came."

"I have to pass on the way home. Doctor Picton is out this evening, so I offered."

Gale finished drying her hands, jerking at the cloth. "You'd better come in," she said. She led the way to Josh's sitting room. "I'll see if he's well enough to see you."

"Miss Steel, I am a nursing sister," said Isobel quietly. "Many of my patients are quite ill."

"He might be asleep," said Gale, and closed the door hard behind her.

Isobel took off her coat and hung it over a chair back. The navy cotton uniform heightened the severity of her expression and the paleness of her hands. All day long, since the phone call to say Josh was ill and would not be coming to work, her heart had been thumping. Her answers and her temper had been short. You're behaving like a teenager, she told her-

self. You know he doesn't care . . . but he makes a fuss
of you and he kissed you. She searched for traces of
him in the room. There was a motoring magazine on
the floor beside his chair, a very poor snapshot of a
dog on the desk beside a studio portrait of Sarah,
and two cigarette butts in the ashtray which she
wanted to pick out and touch where his lips had been.
Gale came back.

"You can go up," she said abruptly. "But he's tired.
I'll show you the way."

As they climbed the stairs, Isobel asked, "Is Sarah
with him?"

"N-no. She had to go out urgently, but I'm sure
she'll be back soon." She led the way into the bedroom. It was cool and bright from the dipping sun.
Josh was holding his hands up to make shadow pictures on the wall.

"Woof! Woof!" he said. "Look, there's a swan. What
noise does a swan make, Isobel?"

"I don't know."

"Sit down. Pull up that other chair, the straight one
is as hard as iron." He dropped his hands outside the
covers and Isobel saw his fingers were shaking. Gale
hovered inside the door. "Dear Aunt Gale," added
Josh, "Isobel's just come off duty and would love a
cup of tea, and so would I. Would you please be an
angel?"

Gale folded her tea cloth exactly edge to edge and
stared severely at Isobel, then more gently at her
nephew. "All right. I won't be a minute."

When she had gone, Josh smiled at Isobel. "Don't
mind Aunt Gale," he said, and his voice was quiet
and rough. "She's a dragon, but quite tame. A pet if
you scratch behind her ears."

243

"She doesn't like me to come here," said Isobel. "But I thought someone from the hospital should come, and Jim's busy tonight."

"I rather thought he would be. How are you, Isobel?"

She smiled at him through her worry. "It's you that's ill. What did Doctor Gordon have to say?"

"Nothing." He looked mischievous. Isobel saw how the clavicles showed through the skin at the base of his neck and how the tendons stood out and his jaw squared. He tried not to frown with the pain but the corners of his mouth pulled down. "Doctor March says I have pleurisy."

Isobel wanted to touch him. Her nerve ends reached out and she sat with her leg muscles taut, her thumbs rubbing over her curled fingers. "I shouldn't have come," she said.

"Why not, my dear girl? Would you have me suffering all alone with no soft voice to soothe me or cool hands to caress my fevered brow?"

"You're talking too much."

"I know. It's silly to have to breathe in such shallow little puffs."

Isobel frowned at her fingers that longed to stroke the gold-brown hairs on his forearms. "Sarah should be here," she said. "People are talking enough already. No wonder your aunt dislikes me."

Josh shook his head, coughed and doubled up with a groan. Isobel's professional concern allowed her to touch him then. He was warm and helpless in her arms and she hated herself for the part in her, the lonely part that enjoyed his need and took comfort from it. Even when he relaxed again she kept her fingers round his wrist. She stared at the second hand of the watch pinned to her breast and could not count the seconds nor the flying pulse beats. His skin was so smooth.

"Would you pass me one of those pills and the glass of water," said Josh.

She did so and when he had swallowed the tablet he folded his hand away out of her reach. Isobel's eyes noticed and shuttered down. A silence grew in the room so deep that the roses on the wallpaper seemed noisy. "Do you know how long you'll be away, Josh?" said Isobel, frightened of the quiet.

Josh blinked at her wearily. "No. I don't know. I guess this should clear up in a week or two. Can you manage without me until then?"

"I've managed all this time."

He reached for her hand then and tried to squeeze away the damage. "I'm sorry," he said softly. "I think you should try to forget it."

To her knees she mumbled, "Forget what, Josh? I hope you don't want me to forget our friendship."

"No, but are you a person who can be a friend and just that? It's easy to misread intentions, Isobel."

Gale came in with the tea. She put the tray on top of the bureau, poured three cups and passed two. Josh rested the saucer on his chest and raised his head to drink. The two women watched his exhausted face. "Get out the candles and the black veils," he said, smiling. "You're watching me as if I might expire."

"You talk too much," said Gale. "When you've drunk that you must get some sleep."

"And I must go," said Isobel. "I'll come again later in the week, if I may?"

"Of course you may. I'll look forward to it."

Gale slammed down her half empty cup. "I'll show you out," she said, opening the door. Isobel left her tea and followed.

Gale gave her her coat and said, "What did you think of him, Miss Kenny?"

Isobel turned away, fumbling with a button. "I'm not sure," she said hesitantly. "He seems bright enough, but he's obviously in pain and he looks ill."

Gale's eyes were bright as she looked at the young woman, and pitying. "You shouldn't speak of him," she said quietly. "You give too much away."

Isobel did not reply. She picked up her bag and went to the door. "Thank you for the tea," she said.

"Forgive me, my dear. But it is plain to anyone with half an eye. I'd advise you to try to forget him. A lot of young women have fallen for Josh, you know, and they've only hurt themselves."

"I'm sorry, Miss Steel, but I don't understand you." Isobel went out with her head up and her world foundering. Gale went back upstairs.

"You might have let the poor woman finish her tea," said Josh. "She knew exactly what you were doing, Gale, she's not a fool. Now, I have something to say and I'm not going to argue with you. Sarah is out and you and I both know who with, so while she's out I want you to do something for me." His aunt screwed up her hands and tried to interrupt but his eyes silenced her. "I want you to fetch the telephone so that I can arrange to go into the clinic while she is away for the weekend. She probably won't want to go now, but you and I are going to persuade her. Okay?" He gasped and sweat ran like tears.

"But Josh . . ." Gale stopped helplessly. "Why can't you be treated here? Why won't you tell Sarah about this bronchi—whatever it is?"

"Because I say so!" His face was wet and his lips were white. "Now, please! Do as I say!" He looked so frighteningly weak and was so strong in his heart that Gale nodded quickly and went to get the telephone. It was half an hour before he could use it, but when he did the clinic was as efficient as only well-greased institutions can be. He would be collected at nine-thirty A.M. on the following day.

Shortly after ten o'clock Gale insisted he take sedatives, and by the time Sarah arrived home he was in an uneasy sleep filled with dreams of drowning. Gale woke him, even though she opened the door with great care. "Sarah?" mumbled the figure in the bed.

"It's me. Sarah's home. She asked if you were worse and I said you seemed the same; so she's going to London tomorrow. I thought you'd want to know before she came up."

"You see? She's not unhappy. I'm glad about that."

Gale said "Hmph!" through her nose, then whispered to Sarah who was coming up the stairs, "He's almost asleep, dear."

Josh heard his wife reply, "I'll just say good night. I'll sleep in the next bedroom tonight to save disturbing him." She went into the room where he lay, bringing the scent of honeysuckle to sweeten the sweat-soaked air. He breathed it in and his chest did not hurt because so much old happiness flowed in with the perfume memories. "How are you, Josh?" She switched on the small shaded lamp beside the bed.

"Better, I think," he mumbled. "My chest doesn't hurt so much. Did you have a nice evening?"

"Yes, thanks. Would you mind if I still go away tomorrow? I need to see Joan, I think. There's such a lot to talk about."

"You go," Josh said. "Gale will see I'm okay."

She sat on the bed for a moment, looking remotely

247

at him. "I suppose this is how it is meant to be," she said. "I don't understand it, or how it came about, but the circle must turn."

"Your theories again, wife?"

"My life, husband. The way things must be. Good night, Josh."

Somerfield knew of Joshua Steel's illness before the first day of it was ended. The staff of the Cottage Hospital knew and took the tale home to their tea tables. The milkman knew, and the Co-op baker who delivered to almost every door and passed the news with the daily bread. Even newcomers knew though they only recognized the young doctor by his car and his aunt, Miss Steel. Mr. Kingsley, the vicar, knew and prayed conscientiously for a quick recovery, between prayers for Mrs. Jankowski, who had osteoarthritis, and Mr. Greaves, who drank too much and beat his wife and children. It had been seven years since Somerfield had had its own police station, so there was no kindly and respected local sergeant to know. The Panda cars that occasionally passed through from Shepton Mallet were driven by remote robots who did not care to know. The village to a man would have clammed up to silence had they stopped and asked. But the school children knew and little Veronica who said she had listened to his heart, and Jemmy Allen, who had replaced Cider 'Arry as village idiot, knew because he knew everyone and everything in his slowly whirling brain.

There were raised eyebrows and knowing nods of heads among the shop customers as the news passed, expressions meant to show sympathy but always with the rider, "That's what you get for fooling around with other women." There were suggestive suckings in of breath when pleurisy was mentioned, and old wives' predictions, and Miss Vivian told how he often came in for cigarettes and how he was pale and polite. The village took the news no more seriously than when Alec Grove's cows broke out and ate Mrs. Lock's garden that was entered for the Best Garden of the Year, or when Mrs. Bassie the news agent's wife had run away with an Indian brush salesman. Anything that happened was news.

Four or five people called at the house on Saturday with nosey best wishes, and Gale thanked them and fended them off. When Mrs. Corbey asked why the big navy car had been in the lane, Gale said it was a friend of Josh's from the hospital. Mrs. Corbey nodded and did not believe her.

Josh returned from the clinic on Sunday evening, weak as water but better. He lay on the settee in Gale's room and stared about with brooding eyes, one finger rubbing gently at the bruised veins of his left hand. His lungs were empty of fluid and he could breathe easily, but all the time his head sang with a murmur like an electric current. Gale fed him soup and told him of the visitors.

"But they don't know me," he said.

"A lot of them remember you from when you were small; and your name has been bandied about recently."

"Nosey lot of buggers."

"That's unfair. People in villages gossip, but those that came genuinely wanted to help. They came out of their way to wish you well. You've been too long in big cities, Josh."

He drank some soup and chewed a piece of chicken thoughtfully. "Why don't they talk about Sarah?" he said.

"Who says they don't? They wouldn't talk to you,

249

would they?" Gale lit a cigarette and blew smoke away from Josh. "She knows the village better than you do, anyway. People like her."

He laughed. "Better than me?"

Gale saw nothing funny. "Naturally. She's on a different level from you. I'm sure there have been rumors, but Sarah is a discreet person. Even if she had something to hide," she ended sternly.

"You really think my wife is purest white and I am Sir Jasper with a big, black moustache like in the old movies? Gale, where is your common sense?"

"I have to believe something, otherwise I'll walk out of here and let you rot. Both of you, all of you. And I'm not going to do that when it's my house." She took the soup bowl out of his hands and left him to think. Josh did not reflect on her words. People's words left him unmoved now. The river was slowing, the estuary was in sight, and beyond that the beckoning sea so big that all thoughts could drown in it. When Sarah came home he knew she would have her future actions planned, and unless Joan had let him down by stepping right out of character, he knew what they would be. A peace filled him, a gray lonely peace. Now he could remember the loving of her and the glow of her loving and that was dreaming and this was real. Gale had been right. Aloud, he said, "Gale, you were right. I've changed us all and I can't go back either." The wall around his caring was complete. Experimentally, he said, "I love you, Sarah," and the sensation was blunted and dull. "I don't know," he said, and his wide eyes stared up at the wandering river cracks in the ceiling. He was quite alone.

The morning Josh returned to work was sunny with a stiff breeze from the north. The beech trees roared their near black leaves and tiny apples, hard as marbles, blew down from the Bramley in Gale's garden. Sarah took her book and folding chair to the angle formed by the house and the garden wall and sat in the sun. Her eyes flew away from the pages and she could not read. She sat instead with her eyes quite vacant and her hand curled under the book across the base of her stomach. Her fingers moved gently from time to time and once she pressed her upper arms forward together and felt the slight ache in her breasts.

If you talk about a dream it will make it ordinary. Josh had said so; but then, the weekend with Joan and Alan and their son Donald who had been home from boarding school was not a dream. Yet it could have been because it was completely outside the reality she had come to accept. Her lips moved as she went back over it. They had asked about Josh, of course, and she had said he wasn't well. After his name had been mentioned twice more Joan had sensed something wrong. Sarah had gone there to talk, so she talked while Alan took his son to a friend's for tea.

"He's got another woman, has he?" said Joan. "Bloody men! You feed them, work for them, bear their brats, wash their dirty socks and underwear— and what for? If I had the chance again, Sarah, I'd never get married. Have them while they're still keen, but as soon as the roses and chocolates stop, drop them. The men I mean. Who is she?"

"She's nice. I like her. The four of us have gone out together quite often. She's a sister at the hospital."

"Like her? I'd put a knife in her guts after what she's done."

"Oh, you wouldn't. And I can't help feeling it's not all her fault, there's something strange about it."

251

Joan screwed up her face in indignation. "Don't ever blame yourself," she said. "Even if it is your fault. Tell him that and you're mud on his boots forever. Have you been seeing someone else, Sarah?"

Sarah nodded. "Good for you!" Joan slapped her knee. "That'll wake his ideas up. Look, love, men are like dogs in all senses. They are sometimes pretty, always randy and sniffing around, but when they've got a bone, even if they're not chewing it, God help the dog who tries to take it away."

"I wonder whether you believe it's that simple. I'm certainly not getting the chewing."

"Of course it is! Men are simple. Very cunning, but simple. You wait; when Josh realizes what's been happening he'll come running."

"He hasn't. He's known for a couple of months. I even think he's encouraged it. Joan, I didn't come for advice. I think I came to say things aloud to see how they looked. You see, he's been so cold so long and I don't know why, he's changed so much but so gradually I only notice when I say it in words. I don't even know how I feel about him any more."

"He must be mad," said Joan coldly. "Are you sure it wasn't you who started it? I mean, could it have been this other bloke that turned Josh off you?"

Sarah shrugged. "I don't know. But I think I'll leave him, Joan. I think I'll have to, but I can't while he's ill. What would you do?"

But Alan and Donald had come back right then and Don had a new badminton set he wanted to christen.

Later in the evening when the boy had gone to bed, Joan returned to Sarah's problems. "D'you remember I read your hand, ages ago?" she said. "And Joshua's."

Alan interrupted. "If we're going to have astrology

for supper I'm going out for a pint before they close,"
he said.

"Good. Push off," said Joan. "And don't come back
here Brahms and Liszt or you'll be sleeping with Don
tonight." She turned to Sarah and ignored Alan completely.

"I said—shall I bring you back a bottle of stout?"
he shouted.

"Stout? I've got a bottle of gin. Bugger the stout.
You could bring us some crisps though." Her husband
sighed, winked at Sarah and went. "About Josh," said
Joan. "I think there was a lot of change in his hand,
and an illness, Sarah."

"Was that all?"

Joan scratched her head. "It was a long time ago."

"I remember it," said Sarah suddenly. "I remember
being cold, very cold. Was it something you said?"

Joan tried hard but could not remember. "What's
more important is what you're going to do," she said
finally. "If you leave him, it doesn't have to be irreversible. Lots of couples split up, then go back together. But be careful you don't ruin your life and
get left with nothing."

"With Josh it would be irreversible, and if I run to
Jim I can hardly run away from him later, can I?"

"Why not? Treat them like dirt, gal, and they love
you for it."

"I don't know if I want to be loved right now," said
Sarah quietly. Behind her eyes another problem was
winging round, but she could not talk about this one.
She did not even dare think of it.

The north wind whirled into her corner and flicked
over the pages of her book with impatient fingers
before it left. Sarah closed the covers. She was back

J. J. McKENNA

at square one, rubbing at her frown. Soon it would be
lunchtime, then after that dinner, and Josh would be
home and perhaps Jimmy would come. She found
that she wanted yet dreaded Joshua's arrival, and the
thought of Jim left her warm but not thrilled.

Doctor James Picton was finding the going tough.
He was obliged by pressure of work to be in his room,
and Joshua sat across from him with his feet on the
desk and the *Lancet* in his hand. The room was silent
but for the turning of pages. It agitated James when
other people had nothing to do, especially when he
was busy. James was agitated often lately, but kept
pushing away the one big reason in favor of a lot of
little ones. His tidy mind hated uncertainty and loose
ends, and his honesty made the love he harbored in
his heart a sinful thing.

"You might just as well have stayed at home," he
said to Josh's feet.

They changed position, one over the other. "Uh huh.
There's a very interesting article in here about herpes
labialis. Have you read it?"

"What time have I had."

"You've been busy lately."

Jim breathed hard in and out through his nose.
"This *is* a hospital and I *am* resident house surgeon."

Joshua's head appeared over his shoes. He grinned
affably. "Not so much time to be entertained these
days, eh?"

The other man rumpled his corn-colored hair.
"Bloody busy," he said.

"What are you doing?"

"Now?"

"Yes."

"Putting relevant details from these case notes on

254

to general index cards. It's for my own purposes, I like to keep a record of anything interesting."

"They'd be better typed."

"I know, but I can't type and I can't ask anyone in here to do it. They're far too busy with official work."

"Ask Sarah. She'll do it for you."

James clenched his fists and stared at them in angry embarrassment. Suddenly he wanted to be straight. "Look—" he said, and found himself glaring into Josh's understanding eyes. Did they hold a taunt or not?

"Yes, James?" It was not a taunt but a dare.

"Nothing," he muttered. "I'll ask Sarah sometime."

"I'll ask her for you. She'll be delighted to oblige, I'm sure."

And James could not for the life of him tell whether he was being mocked or whether the pale face on the other side of the room was full of genuine helpfulness.

He asked Sarah one evening later in the week. The small cinema was almost empty and held the peculiar smell of disinfectant and old upholstery. The film was very bad. "Does Josh know about us?" He had his arm about her shoulders and his mouth close to her hair.

"I should think so. Joshua may be an awful lot of things but he's not an idiot. Does it worry you, Jim?"

"Of course it does. I work with him. In the same room. If he knows he never lets on."

Sarah smiled. "You'd hardly expect him to shake you by the hand and say, all right, old chap, you can have her with my blessing, would you?"

"No, but oddly enough that's what he seems to be saying in a roundabout way."

Sarah lost her smile. "That's strange," she said. "That hurts. I knew it, but that really hurts."

The film rattled on and the good guy killed a bad guy at fifty yards with a pistol. "I've been looking around for another job," said James later. "There could be one coming up in Yeovil soon. Even—even if things don't work out with us I think I shall still move. It gets harder by the minute trying to avoid Josh. He just sits there and looks blank and smiles occasionally. I don't know what to make of him, he used to be so talkative and amusing."

"I wonder why it hurts," said Sarah to herself.

"Pardon?"

"Jim, I might leave him. Would you have me . . . ?"

"Like a shot." He tried to kiss her but she held him away.

"There would be a lot of degradation. Divorce court, private detectives, sordid things like that. What about your reputation?"

"We could move farther afield than Yeovil. Somewhere where no one would know us." Sarah laughed a little. "What's funny? You are as bad as Josh for laughing at nothing."

"Yes, I am, aren't I?"

Joshua decided to push the boat out. He knew he could not hold out much longer. The pains were worsening every day, and keeping them out of his face was becoming impossible. Sarah might want to take her time about deciding and the sands were almost through the glass. So one night as they lay in bed, he chose his words and nerved himself to say them.

Before he could speak, Sarah said, "Josh, I think I'm going to leave you."

It almost made him physically sick to be filled with a fountain of agony and relief. Experimentally, he said under his breath, "I love you, Sarah," and the sensation was sharp and bright. You're just frightened, said the middle voice. You've got your way and you're scared to be alone, that's all it is, all it is.

"I guessed it must come to this," he finally said out loud.

"What will you do?"

He was glad the light was off and there was no moon. "Does it matter?"

Sarah lay on her back, flat and straight, her feet together. Her hands rubbed across her stomach at a faint, dull pain. "It ought not to, but yes, it does."

"It's all right, Sarah. What will you and Jim do?" How those words rolled round like thunder in a tin room.

"I haven't told Jim my decision. I don't want to push him."

"He won't need pushing."

"Don't you mind?"

"I have no right to mind. It is my fault as much as yours."

And so solid was the plan that Sarah accepted her part of the blame without question. "Would you like a cup of tea?" she said.

"Yes. Yes, I would." By the time she came back the wave of loss had rolled over and left him flat.

They drank tea and smoked together in a comfortable silence. For the first time in months they relaxed. Josh thought that it must be that human beings are basically good. Why else should honesty give such relief, almost lightheartedness?

"When will you go?" he said.

"When Jimmy gets a new job, I suppose. He's onto a virtual certainty so it shouldn't be long. I'll move out to a hotel or lodgings anyway."

257

"No need to, goose-bump. You can stay here."

Sarah looked uncertain. "Won't that appear odd?"

"Who will know? There is a spare bedroom."

"Well . . . I'll think it over."

"Do you want to move in there now?"

Sarah said, "If it wasn't so bloody serious I'd laugh."

Isobel Kenny decided to try just once more. She caught up with Josh in the parking lot. He was swinging his heavy briefcase into the back of the Morgan. "Hi, Isobel," he smiled. "Can I give you a lift?"

"Yes, thank you. That would be nice."

As they drove she glanced often at the side of his face and his hands on the steering wheel. There was a pain beneath her ribs and her heart thudded in her throat and tried to choke her voice. "I haven't seen you much since you've been back," she said. "Are you feeling better?"

"Much. Good as new."

"You look ill, Josh."

"Nonsense. I need to sit in the sun, that's all. It's about time I had a holiday."

Isobel was not convinced. "My mother is away on holiday," she said. "With my Aunt Krissie. They've gone to Holland."

"Nice," said Josh politely. There was a prolonged silence. They drew up outside the Kenny house and he leaned across to open the door for Isobel. She caught the scent of his aftershave and thought it the best perfume in the world. She could see the shadow of shaved hairs on his upper lip. She sat still. "Would you care to come in for a drink?" she said.

Josh looked into her eyes for a moment. He could not see what their richness hid, but they were beautiful. "Thank you. But I'd better not. Sarah will have dinner ready."

Isobel creased the hem of her uniform, then straightened it out again. "It's a long time since we've been out together," she said. "How is your wife?"

"Well, and I think quite happy."

"She doesn't love you." Isobel scared herself with the abrupt words. She had no right.

"Perhaps not, my dear."

"You don't know! You don't know at all. You're being taken for a fool. I don't know why you put up with it." Isobel tried to bite her tongue, but it had already run away. "She's using you."

Josh said, "What else should she do? What else should I do, Isobel?"

"There's always—always someone else."

"That's childish. You're not a little girl, things aren't that simple. Whatever you may think, I love my wife." He said it very gently.

Isobel sagged. It took all her strength to get out of the car. "Maybe I'm still a little girl," she said. "I couldn't help myself. I never liked a man so much before." She walked away up the path and let herself in through the front door. Inside, she went straight upstairs to the bathroom. She locked the door and leaned against it. She wanted to cry but no tears came. She heard the car pull away outside and thought of Josh driving home to Sarah. She moved slowly to the cupboard that held the clean bath towels and pulled out a pile of five or six. On the windowsill beside the wash basin lay a small razor. Isobel thought about the uselessness and the pointlessness, about the life wasted, about the lost battle. She even thought about her mother and felt only a pale sadness. Then she sat on the laundry basket beside the bath and her deep hazel eyes watched her hands with fear.

Sarah's waiting was uneasy. She was waiting for two or three events. She was waiting for a letter and upon the letter's contents would be based the rest of the waiting. She felt cold. The weather outside the open window was golden, a buttery evening with roses. Samson in the sun dozed. "They shouldn't have shorn him," said Josh. "He doesn't know about the delights of Delilah."

Sarah chewed at a fingernail. Three days now spent in waiting; three suspended days when life had stopped and feeling with it. She felt cold and tired and watched her husband at the window. His hair had fallen into his eyes, it needed cutting. Her breath caught in her throat.

"Pardon?"

"Nothing. I didn't speak, Josh."

He pushed his hair back, he had a way of doing it, always the same.

The clock on the mantelpiece ticked round to seven o'clock. Josh turned a page of the magazine he was reading, but his gaze darted away to the garden. The velvet black and baby-brown flowers danced across his eyes. "Where's Gale?" he asked absently.

"I don't know. Have you told her yet, Josh?"

"No. Have you?"

"No, but I suppose she knows. I think it's worse for her. She doesn't accept changes. She's fighting knowing all the time." Sarah watched Josh. In the thin face were eyes she did not know, lines she did not recognize, and a hardness of the mouth. She did not know the man, but she was waiting. "I hope it won't be too long," she said.

"Are you in a hurry to go?"

"I don't know. You might be glad to get rid of me."

Josh did not reply. The sensation was still sharp and bright, almost intolerable now.

Gale came home with the news half an hour later, just as the clocked tripped a tick and began to chime. She came in slowly with a determined step and looked for a long time at her nephew. Then she said, her eyes straight ahead, "They've just found Isobel Kenny."

When Josh heard the story, the poor little story, his mouth opened and his eyes were wild and disbelieving. "She can't be," he said.

"She is," said Gale. "She knew what she was doing."

Sarah went to her husband, meaning to take his hand, touch his hair, anything, but she could not. He only frowned and shook his head like a drunken man. She stood in front of him but spoke to Gale. "Why did she do it?" she said softly.

Gale shrugged hopelessly. "What can I say?"

Josh went out of the room. In the hall on the small table where a vase of flowers always stood, lay a small green book. He picked it up and threw it with all his strength at the kitchen door, and the spine split and a few pages of poems drifted out of the broken remains. The women came out to see what the noise had been and Joshua was running up the stairs two at a time, right to the room at the top of the house.

"Did he love her?" said Sarah.

"If he did it wasn't enough," said Gale.

The three of them went to the funeral three days later at the Church of St. John. James Picton went too but Sarah only nodded to him as she and Josh followed Gale into the tiny cold church. The Cottage Hospital had left a skeleton staff and all those who could come wound their silent way between the yew trees and into the black pews. Somerfield left its shops to watch and sigh and nudge, and Jemmy Allen leaned on the wall outside with his cap under his hand and his black hair haloing out. "I didn't realize she had so many friends," wept Mrs. Kenny as the grave was filled.

"Lot of good they did her," muttered Mr. Erroll the publican, but only Josh heard because he was standing close. He turned away and took Sarah and Gale back home.

"It was a nice service," said Gale, taking off her black hat and reaching for the kettle. "Poor Sylvia Kenny cried all the time. It must be dreadful to lose your only child."

Josh gave her a glazed look she could not interpret that made her shiver. "I don't think I'll have tea," he said. "I'm going up to get changed."

When Sarah followed him a few minutes later, he was lying on the floor beside the bed. He had hung up his dark suit and the black arm band was on the bureau top. His face was waxy and his breathing shallow. Sarah went on her knees beside him. "Oh, no Josh," she murmured. "No, please, no . . . " Then she called for Gale.

Sarah went into the bedroom the next morning with an opened envelope in one hand and a cup of Aunt Gale's milky coffee in the other. Josh knew Sarah's range of expressions from A to Z but her morning face did not fit any of them. She was, for the only time he could remember, blank. Even in sleep she had faces, but today, wide awake, her eyes held nothing. She set the cup on the table beside the bed, then sat on the small hard chair that Josh had used

as a child as a balance while he pulled his socks on.
It was a spiteful chair. Their eyes meshed for a moment, then he looked away. It was a day for firsts. He
didn't recall ever having been totally confused by
Sarah before. He waited.

"Drink your coffee," she said quietly. He picked up
the cup with a hand he momentarily mistook for
someone else's, the way it shook and was so thin. The
steam from the coffee condensed on his eyes. Sarah
hesitated. Nothing she did with her hands or her
voice, but he felt her thoughts hesitate. "You're quite
ill," she said. "Gale told me. I made her. It was a
relief, she'd been very worried."

Her little bursts of words were like bullets and they
were all on target. "Poor Gale," he said. "What did
she tell you?"

"You've known for a few months that you are ill. I
suppose I might have known if we'd still been close,
Josh, but there was Jim and Poor Sister Isobel and so
I thought it was . . . I still don't know." Her voice
went all scratchy and broke up. He tried to move
toward her and couldn't. The coffee he'd drunk rose
in his throat and left a taste so bitter he choked, then
it seemed hours before the paroxysm wore off and
Sarah was wiping his face and there was blood on
the face cloth. "How ill are you, Josh?" she said, sort
of breathless, folding the face cloth so the red brown
traces didn't show. "Gale didn't say, but . . . "

"Not too bad, I'll survive."

"Doctor Gordon's coming soon. He's back today."
She looked down at him. "You were made to be a
patient," she said suddenly. "I have never seen such an
angelic face. You don't care so much about me now, I
know. You've made that plain for the past few months,

and now I've said I'll leave you, but things have changed and you are ill and I don't know what to do." She said it quite expressionlessly.

"Whatever would make you happy," croaked Josh.

"Are you really so selfish or so uncaring, Josh? Which is it?"

The silence pushed the walls back with its weight. "Whichever suits you best," said Josh finally.

Sarah creased the brown envelope in her hands. "I think I have to know more definitely than that," she said. "I'll stay now because you're ill; I couldn't think of leaving. But when you get better, what should I do then?"

"You already decided. This makes no difference. Go now if you want to."

"It would put too much on Gale, had you thought of that? And there's another thing, too; you'll have to help me because I'm uncertain, Josh." She waved the envelope gently. "This says I'm more than three months pregnant."

Then she walked quietly out of the room.

CHAPTER
ELEVEN

Sarah drove Josh to Madison's clinic as silently and carefully as she had been doing everything for the past two days. Alec Gordon, with whom Josh was on nodding terms at the GP unit in the hospital, had come in on the day of his collapse, his bushy eyebrows dense with professional concern and his gruff bedroom tones almost inaudible as he discussed the case with the patient.

"I'm sorry you were troubled," Josh said. "My wife doesn't know about my condition, otherwise she would have called Madison straight away."

Gordon was shaken. His hands jittered as he folded the stethoscope into his black bag. "Then you know what your disease is?"

"Of course. I've known and been treated for six months. It's acute monocytic, if you're interested. I've had four remissions. I guess it'll be a miracle if I get a fifth."

"Has Madison—?"

"Everything, Doctor Gordon. Except irradiation,

and that's unlikely to have been effective, even if it had been practical. I didn't want my wife to know. Now she must." Oh, the best-laid plans.

"But man, you couldn't have hoped to keep it from her."

"But I did. Yes, I did. And it almost worked. Even this lot could have been explained as serious but not fatal. Not now, though, not with the baby."

Gordon was a wily old bird with pin-black eyes beneath the bushy brows. He had dealt with human nature for more years than Josh had lived and probably practiced medicine with as much intuition as skill. "She came to Doctor March a week ago," he said slowly, walking to the window and playing with the pebbles on the sill. "She must have had the result today." He turned, rubbing the pebbles together in his palms with that dry seashore sound. Josh nodded, the sudden pain in his chest catching his words. "Then you'll be worried about her?" added Gordon.

"She's my wife, Doctor. Tell me; am I right in thinking that my leukemia is unlikely to affect the fetus? I remember reading a paper somewhere ages ago, but the details . . . "

Doctor Gordon rearranged the eggs of granite and quartz on the sill. "I don't think there's much chance of it," he said. "But I'll look it up and let you know. There's bound to be something in the stack of medical journals I keep. Never throw anything away. My wife complains bitterly sometimes. I'll phone Madison about you today and no doubt he'll want you in. All right?"

So they were going to Madison's clinic, Josh's bag containing brand new pajamas and old dressing gown, toothbrush and razor, bouncing against the back of the car seat. Sarah was driving more slowly than usual.

She had refused to let an ambulance collect her husband.

"You've been crying," said Josh. "Your eyes look all sexy, they always do when you've been crying." She would not smile. "There's nothing I can say to you now," he said. "Is there?"

"So have you," she said. "And there's plenty you can say, but after you've seen Mr. Madison and after you are safe in one of his beds." Two orderlies lifted Josh onto a stretcher and the white of his knuckles trying to help himself made Sarah grimace and turn away. "I'll be along soon," she said steadily. "I'm going to see Madison now." Despite Josh's call she walked walked away to the entrance marked *Reception and Enquiries.*

"I'm Mrs. Steel," she told Madison in his elegant office. "I came with my husband."

"Uh, good afternoon. Sit down, please." There was a prolonged silence while he toyed with the carnation in his buttonhole and his eyelid flickered like a neon light. He prepared to deal with the hysterical little woman, and cursed Steel's insistence upon secrecy. "Can I help you?" he said finally.

"Can he be cured?" said Sarah, and her voice was as small as the hope in the question.

"Well now, Mrs. Steel—"

"What has he got?" And her voice was as big as the demand.

"I'm afraid he did stipulate that you . . . Look my dear, we shall do our utmost to treat . . . " He had to stop. The great gray eyes called him coward yet wanted reassurance, dared him to be brave yet asked that he lie. He watched their light fade.

"He's dying, isn't he?" she said. "I know it. I've been connected with the medical profession long

267

enough. I thought at first it might be TB, anything . . . tried to believe only children suffered from it, not grown, healthy men like my Josh. But when I heard who had been treating him . . . You and your specialty are well known, Mr. Madison. It's late, too, isn't it? Late." She stood up and was tall and tough and weak inside. "I must see him now," she said. "We have a lot to talk about."

As it happened, there was not much said. Josh lay in bed in his tastefully green room, dressed in the new pajamas and looking small and lost and very ill. There were no flowers or cards yet, nor grapes for the visitors; just the razor and toothbrush and face cloth left by the nurse on the locker shelf. Sarah went to the window, and Josh realized how often it was that when people had something to say they said it out of a window; as if, privately, they wanted to broadcast it because it felt important, yet could only whisper it to the panes. All the important things, he thought, are said not face to face, but face to pale reflection, because truth is too naked for people to share.

"I love you, Josh," said Sarah to the window, not seeing the irises glorying in the sun below. "I know why you did what you did."

The man struggled up against the frail hold of the bedclothes and would not give in until his back was straight, his head erect, his face gray-white and dripping. "Sarah, my daffodil, Jimmy loves you. Even when I get better—"

"Shut up! Don't make it worse, Josh. I know, don't you see, I know. Oh, why didn't you tell me, you great, noble fool! Do you think I'm so insensitive, so—so lacking in love and understanding and intelligence that you couldn't share it with me? Don't you know me at all? Did you never understand what I feel about living and dying, how I wouldn't need consolation and compensation? Who do you think you are? Some lonely hero on a mountaintop?" She wiped the rain of her eyes from the windowsill with an angry hand.

There was a century of silence. "My world is getting smaller and smaller, Sarah."

"Uh?" She turned to him and he was gray-white and dripping.

"It was what I wanted for you. I hadn't looked. To make you happy, you see."

"And you."

"Yes, mostly me. See what I mean, butterfly? Smaller and smaller. My fault." His head sagged and he pulled it up with a grave effort. "Now you have the baby. That will be consolation and compensation whether you like it or not." He smiled and she saw the sweat run into the lines. She went to hold him in her arms, rocking him gently, clenching her teeth.

A sister and a nurse came in with a trolley of gadgetry to put up an i.v. Sarah kissed her husband's cheek and smiled for a moment into his eyes. "I suppose I ought to thank you," she said. "I'll be back soon. These ladies have a stern and busy air." She was still smiling as she closed the door, but outside in the long, cool corridor the animal agony spoiled the asepticism like the invasion of a warm, incontinent little pup and she had to run so he wouldn't hear the noise in her throat.

Jimmy Picton called at the house that evening, still wearing a black tie but bright and breezy and oblivious, expecting the door to be answered by Josh. Gale let him in with a vacant smile. Her back was ramrod and her pearls plumblined and her neat pleated skirt uncrushed, but she was a million miles away. "Sarah's in the sitting room," she said tonelessly, then went away to her own room to stare blindly at Samson and see only Josh's face.

"All by yourself?" Jimmy asked Sarah. "Good. I can present my lovely lady with chocolates and not feel her husband's eagle eye upon me." He stopped in the act of producing Black Magic from his coat pocket. "You look unhappy, Sarah. Had a row?" There was a touch of hope almost hidden in his voice.

Sarah, sitting in the armchair, Josh's armchair, with her hands folded in her lap, said nothing. All afternoon she had been wondering whether to cancel Jim's visit, whether to go on simply canceling all his proposed visits until he gave up. Even now, she was undecided. "Have a drink," she offered, indicating the half-empty bottle of wine on the coffee table. "Pour me another too, a small one." Nothing must hurt the baby now. No strong liquor, cut down smoking, reduce stress. Huh. But even if it meant tranquilizers by the handful, the baby must not, would not, be hurt.

As he passed the glass, Jimmy noticed the pallor of her face and the dark shadows in her eyes. "Where's Josh?" he said. "He told me he'd be in tonight. Sarah, what is it?"

"Did you know?" said Sarah. "About Josh?"

"What about him? I really don't understand him too well. I always feel I only know his surface. Has he hurt you, Sarah? If he has I'll—"

"No! No . . . no. Joshua has never hurt me intentionally—or was it?" She caught her breath quickly. "He's done everything he could to save me from pain,

Jimmy. Silly great fool. Taking all that alone. I think he still doesn't realize I know. His eyes weren't right, you see. I never really believed it all because his eyes weren't right. And yet the facts were before me, the coolness, the sudden lack of tenderness, the way he almost threw me at . . . " She stopped, glancing up into James's bewildered stare. You look like that forlorn little chimpanzee we saw on TV the other night, she thought. Lost its mum and all alone. "I'm sorry. You don't understand a word, do you, Jim? Listen to me; would you go now and never come back, just because I ask you to? Do you trust my judgment enough?"

"But Sarah, what are you talking about? Last week you were talking seriously of leaving him. You said you cared about me. You can't mean it."

The woman dropped her stare. How could Josh have stood to see the same look in her eyes, the same perplexed resentment. Why hadn't he known? Why hadn't he known? "What has happened, Sarah?" Jimmy ran a hand through his hair, confusing his appearance to match his feelings.

"Go away, Jim," she said softly. "You've been used, I think. I never knew my husband could be so devious. Or such a good actor. Poor, poor Joshua. I think you'd better go away, Jim. There's nothing here for you." She did not have the strength to watch his hopes collapse. She thought of the tiny being secret inside her, stood up and walked out of the room without a look.

Sarah Steel was helping her husband's aunt by cleaning the bedrooms. Gale gave her a cloth and the polish with a quizzical, worried look, but Sarah's eyes gave no hint of her feelings, not even as her mouth smiled an attempt at reassurance. In her bedroom she stared at the empty wide bed, the cloth in one hand, polish in the other. Her gaze floated to them and she had forgotten what they were for, why her hands held these alien objects.

Something in Sarah Steel was strong as her name, but the metal of her was suffering now, beaten thin as tin foil, bending and folding. She sat at her dressing table and her reflection was pale and vacant. She felt dreadfully tired. Always when some mental disturbance attacked, she felt a huge need for sleep, though sleep would rarely come. Now she was so badly torn there was no relief. She dropped the cleaning things and tucked her hands across her belly, her fingers warmed by the new life she held. If she could only enjoy it. But Josh was dying and he would never see their child.

She bit her lip. Her son would have no father; she could not bring herself now to think of Jimmy as his stepfather. Maybe later, years away, but until then her child would be raised on memories, would see the loss in his mother's eyes and wonder why, would be embarrassed when she caught and held him because the turn of his head or the expression of his mouth reminded her of a man remotely glimpsed in a photograph of "father." For a fleeting moment Sarah considered an abortion. It would be killing Josh twice though, wouldn't it . . .

Gale heard the wail and dropped the potato she was peeling. She moved through the house so quickly the familiar rooms passed in a blur, the stairs fell away two at a time, and still the noise echoed, filling every corner with piercing thickness. It broke, then started again on exactly the same pitch. Gale covered her ears as she ran but still the noise assaulted her brain. She found Sarah seated before the glass, her mouth open and the scream coming out. Her eyes were wide and frightened as if they could not understand what was happening, her hands folded across her belly. Gale shook her shoulders and shouted, "Sarah, what is it?" but she might have spoken to a wailing statue. She shook the girl hard and the noise wobbled but did not fade. Finally she slapped Sarah smartly across the face.

The silence that followed was worse than the scream. "What is it, child?" Gale said gently.

"I don't know," said Sarah calmly. "I couldn't help it. Oh, Gale, what is to become of us? This baby doesn't soften the blow. It is many times worse."

Gale sat on the bed shakily, her legs like water. "It may not be so bad," she said, but Sarah's look left her no hope. "At least you will not be alone, is that any comfort?"

Sarah turned her head slowly away and her eyes were dead. "No," she said. "There is no comfort. I will want to be alone and lonely, it would be right that way. It would be right for Josh that way. I'm afraid I will lose his face too quickly because the joy will dilute the pain."

"I don't understand."

"Neither does my Josh."

As she entered the clinic, unimpressed by the decor, soft carpets, and vinyl walls, Sarah arranged her face and set her shoulders. As she passed, the receptionist watched and commented to the nurse at her side, "That's his wife. Doctor Steel, you know. Looks a bit of a bitch, doesn't she?" Sarah heard and faltered, then walked on by. There was no time to waste and no point in wasting it.

"Hello, Josh." She put the bag of fruit on the locker. "How are you?"

"Fine, but I wouldn't advise the fruit, poppet. I'm on Codeine sulfate already."

Josh was propped in the bed, flattened against the pillows as if a hammer had laid him there. The i.v. still hung and his left hand clenched the slab where the needle went in. Sarah had thought her husband handsome before. Now he hurt her eyes with his pale glow. He looked more than dead already because there was no peace in his face.

"How are you, my daffodil?" he said. "Is Gale taking good care of you? And Jimmy?"

Sarah squashed her anger. "Don't be clever," she said. "Whatever you have contrived, I don't love Jimmy Picton, even though I am fond of him. I've decided not to believe you, Joshua, so forget it. I love you, no matter how you feel about me. Don't torment me."

"Okay, rosebud." The words were very light. He coughed and coughed and the pain in his chest and back made the frown come and the sweat break out. When he could speak, he said, "Sarah, it won't be long. Oh, Christ, these bloody drugs! I shouldn't have said it. Sarah, sweet Sarah, say you'll marry Jim. Give me peace of mind."

"Wasn't Isobel enough?" His wife shook her head. "I'm sorry, I'm sorry. But I won't lie. I'll make no promises, not even for your peace of mind. You'll leave me with money and—and something far more precious. Listen to me. Hear me, just once. We've done it your way and it didn't work. Let's be true now." Josh closed his eyes and sighed and it seemed to Sarah that he gave up then. "Do you want to come home?" she said.

He looked at her hopefully. "It would be too much trouble."

Sarah wondered why his eyes did not spill over his face, they were so large and liquid and his cheeks so insubstantial. "There is no such animal," she said. "I don't think they can do more for you here than we can. Come home with me, Joshua."

Madison allowed it and the allowing set the seal and brought reality home to roost. The specialist would never have countenanced the removal of his patient had there been the slightest chance of his recovery at the clinic. Although Gale fought it valiantly, the inevitable was borne in upon her by her nephew and his wife.

"They're so resigned," she told Mrs. Corbey. "They leave no room for hope. I don't understand it."

Gale and Sarah were in the kitchen, Sarah watching the kettle and Gale rolling pastry. Her pastry was famous in the village; it had won prizes for its crumbly yellow delicacy at every Women's Institute competition. "Do you think Josh would like some steak and kidney pie?" she said.

Sarah said, "He'd love it, but Gale, he can't keep it down. Even this Complan makes him sick." She stirred hot water into a cup.

Gale began to sniff. Her pockets were always full of damp handkerchiefs now, her eyes always puffy. Even her straight back stooped. "He's like a son," she said. "The only one I ever had. Why him, Sarah? Why does God say it has to be him?"

"Don't, Gale." Sarah went to her and held one of her

275

floury, freckled hands. "You've said it all before. I can't give you answers. Ask your God, not me. I just don't know."

The older woman pushed the hand aside. "You! You should have helped him, not gone off with that—that Picton! How can you bear it, how can you be so un-moved!" She covered her face and the flour on her hands turned to paste with tears.

Sarah sat down. Her pregnancy was beginning to show in this, her fourth month. She was often sick in the mornings and her legs ached from running up and down stairs. A woman with child is usually calm and placid, she knew, but this calm was more like the im-movability of fear, and the placidity was the center of a hurricane. One step outside it and she would be destroyed completely by the cylinder of winds. "I can't cope unless I'm cold," she said quietly. "Do you know how often I have to run from his room after he's vomited, Gale? How many times I've passed out washing bloody towels and dirty sheets? I love him so much I can't be anything but cold."

Gale wiped her sticky face and stared. "Sarah, I didn't realize. I'm so sorry, child."

"I shouldn't have said it. It was only to be unkind. There's something nagging at me about Josh; some-thing else. It all gets to be a little too much at times." She stood up and picked up the cup.

"What is it, about Josh?"

"I'm not sure. He hasn't told me. I feel he wants to, but he thinks I'm cold too, so he's afraid. And most of the time he's too ill to say very much." She took the cup upstairs.

For three weeks it continued, and the man in bed upstairs lay shrinking and weakening, staring for long hours at the ceiling. His body had become smaller and his mind bigger. When Sarah came he always smiled and hoped for an answer, but she rarely gave it. She tended him carefully and thoroughly and she was behind a glass wall several feet thick. Hemmed in, he lived with the shadows of pain; there was the dog he'd accidentally burned in the shed and he heard its howls, the children in Africa he had not been able to cure and he saw their stoic smiles. But they were ancient, soft shadows. They reproached, but they had forgiven. The big pain shouldered in and sat beside his bed on the hard chair and obscured the rest. It had a presence and a voice that said, "You are blind." And its big backside did not feel the iron of the chair, so it sat always, day and night.

Doctor Gordon came and went regularly, and he always came jovial and went away sad. Once he told Josh, "The baby should be perfectly normal. I looked it up. I've given your wife some tranquilizers and she's promised to take them. They might make her a bit vague."

"She is already. She's all locked up. Alec, I need to to talk with her." His facial bones stuck out with needing and his knuckles were desperate.

In the kitchen, Sarah made tea. "It won't be long, will it?" she said. "Doctor Gordon, don't let him feel pain. Don't let it be agony for him."

The old man pinched the skin over the bridge of his nose and his bushy eyebrows came down. "I don't think that is what bothers him. There's more than one kind, Mrs. Steel."

She poured the tea into Gale's thin china cups. "I do all I can. So does Gale."

"My dear," he patted her thin fingers. "You must give in to yourself, you must relax your hold. That man up there is your husband. He needs comfort for his soul, I don't know how exactly, but he needs it. You do all you can for his body, I've seen that. I'd hate to say it's not enough." He squeezed her fingers and found they held onto his.

Sarah dropped her head. "I know," she said. "I suppose I'm running away. If I don't talk it isn't real, it isn't happening to us. I can't let go, can't feel."

"Why not, my dear? It's perfectly natural."

"I *know*. Don't you understand, I know it. I'm not in control now, it's gone too far, it's got a hold of its own like an animal. It's outside me. You tell it to stop, Doctor. You give me a miracle pill so I can feel again!"

Alec Gordon looked for tears and there were none. Like other men before him he found Sarah's eyes astonishing; he avoided them. He shrugged his heavy shoulders. "You should get more rest," he said.

Sarah smiled. As she watched him go down the back path with his bent back and shuffling steps, her mind was already on Josh's next wash, change of clothing, liquid meal.

Visitors came from the hospital at first, but having seen Josh once, went away with shaking heads and feet quickened by the need for fresh, healthy surroundings. Matron Dixon came and was bright and encouraging. She never mentioned Isobel Kenny once. Staff Taylor came with a bag of apples Josh couldn't eat, and could think of nothing to say. James Picton came, too. He did not ask to see Josh but Sarah took him up.

The figure taking up so little room in the wide bed was hardly recognizable until he spoke. "Hello, Jimmy. How are you?" His voice was soft and strained. "How are my patients?"

James fidgeted. He tried to speak but his words could not get past his stiff lips. He sat in the chair Sarah had pulled up for him and waited.

"The entertainment is off," said Josh, smiling. It made thin, hard lines each side of his mouth. "You'll have to put on an act for me."

"I'm sorry. I—I don't think I can."

To his bowed head, Josh whispered, "I like you, James. You must never feel guilty. I'm glad you love my Sarah. Keep an eye on her for me, she'll need a good, strong arm soon."

James shook his head. "I shouldn't have come. Sarah told me not to, but . . . "

"Thank God for that 'but.' I'm glad you did," then, in a decimated baritone, "Good-bye, Jimmy, good-bye."

"You can't sing! Not now."

"Never could. Seems there is to be no last minute miracle. Still, there must be other flat notes in the heavenly chorus."

Sarah showed James out. At the door, he said, "Josh asked me to look after you."

"He won't give up, will he? So long, Jim, thank you for coming. Thank you for everything." They shook hands and locked eyes and Jim saw Sarah's were lost. She went back to Josh. As she plumped and smoothed his pillows, Josh reached out and touched her glass cage. His palm flattened against her stomach. She hesitated, then sat on the bed. His hand moved gently over the warm cotton of her dress. Very slowly, she brought her hands up to cover his.

"It's so long since you touched me," she said.

"I wasn't sure I could any more. Sarah, the baby is mine, isn't it?"

Anger flared in the woman, the first real emotion to emerge from the heavy gray mass of self-sedation for several weeks. Lifetimes, they seemed. Her nails dug into the back of Josh's hand and left small red parentheses in the yellow-white skin. "No one has ever . . . not since you. You should have known that, Joshua Steel. Don't you know me at all?"

He sighed and his lungs gurgled. "I thought I did. But I changed us all and it got beyond my control. I just wanted to be sure. Alec says the baby will be all right."

Sarah smoothed out the marks she had made. "So you asked, as if you knew you were the father."

"Yes. It was only a tiny doubt, my mother of the earth. Forgive me."

She looked at his face. It may have been ugly in its ravaged lines and hollows, but to her it was a child's face. She lifted his hand to her breast, then her lips. His skin was bitter-salty against her mouth. "I think you're allowed a doubt or two," she said. "But don't doubt me. I can't let you do that."

"Will you lay your head on the pillow by me? I want to know things of you, Sarah, and I can't talk loudly."

"But Josh, I have—"

"I may not ask these things again."

She lay on her side outside the covers and smoothed his hair as he whispered, "I feel so bad, my darling rosebud-bump."

"Is it the pain? Should I fetch the injection?"

"No, no. I don't seem to have a body. Sarah, do you despise me for what I have done?"

"Sometimes. Sometimes I lie awake at night and get

furious at you, but it passes so quickly when I remember why. It must have been bad for you too—worse, because you knew what was happening and I didn't. How could you stand it, Josh? You're such an honest person."

"But I'm not. I lived a lie for six months. I got used to it. I even began to think I did not love you. I guess it was a kind of brainwashing. I'm scared, Sarah."

She stroked his hair and ached. "Why, Josh? Does . . . does dying scare you?"

"Yes, and I've no way to repay. Isobel. I didn't know about Isobel. I thought—I thought she was nice, I guess I thought she was a pawn with a stone heart. Sarah, what can I do about Isobel?" His words came out thin and strangled. He turned his head and their eyes were only inches apart. Sarah saw how dark brown his were and how big and black the pupils, and how intense, more than they had ever been. She saw how the eyelashes framed them so they looked starry and how the whites had tiny veins across them, and how furrowed was the forehead above them.

"You can't do anything," she said. "Except hope that the next time round you remember and make a better choice . . . But you don't believe me, do you?"

The lids came down and hid his eyes. "I don't know. I want to, but it doesn't ring true with me. If there is a next time there must have been a last, and I don't remember that. A dreadful circle where I go on making the same mistake over and over seems worse than some religious eternity with wings and harps."

"Or shovels and pointed tails," said Sarah. "Don't be too literal, my Joshua. It could be there is no black and white, only shades of gray. What is done, is done.

Torturing yourself won't change it. Or me. I think I'm going to cry, isn't that strange." He took her hand while she sobbed and wished he had the energy to pull her close to him.

"Not for me," he whispered. "Don't cry for me. Once, early on, I wanted you to mourn me, my child-wife, but that was before I really knew. That was when I still believed it couldn't happen to me. Now, you see, it hurts to have you in sorrow."

After a while she wiped her eyes on the hem of her dress. "I'm sorry I am no comfort," she said. "What I believe in comes from me, from things I've experienced which are more real to me than—than being here now. Our inner selves are never wholly shared, are they?"

"Sometimes, my love, sometimes. We peek at each other's souls through chinks in our words, through tiny holes in our skins."

"You're exhausted, Josh. Will you sleep now?"

"Would you read to me? I miss my books. I can't hold them up and I can't concentrate. Read to me, please."

Sarah fetched a small green book. It was stuck together with brown tape and one cover was broken. "Maybe this will help say what I mean," she said, opening it. She read Donne's "Valediction: Forbidding Mourning."

Josh joined in the last two lines with a quiet smile. "Thy firmness draws my circle just, And makes me end, where I begun."

The clock ticked in the room, each tick a composition of crack, buzz, echo; crack, buzz, echo. The ticks filled the room to its corners. Samson sat in the window and laid his faint shadow on the wall above the sideboard between the azalea and the willow-patterned vase. The blackbirds fed their big young on the lawn outside, but the cat cared nothing for them. It drizzled and he hated to get wet.

The clock ticked louder. Gale watched Sarah dozing in the chair opposite. They sat each side of the empty hearth like tired stone lions guarding a doorway. Gale hurt numbly right down to her toes. The clock coughed and caught its breath to chime, and as Gale looked up at it she could have sworn the notes came out in metal bubbles that drifted one by one to the floor and burst silently on the carpet.

Sarah stirred uneasily. "It's four o'clock," said Gale. "I went up just now and he's asleep."

Sarah rubbed her eyes. "How long since you saw the outside world?" she said.

"I went shopping this morning."

"But did you see anything?"

Gale shook her head. "I know what you mean. We revolve around him, don't we? What shall we do when he's—he's not here any more? Sarah, what shall we do?"

The younger woman sighed. "That doesn't matter. Josh matters. He's worried, mostly I think about Isobel. It was his fault, you see."

"Oh, Sarah, how can you! She was that sort of girl. She would have done it anyway. It wasn't the first attempt."

"Nobody does it anyway." Sarah was kind and angry, too. "Gale, why hide from the truth? Josh has done it, you do it, Jim does it, Isobel did it good and

283

proper. If Josh had been honest, Isobel would not have done what she did. He knows it. You and I know it. Don't you see? Deceit is the worst of all."

"We don't even know what Isobel's reasons were. She didn't leave a note or anything."

Sarah's voice went as hard as concrete. "Deceiving yourself is the worst of all," she said. "Josh has stopped doing it; can't we? He needs reassurance, help. We can't give him that unless we admit he was wrong."

"Huh! Anybody would think you are a lily white angel."

Sarah crossed her feet and studied her toes. "To him I am," she said. "A human, imperfect angel. That's why I can tell him the truth. We were never jealous of each other, Gale, we never resented the good or bad we found in each other."

"I don't understand you," muttered Gale. "I never did. There's the poor man up there blaming himself for something which probably wasn't his fault anyway, and you say all right, let him blame himself. You should be up there comforting him, making it better!" Tears began again. Since she had known, it had been raining in Gale's heart.

Sarah said, "It would be a lie and he would know it. He is Joshua, he is not you or me or anyone else. He is Joshua, alone. No force in the world can change that, no words or deeds, dear Aunt Gale. He will be Joshua and the sum of all his Joshuas deep inside himself, no matter what we say."

"Oh, I'm weary," said Gale, dropping her head back and letting the tears drop from her chin to become pearls among her pearls. "I'm so weary."

"I know," said Sarah. "I'm weary, too. But there is life in me even against my will." Her hands folded gently across her stomach and her upper arms pressed against the ache in her breasts.

The clock ticked into the silence, each tick a composition of crack, buzz, echo; crack, buzz, echo, and the ticks filled the room to its corners. Samson washed behind his ears, a sign of rain to come, they say, but he had always been a pretty useless cat.

CHAPTER
TWELVE

"Josh, can you hear me? Can you talk?"

He had been away, journeying through every corner of a nightmare; men with black beards and shapeless faces were his companions, cruel jesting men without words, dragging, shoving, tearing men with the strength of mammoths. They had borne him along through hot red rivers, icy snowfields under green lights, strange cities designed by a mad Leonardo; and him in a long white nightgown of voluminous calico whose rough folds billowed and constricted. Was he to die now, then? Was he dead already? Was the end of the journey here, with a woman's voice, gentle as angels?

Sarah left one hand folded across her stomach, warm and knowing, while the other brushed over her husband's forehead. Warm-cool, warm-cool, infinitely soothing. She felt his torment leave through her fingers, sensed the sudden change as his skin relaxed and his body stilled, and the hand on her belly moved caressingly as if she took life and gave it through her palm, as if all three united in her and became whole for a suspended moment. Joshua opened his eyes and they were clear and lucid and hopeless. They stared at each other, the man and his wife with the baby in her, and Sarah's heart pounded and the world was two wide brown eyes. The beauty of the eyes moved her, brought tears to her like the tears of great music or words. I think I cannot bear it, she said inside, I think I cannot lose this Joshua who is so good, who tried so hard to leave me happy.

"Poor sweet Josh," she said, cool-warming his forehead all the while. "Poor sweet Josh, you didn't understand, did you? You didn't hear me when I told you how I believe. You were all the time looking at Josh; it's your way, it makes you real." But now you don't look real at all. Now with your skin so white and your eyes so huge.

His voice was soft and cracking, like a rustle of leaves. "Sarah . . . Sarah, what day is it? Was I talking nonsense again?"

"It's Thursday. Doctor Gordon will be here soon. How is the pain?"

"I don't know. Sarah, forgive me . . . please."

She stroked again, cool-warm, warm-cool. "You kept mumbling that," she said. "I have found nothing in my heart that is hurt, so there is nothing to forgive, nothing wrong in the whole world to forgive."

"Sarah smiles, there's no time now except for truth." He moved and groaned. "Tell me . . . tell me."

"What, Joshua? That I love you? I love you, my Joshua, and I will find you again, always."

"That's it . . . tell me." It was a last-minute agony greater than pain, like boarding a train that is going, but with no destination.

She took his long, thin fingers in her hand and pressed them to her belly. "I don't know how. Once I dreamed, and in the dream I discovered the secret of life and death, Josh, how it goes, why it is. It was so simple, so very, very simple. But I forgot in the morning. I tried very hard but I forgot in the morning . . . But it's there, I know it's there. I just forgot, that's all."

"Sarah, I'm scared." The whites of his eyes showed all round like sometimes when he had been angry. He would not be angry again. The woman's hand across her rounding stomach spread and stilled, pressing away the fear that sprang up in her.

"He will have brown eyes, Josh. I shall call him Joshua Matthew."

"And he'll break your heart, too. Boys always do, they say." The man smiled. "We all break each other's hearts."

Sarah shook her head firmly. Josh watched her with a clear vision, a vision which gave the room a dream-like quality, too vivid, as if the sky at the window were solid and all the objects seen through holes in it. He saw more than he had ever seen. The tiny blue veins on the backs of her hands, the vitality of her body contrasting with the weary sorrow of her face. "Ladies are so valiant," he said. "Never say die, eh, Sarah-bump? Never say die, ought to have been a lady who said it. Now I'll never know, one of those things I should have looked up. Tell me again, Sarah, tell me about forgetting in the morning . . . "

"It will be all right, Josh, we'll find it. It's only because it's now that I've forgotten. It'll be there, it will . . . "

He died in delirium later that morning before Alec Gordon arrived. For a long time Sarah sat beside his bed, one hand across her belly and the other around a cold wrist whose pulse had fluttered to a halt, and once she murmured, "So if I dream I have you, I have you, For all our joys . . . " And later she said, "I don't know, Josh. I don't know."

The Story
All America
Took To Its Heart

A
Woman of
Independent
Means

A Novel by
Elizabeth
Forsythe
Hailey

THE SPLENDID
NATIONAL BESTSELLER

"Nothing about it is ordinary . . . irresistible."
Los Angeles Times
"Bares the soul of an independent American housewife . . .
a woman to respect . . . a writer to remember."
John Barkham Reviews

AVON $2.50

THE BIG BESTSELLERS
ARE AVON BOOKS

☐	Adjacent Lives Ellen Schwamm	45211	$2.50
☐	A Woman of Independent Means		
	Elizabeth Forsythe Hailey	42390	$2.50
☐	The Human Factor Graham Greene	41491	$2.50
☐	The Train Robbers Piers Paul Read	42945	$2.75
☐	The Brendan Voyage Tim Severin	43711	$2.75
☐	The Insiders Rosemary Rogers	40576	$2.50
☐	Oliver's Story Erich Segal	42564	$2.25
☐	The Prince of Eden Marilyn Harris	41905	$2.50
☐	The Thorn Birds Colleen McCullough	35741	$2.50
☐	The Amulet Michael McDowell	40584	$2.50
☐	Chinaman's Chance Ross Thomas	41517	$2.25
☐	Kingfisher Gerald Seymour	40592	$2.25
☐	The Trail of the Fox David Irving	40022	$2.50
☐	The Bermuda Triangle Charles Berlitz	38315	$2.25
☐	The Real Jesus Garner Ted Armstrong	40055	$2.25
☐	Lancelot Walker Percy	36582	$2.25
☐	Snowblind Robert Sabbag	44008	$2.50
☐	Fletch's Fortune Gregory Mcdonald	37978	$1.95
☐	Voyage Sterling Hayden	37200	$2.50
☐	Humboldt's Gift Saul Bellow	38810	$2.25
☐	Mindbridge Joe Haldeman	33605	$1.95
☐	The Monkey Wrench Gang		
	Edward Abbey	46755	$2.50
☐	Jonathan Livingston Seagull		
	Richard Bach	44099	$1.95
☐	Working Studs Terkel	34660	$2.50
☐	Shardik Richard Adams	43752	$2.75
☐	Watership Down Richard Adams	39586	$2.50

Available at better bookstores everywhere, or order direct from the publisher.

From the author of
Devil's Desire and *Moonstruck Madness*

THE STORY OF ONE MAN, ONE WOMAN, ALL LOVE!

AND NO LESS THE STORY OF

LAURIE McBAIN

TEARS OF GOLD

Reaching across an unending landscape of human emotion, from Paris to Gold Rush California, Laurie Mc-Bain's long-awaited new romance brings together two proud people:

MARA
She could seduce the moonlight . . .

NICHOLAS
A man who took what he wanted,
when he wanted it . . .

Through breathless adventures and dangerous charades —from vast, sunbaked ranches where Spanish land barons beckon with kisses flavored of wine, to a lush Louisiana plantation where they unite in a blaze of joy and pain—their destinies were one. For though Nicholas had sworn to kill her, she was the love he would die for!

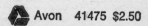 Avon   41475 $2.50

TEA 4-79

AVON ◆ THE BEST IN
BESTSELLING ENTERTAINMENT

IN HOLLYWOOD, WHERE DREAMS DIE QUICKLY, ONE LOVE LASTS FOREVER...

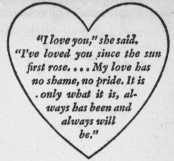

"I love you," she said. "I've loved you since the sun first rose. . . . My love has no shame, no pride. It is only what it is, always has been and always will be."

The words are spoken by Brooke Ashley, a beautiful forties film star, in the last movie she ever made. She died in a tragic fire in 1947.

A young screenwriter in a theater in Los Angeles today hears those words, sees her face, and is moved to tears. Later he discovers that he wrote those words, long ago; that he has been born again—as she has.

What will she look like? Who could she be? He begins to look for her in every woman he sees...

A Romantic Thriller
by
TREVOR MELDAL-JOHNSEN

AVON

41897
$2.50